Tales from My Closet

Tales from My Closet

JENNIFER ANNE MOSES

Scholastic Press

NEW YORK

ISBN 978-0-545-66811-8

10 9 8 7 6 5 4 3 2 1   14 15 16 17 18

Printed in the U.S.A.   40
First edition, February 2014

The text was set in Apollo MT.
Book design by Natalie C. Sousa

For Rose

CHAPTER ONE

My Life on Planet Toilet Paper

• Justine •

I hate being the new kid at school. Just. Hate. It.

And I always am. Okay: maybe not always. Maybe not *every* year. But almost. Or at least it seems that way. First Houston, then Germany, and then Saint Louis, back to Germany, and then, for two whole years, San Francisco, and now I'm in tenth grade and starting all over again, this time in West Falls, New Jersey, which my mother says is, quote, "so sophisticated," and my father says is, quote, "close to everything." By which he means: (a) his office and (b) an airport.

"Don't worry, Pooky," he emailed to me from his office downtown on the day after he'd broken the news. "They have shopping there, too."

Ha. Ha.

He gets transferred around a lot. He also travels. The rest of us — which is me, Mom, and our cat, Skizz — follow. Before she'd had me, Mom had been a dancer: She'd been a member of a company in Boston. Now she jokes that she's his senior staff and I'm his junior staff.

Our New Jersey house, which I'd secretly named Homely Acres, has three levels, connected by half flights of stairs, and a two-car garage. The room my parents chose for me is on the second level, same as theirs, but unlike theirs, mine is painted a pale, sickening lavender-pink and smells vaguely of sugar, like maybe there's ancient spilled Coke that soaked into the floorboards. There's no point in getting it repainted, either — not the way we move around. "You'll love it," Mom said.

We moved in early August, just in time to arrive in West Falls for my fifteenth birthday, which I celebrated with Mom at a not-very-good Chinese restaurant, because even though he'd promised me that he wouldn't miss what he called my "big day" for anything, Dad ended up working late, calling me on my cell phone while I was in mid-sesame-noodle-slurp. "I'm so sorry, Pooky," he said. "I'll try to make it up to you soon, okay?"

West Falls itself was dead, and that's because everyone over the age of two and under the age of ninety was at the beach. As for people my age to make friends with? It was as if they'd all been vaporized and sent to another planet.

"Don't worry," Mom said. "Once school starts up again, you'll be back in the swing."

I hated when she said that: *back in the swing.* What did that even *mean*?

In San Francisco I'd fallen in with a bunch of nerdy brainiac types, and through them I met my best friend, Eliza. Mainly we hung out at the beach and, on weekends, explored the Castro or the Haight or any other neighborhood that, once upon a time, had been utterly cool. It was on one of these excursions that I discovered vintage. It was a whole new look for me, a mash-up of hippie and gypsy and blues singer. The look made me feel not just *visible*, but also like a person in my own right, and not just an extension of my parents' ideas about who I'm supposed to be.

Neither one of them was exactly crazy about my new look, though. Mom told me straight-out that she thought I looked better in what she calls "normal" clothes. Dad barely noticed at all. Even when it came to my going-away party, he barely glanced up. It was cold and misty, so I wore my absolute favorite dark-green velvet hip-hugging bell-bottoms with black ballerina slippers and a pink silk top, bona fide vintage Pucci.

"Have fun, Pooky," he said from behind his computer.

I'm Justine. The story they told me was that I was supposed to be *Justin*, like my grandfather who died before I was born, but then I turned out to be a girl.

Justine Ruth Gandler.

The. Worst. Name. Ever.

Another thing Mom thought was just swell about Homely Acres? It was right across the street from a girl exactly my age and her little brother. Only they were at the beach. "Everyone says they're very nice," Mom said. "And there's another girl who lives just up the street, too, who goes to your high school. She's supposed to be very nice, too. Everyone said so."

"What do you mean, *everyone*? We don't know anyone here, remember?"

"That's not exactly true, darling. I talked — at length — to the people we bought this house from. Very nice people. Very nice. They told me that we were in luck because of the nice girls across the street and up the road. I'm sure they can't wait to meet you."

"Goody," I said.

I didn't know which was worse: August with no one around other than my mother (because Dad was already working 24/7) and nothing to do but lie on my bed in my puke-pink bedroom with Skizz sleeping on my stomach missing Eliza, or starting a new school. Again.

"What are you going to wear?" Eliza wanted to know.

"I'm not sure," I said, though I'd been obsessing about it for days, trying and rejecting half a dozen different outfits, including movie-starlet-style cutoffs with a white button-down cinch-waist blouse, a vaguely Indian-looking printed silk maxi skirt with ankle boots and a black tank top (it was from the Gap, but it still looked great), and a black classic sixties one-piece mini with a silver zipper up the front, which I usually wore with red cowboy boots.

"*You?* Not sure? Since when are you not sure?"

"I know. But it's different here. For one thing, it's hot."

"Of course it's hot. It's summer."

"Yeah, but here it's sticky hot. Humid. Like the air is filled with spit."

"Gross," she said. Then: "I've got it! What about your leopard-spotted leggings with a big top?"

"You're not listening!" I said. "It's hot here! I'd boil to death. I'd turn into a puddle of leopard spots and someone would cut me up and use me as a floor rug."

"Well," she said, "at least you haven't lost your charming personality."

Precisely two, count them, two days before school started, Mom came barging into my puke-pink room saying: "You're invited to go across the street."

"Huh?"

"You heard what I said. I was out front watering the grass" — Mom was always watering the grass — "and I met our across-the-street neighbors. Not all of them, of course. The mother. Very nice. *Very*. Her name is Meryl. She was walking her dog. They're just back from the beach. Anyway, she — Meryl, the mother — said you should come over right now, that her daughter has been moping around ever since they got home from vacation and has been dying to meet you ever since she heard we were moving in."

"Dying to meet me?"

"She wants to meet you, okay? Which means that you're going."

I rolled my eyes in a way that I knew drove my mother stark raving mad.

"I told Meryl that you'd be there in ten minutes."

"Fine," I finally said, arching my back in such a way that Skizz had no choice but to jump up off of me the way he does when he knows he has to find another bed.

"*Now*," Mom said.

I looked down at myself. Earlier that day, I'd been helping Mom in the garden, and I was still wearing my help-Mom-in-the-garden clothes: a pair of too-big army fatigues with my San Francisco Gay-Straight Youth Alliance T-shirt.

"Like this?" I said, even though Mom never approves of anything I wear.

"Just go," she said.

"And what if I don't want to? What if this girl is a total queen of mean? Or a weirdo? Or hates short people?"

"For crying out loud, the two of you will probably be best friends."

Their house was maybe twice the size of ours, with rose-bushes out front and miles of flower gardens along the sides. It looked like the kind of house you see in a magazine: perfect. I'd already caught Mom leaning against the window and staring at it with an expression on her face that looked like a perma-nent sigh.

"I doubt it," I said.

"If you don't move your butt over there, I'll just have to invite the young lady to come over here." She looked like she was about to cry.

"Forget it, Mom," I said. "Nobody does that."

"Please?" she finally said. "For me?"

Dragging myself across the street, I met my neighbor Becka, who was, and this is the honest truth, absolutely beautiful. Black eyes. Black hair down past her waist. Her figure was perfect — like a model's. Not one ounce of blubber or extra anything on her, not anywhere. And her skin was tanned. She must have been six inches taller than me. She was wearing a blue sleeveless minidress and, even though it was hot, a pink-and-gray silk scarf with little flecks of green, so light it was as if it was made out of clouds: pink clouds, the kind that come out at sunset. We were standing in the enormous hallway, just inside her front door, surrounded by modern art. I felt like I'd landed inside the glossy scented pages of a high-end magazine.

"Hi," I said. "I'm . . ." And then, I swear to God, I didn't know what to say, not with this Becka girl staring down at me with her black-black eyes and perfect straight black hair and golden — as in honey-colored — skin. "Um," I said.

"Hi, Um," Becka said.

"No," I said. "My name's not 'Um.' I was just —"

"Kidding," she said. Then, when I didn't say anything, she said: "Cat got your tongue?"

We stood there like that for a little while, under the chandelier, and then she said: "Where are you from?"

"All over."

"I've never heard of Allover. Is it in Europe?"

"What?"

"I went to Paris in July. It was *très, très jolie*!"

"Huh?"

"To study. I was at the University of Paris. *Je l'ai aimé*."

"Nice," I said.

"No," she said. "Not Nice. I was in Paris."

"Huh?"

"*Nice*. It's a city in the South of France. But it's not nearly as *jolie* as Paris."

"Oh." I felt like a moron. Becka was staring at my Gay-Straight Youth Alliance T-shirt as if it were coated in bird doo.

"I'm not gay," I blurted out.

"Who said you were?"

"Not that I have a problem with gay people."

"Cool? I guess?"

"Because you were staring at my shirt."

"I don't generally notice people's T-shirts."

"Oh," I said. I was getting stupider by the second.

"Are you hungry? Want some juice or something?"

"I'm fine."

"Do you like New Jersey?"

"We only just got here."

"Are you going into tenth?" she said.

"Yup."

"Me, too. But I'm going to try to do eleventh and twelfth together, next year. I already have extra credit, from the summer program I did. In Paris. I only need nine more credits to be able to graduate early."

"I used to live in Germany," I blurted out.

"Was it *très jolie*?"

I just stood there staring at her with my mouth wide open like a dead fish's, while Becka stood tall and regal and tan and terrifying, smiling down at me with her terrifying black eyes, her left hand playing with her pink-and-gray scarf.

Me, I'm more in the short and not-exactly-thin category. Plus my hair? It's red, curly, and generally uncooperative, which suits my skin, which is white and freckly. (My mother used to tell me that I looked just like Bette Midler. Thanks, Mom.) My best feature is probably my eyes. I'm not ugly, it's just that I'll never be in the first or even the second rank of pretty girls. The best I could ever do was hold my place in the almost-second rank by wearing cool clothes and making sure that I didn't turn into a giant freckle. Versus girls like Becka, who are born knowing that they'll always be at the very top of the heap.

Trying not to do something completely and terrifyingly geeky, like drool on myself or trip, I gave her a little wave and, saying, "Well, nice to meet you," made my way out the door.

When I told Eliza about her, she said, "Yeah, but Becka's just one kid; they won't all be like that," which was freaky, because it was pretty much, word for word, the same thing Mom had said. Versus on the morning of my first day at Western High, when Eliza said (on Skype): "YOU LOOK HOT!" Actually, it was Eliza herself who had suggested the outfit, right down to what color fingernail polish I should wear (a pale aqua blue) and whether or not I should wear matching blue eye shadow. (No. Too much.) The one thing we agreed on, makeup-wise, was lip gloss. My lips look like pale worms without it.

The thing is, when you're the new kid in school, you have to show up on the first day looking like someone — because if you don't stake your claim to your *you*ness right off the bat, you'll not only be a solo-tard for at least several weeks, but also, you'll be an invisible one. Just another kid wearing a T-shirt and jeans and sandals, going the wrong way in the hallways. I knew I couldn't compete with Becka, and, like, why would I even try? She and I would never be friends. Even so, meeting Becka had had one positive effect on me: I became more determined than ever not to be one of those kids who fade into the woodwork, just one more Gap-swathed shadow with hair on top and sneakers on the bottom. In short, it was crucial that I establish my own brand. And if the dress I was wearing — as authentic, funky, and utterly original as anything I'd ever owned — didn't do it, then nothing would.

"Yeah." I grinned into the computer screen. Good old Eliza: She'd gotten up really early West Coast time to cheer me on. "Thanks to you."

"Yeah," she said. "But you're the one who's pulling it off."

Which is not at all what Mom said when, a minute later, I came down to breakfast. She didn't even smile. Instead, she looked at me, bit her upper lip, and said: "You're not wearing *that*, are you?"

I didn't answer. Instead, I very purposefully, and with as much muscularity as I could muster, rolled my eyes.

Because what I was wearing (thank you, Eliza) could not have been more utterly and astonishingly fabulous. It was: an authentic Scott Paper Caper dress in a black-and-white Mod pattern, cut very simply in the inverted V silhouette and falling to about two inches above my knee. Best yet, it had never been worn before I myself bought it at Treasure Chest Clothing. It was lightweight, it was comfortable, it looked great, and best of all, it was the real deal. How it had survived since 1960-whatever, I have no clue, but there it was, hanging among other brightly colored Mod dresses at Treasure Chest, and the minute I saw it, I had to have it.

Had. To.

And when I pulled it over my head and saw myself reflected in the store's old-fashioned standing mirror, I knew that it had been waiting for me all those years, as if, instead of me choosing *it*, it had chosen *me*. In it, I not only looked slightly angelic — but in this retro rock-and-roll way, like maybe back in the day I'd dated a rock guitarist — but also astonishingly slim. The white of the white paper set off my reddish hair so that it glowed, and the lightness of the material made me feel that I was incapable of sweating. I figured that even my father, seeing me in it, would have to look up and admire me. Except, of course, that he was out of town on a business trip.

Even so, the dress was a miracle, giving me a deep inner coolosity that I didn't otherwise have. An alluring but friendly self-confidence. A hip-hop knowingness to my otherwise every-teen stride.

"Let's go," Mom said, grabbing her car keys so she could drive me as she does every year on the first day of school. We rode in silence until we were two blocks from school and she said: "You know, my mother had one of those things. It ripped the first time she sat down in it."

"Uh-huh."

"You know that those things can catch on fire, right? That's why they went out of style. Fire hazard. Look it up if you don't believe me. By the time I was a teenager it was all peasant blouses and platform shoes and blue jeans."

"Am aware."

"Have a great first day of school," Mom said, lunging over to give me a kiss. "You'll see. It's going to turn out great."

It was the worst day of my life. The. Worst. Day. And trust me, I've had plenty of worst days, not to mention plenty of practice being new.

This is how it went:

First period I had English. Everything was going okay until the teacher gave us an in-class assignment to write three paragraphs about any book we'd recently read. "Pen to paper, students," she said as kids started groaning. "Pen to paper!"

"Hey, what about I use some of this paper right here?" some genius said, poking me in the back with — I guess it was his finger, since my dress didn't tear.

"Get over it," the teacher continued. "Because in this class we're going to have a daily practice of putting your thoughts down on paper."

"That's exactly what I said!" the same finger-jutting joker said, this time patting me a little on the back like I was a pony. I turned around. He wasn't even looking at me, but rather, beaming to the laughter of the class. He had a huge nose and glasses and skin so pale that it looked see-through, but he didn't seem to know he was anything but the world's funniest kid.

So. Not. Funny.

Second period I had chemistry, only because I was the only new kid in class, no one chose me to be their chemistry partner, something that I observed from behind as all the popular kids (you could tell by the way they high-fived each other) partnered up. I had to sit there feeling stupid while the teacher *assigned* me a chemistry partner: John, who was the only other kid left unclaimed after the partner-picking session was over. Wonder why. Maybe it was the eyeliner he was wearing? Or his green-and-pink-striped hair? Or his neofascist T-shirt? Or his tattoos? Or perhaps merely the way he was sitting, just behind me, hunched up over a notebook, by turns scribbling furiously and flicking his pen back and forth like a drumstick. I tried not to hold his hyper-funk-nihilist-grunge-gender-blended-macho look against him, but it didn't help when, preliminaries over, I had to get up to sit next to him at the table he'd already claimed in the far left corner of the room, and he leaned in to say: "Where are you from, anyway — Planet Toilet Paper?"

I tried not to take it personally — after all, he was a guy, as was the finger-jutting jerk from English. Because, and not to put too fine a point on it, as far as I was concerned, in general guys, while occasionally cute, were basically several layers of evolution behind girls. My mom kept telling me that eventually they catch up, but so far I'd seen little evidence of it. "Your father was a teenage boy once upon a time, too," she'd say, which didn't exactly boost her argument.

Just when I was figuring that things had to improve, along comes third period — American History — and, just my luck, there was Becka, sitting next to another extremely pretty girl. Both girls sat with their right legs crossed over their lefts, and as I glanced their way I could see Becka give the other girl one of those subtle, fleeting lip curls that can only mean one thing: They've already been talking about you. Everything about Becka — from her new, simple white button-down blouse, to her perfect pencil skirt, to her toenails, painted a perfect, soft pink, and her sandals, which were flat and excellent, with silver straps — said that she was better, more *expensive*, and classier than other girls, that she was special, a cut above, headed for the heights. Around her neck hung that same delicate pink-and-gray scarf that she'd been wearing when I met her, which she fingered on and off as if it were a talisman. Becka's sidekick was more interesting, or at least she was in terms of sartorial sensibility. First off, her long brown hair was plaited into two perfect braids, so long and silky they were like tassels, and as for her outfit, which was so fabulous I glowed with envy, especially as I knew that, with my shape, I'd never be able to pull something like it off, it was:

On top, a silky blouse with lace, like a nightie.

On bottom, cutoff jeans with fraying ends that came to just above her knees.

On her feet, bright-pink All Star high-tops.

Actually, the more I looked, the more I realized that Sidekick's nightgown-style blouse was in fact a very short nightie, which was something that even Eliza, the queen of creative castoffs, had never tried. But, unlike Eliza, Becka and her PJ-wearing pal were both the kind of high school beauties, tall and elegant as swans, who intimidated grown-ups, so much so that every time the teacher happened to direct his attention toward them, he stretched his neck away from his collar, like he was choking.

Watching him was painful. But otherwise he seemed to know what he was talking about, and the class passed quickly, with nary a snarly comment thrown my way. And then Becka happened. All over again. Lucky me.

"Hey, Um! This is Robin," she said as I was making my way toward the door at the end of class. Then, turning to Sidekick/Robin, she said: "Um just moved in across the street."

"Nice to meet you," the girl said, clearly not meaning it.

"I'm Justine," I said.

"Can I ask you something?" Sidekick said.

"Sure."

"What are you wearing?"

I looked down. "A paper dress. It's an original."

"I think it got leaked on," she said.

I looked down to inspect but didn't see anything.

"In back," she said. "Like, all over. Unless it's part of the design?"

"Um's from San Francisco," Becka said. "She's very original."

"I still don't see it," I said.

"It's all the way in back," Sidekick said, "just below your shoulders."

"Maybe you can cover it up with paper towels?" Becka said. "No one would even notice."

Which is when I felt my face go on fire, and worse, began to sweat, soaking my astonishing dress in blobs of dark stain.

This was so not working out the way I had envisioned it.

So.

Not.

Lunch was next, so I had time to run into the girls' room, where, craning my neck around, I saw it: splattered from my shoulder to my waistline were blobs of blue ink. It was then that I remembered my chemistry partner flicking his pen back and forth while I sat in front of him, at the next-to-closer-to-the-blackboard table, before the teacher put us together as lab partners. He probably did it on purpose, the jerk. I tried to blot it out, but it only made things worse. Now I really *did* look like I was wearing a giant piece of toilet paper.

I was so upset I nearly cried, but didn't. For one thing, I don't cry. For another, there was another girl in the bathroom. Because it's bad enough to cry, but to cry in front of a total stranger, on the first day of school, in the girls' room? NEVER. Plus, I recognized her from chemistry class. She was one of the girls in the front row and had instantly gotten teamed up with some big jock with the kind of all-American looks that belong on cereal boxes.

"Hey," the girl said as she bent to wash her hands in the sink next to mine.

"Hey."

"Cool dress," she said.

"It's paper."

"It is?"

She herself was wearing shorts and a loose top with sandals. She had straight brown shoulder-length hair, muscular arms, and a figure like a hip-hop star — not thin but not fat, either, which, with her height, she totally pulled off. Also, she had a set of perfect big white teeth, and she was smiling at me with them like she was in a toothpaste commercial. In short, this was a girl who *knew* she was pretty and always had. She was probably dating the captain of the football team. She was probably best friends forever with Becka and Robin, and was already planning on telling them about the new girl with the paper dress.

"I don't think I've ever seen a paper dress before," she said, still smiling, but smiling like she didn't mean it, in a way that let me know she thought I was a loser.

"Well," I said, "later." Because, as I exited the girls' room and emerged back into the chaos of the hallways, two things were obvious: first, that Toothpaste Smile girl thought I was a freak, and second, that I'd landed in an entirely different fashion universe from the one I'd come from in San Francisco.

One thing I knew for sure was that if even one more kid said something nasty about my dress I'd be in actual danger of actually crying. Already I could feel the hot burn of tears behind my eyeballs, but I pushed them back with this kind of cranial-sucking-in movement I've perfected, and went looking for a place I could sit where I wouldn't be totally alone or, even worse, unwanted and out of place at some table reserved for this or that clique.

For the first time that day, I was in luck. At a table with a total geek (complete with the too-big tortoiseshell glasses and the sticking-up hair); a couple of vaguely bored-looking girls peering suspiciously at the contents of their lunch bags; a chubby, very pale girl talking with her hands; a girl done up in the classic low-key tomboy uniform of jeans and T-shirt with the classic sassy short hair style, whose one sign of fashion flair was the thin gold bangles she wore on her right arm; and another girl in pure pale-blue prep, there was an open spot at the very end, a seat-gap's length from anyone else. If this wasn't a nonclaimed table, nothing was.

"Hi," I said, sitting down and making a little space for myself with my tray, which I hoped would show that I wasn't trying to elbow in on anyone's lunch routine.

"You new?" Tomboy Girl asked me.

"Just moved here."

"Yeah? Where from?" This time she smiled, lips curling up like she was actually interested.

"San Francisco."

"Must be nice in San Francisco."

"Yup."

"I'm Ann," she said, flashing a grin, which instantly revealed killer cheekbones and dimples. She was built tiny, like a ballerina, and her beautiful skin was the beautiful color of oak. As she reached for her milk, the bangles on her arm made a tinkling sound. I don't know why, but I liked her at once.

"I'm Justine," I said, picking up half of my sandwich.

"Justine, you know you can't eat the food here? Because it'll, like, it's so disgusting, it'll give you cooties — the double cooties."

"Oops," I said, stopping myself midbite.

At that, all the girls giggled.

"Go ahead and eat it," a second girl said. "As usual, Ann's being a tad dramatic."

"You sure?"

"I mean," she said, "it might not be gourmet, but it won't make you sick."

"If you say so," I said.

Then the first girl, Ann, turned toward me and, with the smile still on her face, said: "What's that dress you're wearing? Is that some San Francisco style or something?"

"It's a paper dress," I said it. "Vintage."

"In other words, it's old, right?"

"From about 1968, 1969."

"Is that, like, a trend out there?" the other girl said.

"It's more that I'm personally into the Mod look," I said, actually relaxing into the conversation as the girls beamed what looked like genuine welcome toward me.

But no sooner had I started to explain the difference between "Mod" specifically and "flower power" or "retro" in general, then the first girl, Ann — the one with the beautiful dark skin and ridiculous cheekbones — said: "And if it gets too hot, you can just rip a couple of holes in it and — voilà — instant air-conditioning!" Everyone cracked up.

My face was on fire all over again, so much so that I could feel the heat flaming out of my head and radiating all around my body. Too bad it didn't just incinerate me. It was all I could do to mumble a "Yeah, right" without choking on my turkey on whole wheat with lettuce and mayo.

I ran back into the bathroom, slammed the stall door closed, and called Eliza, whose phone, of course, wasn't on. Then I texted her: "New Jersey bites! I feel like I'm wearing a giant upside-down Dixie Cup!" After I pressed the SEND button I felt a little better, but not enough to stop me from feeling like the world's biggest idiot — a girl who wasn't only plump and pink and a misfit, but someone so desperate that she resorted to wearing clown clothes. After all, my own father barely paid attention to me.

Later, when Mom asked me how my first day of school went, I said what I always said: "Fine." Then I went upstairs, ripped my dress into shreds, and put them in the trash can. But at least I didn't cry.

I swear to God, my mother loves the dog more than she loves me. She calls her "darling" and makes up songs about how beautiful she is. Then, right in front of my face, she'll say: "And unlike some girls, you don't whine when I won't buy you hooker shoes, do you, Lucy?"

"Meryl, I'm almost sixteen. And they're not hooker shoes."

"You're nowhere near sixteen," my mother says, reaching for her ubiquitous can of Diet Coke. "And they are, too."

She's a therapist who sees patients, but mainly, she's made a career out of writing about me. Have you heard of the Daughter Doctor series by Meryl Sanders, PhD — *Navigating the Normal: Tears and Tantrums during the Teen Years,* or *Mothers and Daughters: The Forever Bond*? That's right: They're both hers. And I'm her star witness, her heroine, her guinea pig and protagonist all wrapped up into one. Someone to be dissected and put back together in the pages of her books. "But no one knows it's you!" she says when I ask her to write about something else.

"Not only do I always use my maiden name, but I never use your name at all. Not to mention that the mother-daughter bond is my expertise, and people deserve good, sound advice. Don't you agree?"

"No."

"Honey, I *am* you," she says. "I know you better than you know yourself."

Except she doesn't, not anymore. Yeah, maybe when I was little, and I could tell her everything, and she always knew what to say and how to make me feel better. But now? Forget it. It would end up in one of her books. Which is why, just to take the most prominent example, she doesn't know that while I was in Paris last summer, studying art and French at the University of Paris, I dated a twenty-year-old named Arnaud. When I was with him, it was as if my entire body was made out of magic. Like I glowed, and sparkled, and flew over the heads of ordinary people.

In addition to studying philosophy (and writing his thesis on Jacques Lacan), Arnaud is a poet. He even wrote poems about me. I can't remember how they all went, but here's a part I do remember: *Sa peau soyeuse comme la brume soyeuse/Ses yeux comme le ciel et comme le soleil . . .*

Which means: *Her silky skin like silky mist/Her eyes like sky and sun . . .*

Which sure beats, "My own daughter is a perfect example of a teenager when the unruly passions meet the unruly hormones, and our darling baby girls morph before our eyes into spastic legs, barbed remarks, and budding breasts." Gee, thanks, Mom. I love to be the butt of everyone's jokes.

"Ah, New York, city of dreams!" Arnaud said the first time we met, which was when we were standing in line at the ATM just outside my dorm. I was wearing my NYU T-shirt, so I guess he thought I was a student there. "One day I will go to New York," he said. "Perhaps you can show me around?" I didn't tell him that I lived in New Jersey with my family and was still in high school, but I figured that it was no big deal — after all, it was just a conversation in an ATM line.

"What are you studying?" he continued in English. "Art? Literature? Dance?"

"Art," I said, which was at least partially true. I didn't paint or draw or whatever, but I *was* taking a class on the early modernists, particularly Picasso. I'd already been to the Picasso Museum twice.

"You stay here?" he said, indicating the dorm I lived in with a nod of his head.

"*Malheureusement, oui,*" I said. (Which means: Unfortunately, yes.)

"So much better to have a place of your own, *non*?" he said.

"*C'est bon,*" — it's okay — I said.

As far as the dorm went, though, I really didn't have a choice. It was either live in the dorm, which I knew I was going to hate, or not go to Paris at all; that's how against it Meryl had been. All I can say is thank God for my father, because even though there are days when I don't get to see him all that much (he's a doctor and sometimes has to work long hours), he's always, as in *always*, on my side.

Which is why, in the end, Meryl agreed to let me go to Paris, because Daddo had said that he thought it would be good for me to study abroad, adding that it wouldn't hurt my college prospects any to improve my French.

So I was all set, and everything was *parfait* (perfect), except for one detail: I'd forgotten to pack my raincoat! I could have strangled myself, too, because not only did it rain ALL the time, but also, my raincoat wasn't just any old raincoat: It was this totally awesome Donna Karan that I got for my birthday after I'd begged for it for about a thousand years, and where better to wear something that awesome than Paris? As usual, though, if it hadn't been for Daddo, I never would have gotten it at all, because Meryl had been against it from the beginning. I know because I overheard them talking one night, with him saying, "But she'll probably wear it for ten years," and Meryl saying, "Do you have any idea how much you spoil that girl?" Daddo was just the best, though, and in the end, it had been Meryl who'd given it to me, saying that because I was special, she'd wanted to give me something special. Made of elegantly brushed black sateen, it flared out at the waist and had wide black velvet lapels and cuffs. I'd found it online and was instantaneously obsessed. I'd simply never seen a more beautiful piece of clothing. I was so angry at myself for having forgotten to pack it that I even told my roommate about it. Not that she could care. She studied 24/7 and went to bed by ten. She never said so, but I could tell she was jealous of me. Like when I started seeing Arnaud? All she could say was: "Isn't he kind of old for you?"

I loved Paris, though. I loved the wide boulevards and the old buildings and the way people stayed out late at night, talking and laughing. I loved being able to take the Metro everywhere and shopping at little outdoor stalls. And most of all I loved the sense that I was on my own, free to be myself without Meryl always watching me and breathing down my neck and checking to make sure I wasn't developing an eating problem or didn't have social anxiety disorder or ADHD or wasn't "experimenting" with drugs or all the other things that she loved — just LOVED — to write about.

"Ah, how I would like maybe to live among all the foreign women students!" Arnaud said, grinning a grin so wide that it made his dimples dance. I was like: *No way.* He was the most unbelievably gorgeous guy I'd ever seen! And there was something so charming about him, so — different. Not different as in weird, but different as in *special*.

Okay, I'll admit it: That very first time I met him, I fell madly in love with Arnaud. MADLY! But not in the gross high-school-crush way. Or like I was obsessed with him, sending thought waves toward him in the hopes that he'd hear them and ask me out. (Okay, maybe I was a little obsessed, but at least I didn't go around blabbing about how cute he was and how I just had to make him notice me.) I was in luck, though: Two days after we first met, there he was again, this time going into a used bookshop across the street from the university library. I waited a minute or two, then headed into the bookstore myself. It was dark and dusty inside, with sagging wood floors and a fan propped in the corner of the ceiling, waving the lit dust motes around. I spotted Arnaud three rows back and slowly made my way toward him — but not before I'd picked up a book on Picasso so he'd think my being there was just a coincidence.

"*Bonjour,*" he said as I rounded the corner. I looked at him like: *I'm sorry, but do I know you?* Then I smiled. "You're the guy from the ATM line, right?" I said (in French).

"And you're the girl from NYU," he said. "Someday, maybe I, too, will go there. To get my doctorate! In philosophy, no? In New York! Paris — she is beautiful, no? But New York is *America!*"

He was just so . . . well, I know it's a funny word to apply to a guy, but he was *beautiful.* Slim but not skinny, on the tall side, with light-brown curly hair, slightly freckled skin, and eyes the color of green sea glass. Plus, he had *style.* Not like a gay guy or a hipster or a self-styled bohemian, either: Arnaud's style was very casual, as if he'd picked his clothes up off the floor, not even noticing what they were, but at the same time, completely perfect. His faded jeans were rumpled; the cuffs of his white cotton button-down shirt were slightly frayed, rolled up to just beneath the elbow; and his expressive feet were in brown leather sandals. He carried a beat-up raincoat draped over his left arm, as if it were a cape.

The first time I went out with Arnaud, it started to rain, and there I was, again, kicking myself for having forgotten to bring my raincoat. As we ambled down the rue Danielle Casanova, though, I must have shivered, because the next thing I knew,

Arnaud was taking off his own coat and offering it to me. It was only when my left arm and side were inside the raincoat that I realized that he was still in it — that we were sharing the coat, each of us with one sleeve and one front flap. Because I'm so tall, it fit me perfectly. Arnaud noticed it, too, saying: *"Comment bien vous regardez dans mon manteau! Très belle."* (How well you look in my coat! Very nice.)

Inside, the lining was worn and warm, and it gave off a powdery fragrance, as if it had been absorbing the dusty fragrance of old books for years. It smelled, I realized, like *him*.

We laughed all the way to the café, and when we got there, I noticed people looking at us, smiling. It was like all of a sudden I'd become a movie star, an icon: someone who everyone recognized and wanted to know. It was as if I'd been injected with magic juice.

It wasn't just that Arnaud was cute, either. Lots of guys are cute. But Arnaud had a kind of grace and flourish that was so, so, so, so, so, so different from the stupid, adolescent boys at school and my dreadful, idiotic brat of a brother, who, by the way, thinks he's a drummer. Meryl and Daddo gave him a set of drums one year for Christmas because, in the words of my mother: "Danny needs a healthy way to get his energy out."

"Paris is so quiet in the summer," Arnaud murmured. "Everyone goes away."

"New York's like that, too. By August, it's dead."

"You need to come back in the fall or winter, when Paris is back to normal. When everyone returns. When there's life on the streets. In the summer? Nothing but tourists."

"Like me?" I said.

"No," he said, with a delicious, mischievous smile on his face. "You, a tourist? Never."

Before Arnaud, I'd never walked in the rain singing, never had someone recite poetry to me, never been to a Polish movie with, *mais oui*, French subtitles, never gone to a midnight movie, and never . . . well, you know. Not that we went all the way, or even close. But the truth — and I'm kind of embarrassed to admit it — is that I'd never really kissed anyone before. I mean, guys had lunged at me plenty of times, and I'd tried it, but basically they had all grossed me out. With Arnaud, though, it was different. Everything about him, from his handsome chin to the clean way his skin smelled to his shaved cheeks to the laugh lines at the corners of his mouth made me feel comfortable around him, *willing*. Still, I was nervous. I didn't want Arnaud to know how inexperienced I was. I didn't want him to know that my dad was the most old-fashioned father in the whole world, who'd grown up in a Costa Rican neighborhood going to church every other second, and that I still, on occasion, sat on his lap. Nor did I want him to know that my mother had made a career out of writing about my "adolescent years." After all, he thought I was already in college!

He took me to the rue Mouffetard, which has open-air stalls selling old books, sheet music, china, jewelry, everything. He took me to hear a lecture on the late work of Camus. (It was in French, so I didn't understand most of it.) He took me to his favorite spot on the Seine, where we watched the barges making their slow way. In another flea market — this one in the

Marais — we stopped at a stall that sold nothing but the most beautiful silk scarves, but even secondhand, I couldn't afford to buy one, even though I was dying to and tried on half a dozen of them, just for fun. So you can only imagine how amazing it was when, a few days later, Arnaud gave me most beautiful Hermès scarf I'd ever seen — pale pink, with tiny swirls of delicate grays and greens, wrapped loosely in crumpled brown paper, like he'd stuffed it in his pocket on the way back from the Marais market. As I turned it over in my hands, I noticed that on one end of the scarf was a tiny stain in the shape of a heart, and wondered if he'd seen it as well.

"You must have it," he said. *"Pour toi, la belle fille."*

"Where did you get it?" I wanted to know.

"It isn't important."

"But it's Hermès. It must have cost a fortune."

"Ah, but as you can see, it is not new."

"You went back to the flea market?" I asked.

"It is my secret," he said.

When he put it around my neck, it was like his fingers were angel wings. Right there on the street, we kissed.

Of course he wanted more. Every night, it was like a wrestling contest that would determine which of us would be in control of my buttons and zippers. But it was hard for me to explain why I didn't want to go further, especially since a part of me *did*. It's not that I wasn't grown-up enough, either: It was more that it was such a huge thing, and I wanted to make sure that he was *the one*. Of course, I could have blurted out the truth and told him that I was fifteen, but then what? Thank God that I'd had the foresight to edit my Facebook page, getting rid of certain embarrassing details like where I went to school, and defriending some of the undesirables who I didn't correspond with anyway. I could have taken the whole thing down, but I liked seeing what my friend Robin was posting now that she had gone wardrobe-wild and had (thanks to me) a fashion internship at Libby Fine Design. Finally I just said: "Arnaud, I'm Catholic!" Which was only half true, because though Dad's Catholic, Meryl's kind of nothing.

"I'm Catholic, too," he said, fingering my necklace. "Everyone in France is. This is all merely superstition, how we must stop what our bodies tell us to do. They try to control us with all this talk of sin."

"But . . ." I said, but then, when I couldn't explain, I'd kiss him even more. I'd kiss him and kiss him and kiss him. And then I'd leave to get back to the dorm in time for curfew.

On my very last day in Paris, I skipped my final lecture on Picasso's early cubist work to walk up to Montmartre with Arnaud. It was, of course, lovely. It was also, of course, raining. When at last we reached the very top, with its famous Basilica, it started to *pour*. As in *chats et chiens*. (Cats and dogs.) We dashed inside, where Arnaud, looking very serious, took off his raincoat, draped it over my shoulders, and whispered: "For you. To take home to America. You will wear this at NYU so you do not get wet. *Non?*"

"But what will you wear?" I said.

"That is why you must promise me that you'll return it to me in person."

"I promise," I said as he leaned into me for a kiss.

When I got back to New Jersey, my French was really good and my entire sense of myself had changed. For one thing, I realized that I could never, ever tell my mother anything personal again, because if she ever found out about Arnaud? I could just see her next book: *When Your Teen's First Romance Ties Her in Tangles: The Daughter Doctor's Guide to Unraveling the Knots*. I hung Arnaud's raincoat in my own closet — not in the coat closet downstairs, where anyone, such as my brat brother, might take it. I took my Hermès scarf out of my suitcase and, very carefully, I rewrapped it in tissue paper, putting it away in my underwear drawer as carefully as I could. I looked around my room, at my books, the photographs of Meryl and me together and of my friends from school, at my bed, with its white cover and brightly colored pillows, and wondered whose room it was. I may as well have been someone else entirely, a person who'd never heard of West Falls, let alone grown up there.

There were seven messages on my cell phone: five from Robin, one from my aunt Libby, and one from our old neighbor Mrs. Cleary, who'd just moved to Florida, asking me if I could come over to help her and Mr. Cleary pack. I called Robin back, but she was at her summer internship and couldn't talk. Then I called Aunt Libby, who isn't actually my aunt at all — she's my mother's cousin, and also my godmother, and also Libby Fine of

Libby Fine Design, where Robin was interning. Libby didn't answer, either. She was just about the most awesome person I'd ever known, and in fact had been the one to encourage me to study in Paris in the first place. The only mystery was how she and my utterly uncool mother were related.

Robin came over and told me all about how incredible her internship was, and then complained about the other intern, and then told me about her father, who was, like, always drunk, and then told me again about her internship. But the truth was? I just wasn't interested. Her life seemed so — *teenage drama*. Over the summer, she'd gotten into these really crazy clothing combinations, like wearing a silky cami with cutoff jeans and hiking boots, and wearing her hair like Pippi Longstocking, in two long, straight, tight braids, and while she talked, my brain just kept flipping back to Paris, and how juvenile she seemed compared to Arnaud. *Maybe*, I thought, *I should have gone further with him. . . .*

I was still thinking about Arnaud when, after what seemed like forever, Robin left. But I didn't even have time to Facebook him, because two minutes later the door opened and Lucy bounded in, with Meryl just behind, a glass of cherry soda in her hand. "Guess what?" she said. "We're getting new neighbors. The word is that they've got a daughter around your age. Maybe the two of you will hit it off."

"I doubt it."

"What kind of attitude is that?" she said, putting the cherry soda down on my desk.

It was a stupid thing — the cherry soda, I mean — but when I was a kid, it was my favorite, a treat that Meryl let me have when I was feeling down or had a cold or just because, and even now Meryl kept it on hand for me for when she thought I was "in a mood." For one long, weird second, I saw her as I had when I was little, and she was the most wonderful, understanding mother in the world.

Then she again spoke: "I brought you your favorite."

"I can see that."

"You seem so bored."

"Meryl, it's called living in the suburbs."

"So what I thought was that you, me, and Danny could go to the shore tomorrow or the next day and Dad can join us over the weekend. What do you say?"

What should I say? That I couldn't wait to go to the shore like we did every year, gee whiz, yippee! Maybe I could get some cotton candy and meet a lifeguard! And we could drink cherry soda until we were sick to our stomachs! Instead, I said:

"Does Danny have to come, too?"

"Yes."

"Why can't he stay here with Daddo?"

"Because he can't, that's why. Your father works, for one thing."

My father is a neurologist. That's how he and Meryl met: in med school, before Meryl dropped out and decided to get a degree in clinical psychology instead.

"You work, too."

"I know I work, Becka. But it's August, and I took the entire month off, like I do every year."

"I still don't understand why the Little Jerk has to come."

"Because he does," she said. "And don't tell me that your father can watch him, because he can't. And don't call him 'the Little Jerk.'"

"Danny should be muzzled."

She shrugged. "What will it be? Do you want to go to the shore with us, yes or no? Because since you've come back from Paris, all you've done is mope around, and I, for one, think you could use a little sand and sea."

I didn't mean to be a brat about it, but after Paris, the shore was *lame*. I mean, I *know* how lucky I am to have all the nice stuff I (we) have: nice clothes, good schools, the house in West Falls plus the cottage in Atlantic Cove. My parents rented it out for June and July, and we always went in August, with Daddo going back and forth, depending on how much work he had. Even so, *the Jersey shore*? I was supposed to be all happy about that?

"Oh, good!" Meryl said, even though I hadn't answered. "We'll have such fun!"

By which she meant that she'd try to turn me into a ten-year-old all over again so she and I could go looking for pretty seashells together, or collect seaweed and dry it in the sun, or even (her favorite) ride our bikes to the ice-cream store! She just wouldn't give up. Like, after we got to the shore? No sooner had I put on my bikini, which was the *exact same one* I'd had last year, than Meryl said: "You're not wearing that, are you?"

"It's a bathing suit. I'm not wearing it to school."

"What about your little brother?"

"What about him?"

"Don't you think it's a little — inappropriate — to wear that when he's around?"

"You're sick in the head, Meryl. He's my *brother*."

"And I'd really prefer that you don't call me Meryl."

"All right, Mother."

She crossed her arms, the way she does when she's relenting. Then she said: "All the literature points to girls your age not knowing how provocative you can be."

"Jesus, Mom!"

It was worse when my father wasn't with us, and I missed him. Because at least when he was with us she didn't tell me what to do and how to act *all* the time. He was so cute, my daddo was, with thick black hair that he was always batting away, and a slight Spanish accent from having grown up in his mainly Latino neighborhood in Yonkers. I secretly thought that Mom was jealous of him — because he'd finished medical school and was now a doctor, whereas she was just a therapist.

"Just make sure you wear a cover-up," she now said.

When she was gone, I logged on to Facebook and went to Arnaud's page to look at his photo albums. My favorite was the picture of him wearing "my" raincoat and a floppy hat, and holding a book. There was a picture of the two of us together, too, but it had been taken by one of the merchants at the flea market and was blurred. Another picture was of him skiing. Finally, I went to the beach and let the sun beat down on me.

When I emailed him later that day, all I wrote was: "I'm at the sea with my family. Miss you!" (Except, of course in French.)

And he emailed me back: "*Oui, oui, la belle mer! Beau, la mer magique . . .*"

I'm not an idiot: I was aware that I was only fifteen and that the idea of my sailing off to Paris to live in some kind of happily-ever-after land with Arnaud was a fantasy. But I also knew that, somehow, Arnaud and I would be together again, that the two of us had something special.

So how weird was it that the first thing I did when we got back from the shore was go to my room, open my closet, and press my nose into Arnaud's raincoat? It was the only thing that made me feel, if only for a second, that I was with him again, walking hand in hand down winding lanes.

The Little Jerk barged into my room. "Want to hit some balls with me?"

"No, I don't want to hit some balls with you. I'm busy."

"Busy doing what? Why are you smelling Daddo's raincoat?"

"For your information, it's not Daddo's raincoat. And I wasn't smelling it."

"I saw you."

"You saw nothing."

"Mom says you're grumpy. She says that you must be getting your period."

"What?"

"What's a period?"

"Get out of here before I bash your brains in." I meant it, too. I was bigger than he was — a lot bigger — and perfectly capable of breaking his nose. In case he didn't believe me, I turned to him, my hand balled into a fist.

"I guess I'll Google it," he yelled as he ran out.

The next day, Meryl popped her head into my room and announced that the new girl — the one whose family moved into the Cleary's house across the street — would be coming over soon.

"No," I said.

"Why on earth not? Don't you want to meet this girl? From what I hear, the family's lived all over, even in Europe. She's probably very interesting, not to mention that she's exactly your age. Don't you at least have some curiosity about her?"

"I'm busy," I said, though I wasn't. It was more that I just wasn't in the mood. I'd just gotten an email from Arnaud, and it made me feel farther away from Paris than ever. What was I doing in a place where what passes for sophistication was having your own free-range chickens so you could have free-range eggs and the most exciting thing that ever happened was the annual 10K road race?

Here's what Arnaud had written to me (in French, of course): "I was walking down the lane where we spotted that elderly man — the one who was singing *La Vie en Rose*? And I thought: Oh, summer! Oh love! Oh, *la rose*!"

And I was like: *Oh my God*. Because *of course* I remembered that man, and his scratchy-scratchy voice, and the single red rose he wore in the buttonhole of his black jacket, and how Arnaud and I stood watching him, as if joined together in one long sigh. I was just about sick with wanting to be back in Paris with Arnaud when Meryl started calling up the stairs for me to come down right away because "Justine our new neighbor from across the street is here!"

I could have killed her. Instead, I draped my Hermès scarf around my neck and went downstairs.

The girl was just standing there, looking out of place and like she'd never been inside an actual house before, kind of gawking at the art, and wearing *the* PC tomboy uniform: tight black rainbow T-shirt with "Gay-Straight Youth Alliance" written on it and baggy, badly fitting pants of a style that I can't even call a style. And her hair: like a halo — no, more like an explosion — of reddish-orange curls. Eyebrows so thick she practically had a unibrow, and hadn't she ever heard of *deodorant*? I mean, who was Mother kidding? Does she not know me *at all*?

The girl stared at my scarf, like she *knew*. And even though I was angry at Meryl for forcing her on me, for a moment I got this feeling that, in some weird way, at least the girl wasn't the typical suburban lamiac who can't think of anything better to do than get her nails done or organize a fun run. Sure, I hated her clothes, but at least she had something original going on, something kind of funky and fun, even if it was hideous. But then an expression like a cow's came over her face.

"Hi, my name is . . . um . . . er . . . um," she said.

"Hi, Um," I said. And, yeah, I know it was a kind of mean thing to say. Okay: It was a *horribly* mean thing to say. But it just kind of popped out of my mouth, and once it was out, it was *out*, and I didn't know how to make it seem like a joke. Plus, there she was, just staring at me, like I was a prized pig, when I hadn't even invited her over to begin with! *Meryl had*. Not only that, but I knew from the sweeping sounds that were coming from the kitchen that Meryl was straining her ears to hear every word. As I stood there in the hall, with Meryl probably listening in, and the girl looking at me with her piercing bright-blue eyes, I felt like the world's biggest spaz.

When the girl finally left, I went back to my room to write back to Arnaud. I told him that I loved the scarf and, once fall came, I'd be wearing his raincoat all the time. (I didn't tell him that I'd been *smelling* it, though. I mean, that would have been *pathetic*!) Then the Little Jerk started drumming, *again*, and I went down to his room and told him that if he didn't quiet down I'd personally beat the living crap out of him. Then he went running down the stairs to tattle on me. Next thing I know, Meryl was at my door with a glass of cherry soda, saying that she "wanted to talk." But I didn't want to talk. I wanted to get on the next plane to Paris!

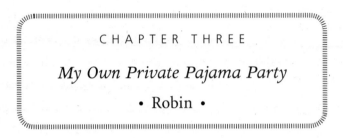

Since I was little and playing dress-up with Becka, I've wanted to be in the fashion business. Which is why, when Becka's aunt Libby (who isn't really her aunt) said I could work for her as an intern over the summer, I almost wet my pants. Which were, by the way, the cutest things ever, even though they weren't strictly pants, in the usual sense of the word. They were bright blue silky PJ bottoms covered with big pink flowers that I'd bought on sale at Anthropologie, which I wore with a black tank top and belted with a wide bright-pink belt.

What had happened was, at the end of freshman year, I'd kind of run up the charges on my mother's AmEx card — *which she'd said I could use!* — shopping online. When she discovered my MISTAKE — which was a MISTAKE and NOT ON PURPOSE, LIKE I TOLD HER A THOUSAND TIMES — first she yelled at me, then she told me that my interest in fashion wasn't healthy, then she cut off my funds, and then she went out and got me a summer job working at the Temple nursery school, even though

I don't much like kids and never have even though I've been babysitting since I was twelve. Anyway, ever since my mother stopped financing my fashion, as in *not a penny more, young lady, until you prove to me that I can trust you again*, I'd been forced to become more creative when it came to pulling a look together, and because I was growing, I couldn't simply rely on last year's fashion crop.

Of course, my mother gave me an incredibly hard time about my new look, but that was nothing compared to the hard time she gave me about my internship.

"You simply have to call Libby Fine back and tell her that you can't take the internship" is what she told me when I burst into the house with my news. "And the sooner you do so, the easier it will be."

"No way," I said. "Forget it. You know how many girls would kill for the chance to intern at Libby Fine?"

"Maybe next year," Mom said. "That is, *if* you can demonstrate the maturity to handle something like that."

"I have plenty of maturity," I said. "The only person who can't see it is you."

"Except that you still owe me four hundred dollars from your last little shopping spree, remember? And now you think it's a good idea to work around fashion all day long? Think about it: First of all, when it comes to clothes, you have no self-control. Second, I already told Mrs. Shankle that you'll help out at Temple, and third, fourth, fifth, and sixth, you'd have to get up early in the morning every morning, which you hate, to schlep into the city, where you won't make a dime, and at the end of the summer you'll still owe me four hundred dollars, and then you'll want to buy new clothes for school, and I'll have to say no, and by the way, you just can't wear what you're wearing to school. Or to anywhere. And certainly not into the city every day! You look homeless."

"For your information," I said. "This look is totally hot right now. It was in *Teen Vogue* last month."

"I don't care if it was on the front page of the *New York Times*. You're not going to take that fashion internship."

When I refused to back down, Mom turned on the guilt machine, saying that she was worried about me and didn't want to see me eaten alive in an internship that usually went to college students. She pointed out that both my twin brother and our cousin, John, had lined up paying jobs over the summer. Then she and Dad got into this giant fight, with Dad telling Mom that she was a hover mother, and Mom saying that someone had to be a grown-up, and they went on and on like that for a while until finally my twin brother, Ben, burst into the room in drag. And not just any old drag, either, but my own favorite skirt and blouse, and a blond wig that he'd probably swiped from the drama department at school. Ben liked to "borrow" things.

"Surprise!" he said.

"I need a drink," Dad said.

"You always need a drink!" Mom said as Dad poured himself a glass of red wine, which is usually what he drinks if he drinks during the day, saying that if everyone in France and Italy can have a glass of wine at lunchtime, then he can, too.

"That's why she's out of control with my credit cards and with this crazy idea she has about going into the fashion business — not because I'm going overboard, but because you have no self-discipline about anything, obviously. You have no will-power, none at all!" Then she looked at me. "As for you, young lady, you need to exert self-control."

"I said I'll pay you back!" I said. "Can't you just be happy for me for a change?"

"I am happy for you," she said. "But fashion? What kind of future could you have in fashion? It's such a grueling world, too. I just don't understand why you'd rather have an internship than a paid position at the Temple nursery school."

"Because I don't much like kids?"

"Oh, and by the way, the Gersons called. They need you to babysit for most of Sunday. I told them you could."

"What? No way."

"You need the money."

"Those kids are *brats*."

"I thought you liked them."

"Last time I babysat them, the little boy put Cheez Whiz in my hair."

"How are you going to pay me back if you turn down pay-ing jobs?"

So I babysat the Gerson brats, and the little boy kicked his next-oldest sister and then threw a bar of soap at me, and the two little girls didn't want to do anything but have me play hide-and-seek with them all day, and then Mr. and Mrs. Gerson didn't get back until almost two hours later than they said they'd be back, and then, as he drove me back home, Mr. Gerson said that he was a little short and would sixty dollars be okay (even though he owed me more like seventy-five), and of course I had to say yes because they were friends of my parents.

"Thanks, Robin," he said, handing me three twenties, and the next day I went back to Anthropologie and bought a second pair of sleepwear trousers — swishy gray loungers with a pattern of small black butterflies, which, thank the Lord, were on total markdown. I needed something incredibly great to wear on my first day at Libby Fine, and what could be more simultaneously outré and fabulous than wearing PJs and passing them off for cutting-edge? Even if my mother said what I knew she was going to say, which was: "I simply can't permit you to wear that to the city."

I swore to myself right then and there that I'd show her — I'd show them all — that I could handle my internship just fine, in my own way, with my own style! Even so, I *was* kind of nervous walking into Libby Fine my first day wearing loose bell-bottom pajama pants (with a skinny black tank top and a simple gold chain), but Libby was like: "Fashionista!"

Libby had warned me that I'd be doing the grunt work, but it didn't matter: I totally loved my surroundings — the way the bolts of cloth looked stretched out on the designing tables and how the phones were always ringing with orders or cancellations or some buyer who wanted an appointment to see the new winter line. I didn't mind running for coffee or taking notes, either, because it meant that I could be part of things a little, listening in at meetings and things like that. A couple of people who worked there said that they didn't even *believe* that I was still in high school. They said that I seemed so much older, more mature.

Which is the REVERSE of what I got at home. I'd only been at Libby Fine for one week when, on Saturday afternoon, Dad looked up from the newspaper and said: "There's an article in here about how hard it is to get into college — the numbers are astonishing."

"So?"

"So I hope you understand that this fashion thing is just that — fashion."

"You must really think I'm stupid."

"No, but I do think that you put frivolity before your schoolwork."

"Earth to Dad? It's summer vacation."

"Is that how you talk to your father?" he said, going red around his temples and eyes.

"What'd I say?"

"My father would have slapped me into Connecticut if I'd used a tone of voice like that."

"But I didn't *say* anything."

"You're being fresh."

"What's your problem?" I said. A mistake — a big, big mistake, and as soon as I'd said it, I realized that now Dad would get even angrier, even scarier, even more red in the face. I didn't know whether to fall at his feet and apologize or run for the hills. All I knew was that, once again, I'd crossed over the invisible line that you can't cross over without getting in a boatload of trouble. I knew he'd never hit me — he never hit anyone — but even now he was pulling himself up from the upholstered chair and crossing the room toward the liquor cabinet, his right hand balled up into a fist and his jaw quivering.

A second later, from the next room, we heard a howl, and my brother stomped in along with our extremely strange cousin, John. John was hopping up and down on the toes of his black-Converse-clad feet. Ben had his head in his hands, saying, "They blew it! They had three men on base and they blew it! What's the point? I mean, can someone just tell me what the point is?"

Dad and I stared at him. He'd recently grown from being shorter than I am to almost as tall as Dad, and was so skinny that he looked like a stick with a head stuck on top of it. Or like someone had come along when he was sleeping and pulled on either end, stretching him like a piece of gum. Also, he has a huge nose. He went around telling people that the reason he's so much smarter than I am is that when we were born, I didn't get enough oxygen.

"Have you started in on any of *your* summer reading, Ben?" Dad said.

"Yo," he said. "No worries, Popster. It's a done deal, yo."

Which was exactly like Ben, because even though he was a goofball, and had a big mouth, and looked like a giant grasshopper, he was so smart that everyone thought of him as being one of the smartest kids at school, and pretty much always had. He was already writing for the school newspaper, including editorials, which everyone thought was this big, huge deal and an indication that he was slated for greatness.

"How about you, John? Have you done yours yet?"

"Most of it," John said.

Dad raised an eyebrow.

"That's more like it," he said. Meanwhile, Mom must have heard the commotion, because she was walking into the living room, saying: "Are you going somewhere, Robin?"

"Just to meet Polly at Starbucks," I said. I've known Polly almost as long as I've known Becka, since second grade. We were Brownies and then Girl Scouts together. But you'd have thought that I'd said I had a date with a terrorist.

"Do you think that's a good idea?"

"Any reason why it wouldn't be?"

"Can you afford it?"

"We're just going to Starbucks."

"But I thought you and Polly weren't really friends anymore."

"Mom? I like Polly, okay? I always have. And just in case you haven't noticed, Becka's in Paris."

"Starbucks is right next to Daphne's Designer Digs."

"So?"

"So you have a little shopping problem. And Daphne's has beautiful things."

"You're saying you don't trust me."

"I didn't say that. Did I say that?"

"No," Ben said.

"Then what did you say?"

When she didn't answer, I left — but just as the door was shutting behind me, Mom opened it again, and, facing me on our front stoop, said: "You can't go out like that."

"Like what?"

"Like that. Like you just got out of bed. You look — I don't know. Like a drug addict."

"Maybe I *am* a drug addict!" I said. "Maybe I'm buying drugs using your credit card!"

There was a pause. Then: "I think you need to talk to someone."

"What?"

"I think you should see a therapist — someone who you could really talk to. Someone who might be able to help you sort out your problems."

"Which are . . . ?"

"You have a shopping issue. Don't wince at me like that. You have a problem, and the sooner you face it the better. This internship thing can only make it worse."

"Mom! I don't even spend a lot of money! What am I *supposed* to wear? Ancient baggy jeans and ugly tops and hideous shoes like yours?"

What was the use? As I turned around and started walking down the driveway, I could hear Dad saying something from inside the house, Mom yelling something back, and the door slamming. Even from halfway up the hill, I could hear the two of them fighting.

But I loved my internship. I hardly ever saw her, but when I did, Libby always said something nice to me or complimented my fashion sense. Everyone else was nice to me, too, saying that I had a good work ethic and a great sense of style. Then Emma Beth came.

Emma Beth, who was already halfway through college, was the *real* summer intern. The first time we met, she looked me up and down, half smiled, and said: "Interesting choice."

"What?"

"Your outfit."

I was wearing, you have to love it, my brother's extralong blue-and-white-striped cotton pajama top, cinched in with a fat black shiny belt that I'd gotten at Target, so the total effect was of updated shirtwaist dress.

"So *you're* the one who got here because you're related to Libby," she continued.

"Well, not exactly," I started to explain, but she cut me off.

"You're in high school?"

"Yes, but —"

"See you around."

Emma Beth had a doll's light-blue eyes and white, petal-shaped face, with hair cut in a forties-style pageboy, and even though she really wasn't that pretty, she had a certain flair, a certain ultradetached attitude that made you notice her. Her look was strictly office-pro: pencil skirts that hugged her bottom half, and a variety of crisp white shirts, with wedges or high heels and ropes of pearls: classy, well-tailored, feminine, and, obviously, expensive. No castoffs or thrift shops or make-it-yourself for her, and sure, I wouldn't have minded having a wardrobe filled with several variations of houndstooth skirts and white blouses, but since I couldn't even afford the knockoff look that you can get at Old Navy, what chance did I have? And she didn't look like a junior lawyer in her clothes, either, not with the occasional rhinestone poodle jewelry that she wore to add whimsy. Which is how Libby put it, anyway, when she stormed into the design room and announced that, thanks to Emma Beth, she wanted to launch an entire new line, featuring poodles. "Such whimsy!" she said in front of the whole staff, myself and Emma Beth included.

Speaking of poodles, by the time I got home, I was feeling like dog doo. For one thing, I was covered with sweat — the city had gotten hot and steamy, the way it does in July, with that New York garbage smell wafting up from the gutters and the acidic burnt-coal smell of the subway grinding up from the vents. With Becka in Paris, and Polly busy with swimming (she's superathletic), and everyone else at summer camp or whatever, I had no one I could really talk to. Dad was in a terrible mood as usual, barely grunting at me when I came home. Plus, I had a babysitting job that night.

Mrs. McCloskey was flat-out nuts, a super–control freak of the freakishly freaky variety. She was waiting for me by the door with a list of instructions, including exactly how much TV the older kid, Tommy, could have (one hour, and it had to be something on PBS), and exactly what he and his brother, the dreadful Matt McCloskey, could have for dessert: a single gingersnap cookie with half a pear. As for dinner itself, she'd already made it: brown rice and peas with melted cheese on top, with a salad.

Matt put his on the counter, grabbed a box of Cheerios and a jar of applesauce, and ate three bowlfuls. Tommy ate his dinner but then proceeded to convince his brother to go downstairs to the playroom to have a burping contest, which he won, but only because Matt got sick and ran to the bathroom, where he threw up all his applesauce and Cheerios, mainly, but not all, into the toilet.

But I just couldn't do it. . . . I couldn't clean up his vomit without getting sick myself, so I closed the door and told the boys not to go in there and to only use the upstairs bathroom. Both boys had lost interest in the burping contest, so we settled in for a nice long night of *Frizzy's Lunch Lab* and *Noah Comprende*, which I alone could *comprende*. (I'm in Spanish III.) I finally couldn't stand it anymore and switched to reruns of *Friends* and then *One Tree Hill* while the boys whined that they were bored and threatened to tell on me. At which point I searched through the freezer where I found, ta-da, a pint of cherry vanilla. I gave each of the boys two giant scoops and took a single scoop for myself, and the three of us sat back down on the sofa in the playroom and ate it. Then both boys went crazy from the sugar and chased each other around the house, both pretending that they were Harry Potter, until at last they collapsed and I told them to brush their teeth and put their pajamas on for bed.

"No!" Matt said. "I want *your* pajamas!"

"Me, too!" his brother piped up.

"These aren't pajamas," I said. "And anyway, they're mine."

"They look like pajamas to me," Matt said.

"Well, they're not."

I didn't get home until almost midnight, where I found Dad fully dressed and snoring on the couch, and all I made, for six hours of those brats, was fifty-four dollars.

Over the weekend my parents got into another huge, whopping argument, mainly about his drinking, until finally Dad stomped out. And the thing is? When Ben and I were little, Dad wasn't like that — I mean, maybe he drank, but he didn't, like, get drunk. Even now, no one — outside our own family, that is — even knew he drank. Or at least that's what Mom said. She said: "Your father's drinking is a family matter, and it's private. No one needs to know. He just needs to exert a little more willpower."

But the fighting escalated so much that over the weekend I took two more babysitting jobs, because even though I really don't like babysitting, at least I didn't have to be home. Ben went out, too, but unlike me, he didn't have to work, and instead contented himself with hanging around with John, watching TV. "Yar, yar, have fun in butt-wiping world," he said as he sauntered out of the house Friday night. But it wasn't so bad. It was just one little girl, and I made twenty dollars for fewer than two hours. But Saturday night it was whine city, a whole family of little bookworms, meaning that I read about a thousand kids' books until at last the parents got home and paid me a whopping huge fifty bucks. When I got home, there was an email from Becka in response to the one I'd sent her about how my family was driving me crazy and Emma Beth was a bitch. Here's what she said: "Hang in there, *chère*!" That was it. Finally, I drifted over to my closet to get into my nightgown, but when I opened the door, there was Ben, waiting for me. "Surprise!" he said, jumping out of the closet and laughing so hard that he went purple.

By Monday I was better rested, and what's more, I'd pulled off the most fabulous of my fabulous loungewear looks yet: a hot-pink Victoria's Secret nightgown of Mom's that she never wore because it was probably three sizes too small for her. Only I wore it like a tunic, over dark-gray leggings, with black ballerina slippers. And did I look fabulous? Yes, I did. Because as much as I wasn't exactly crazy about being taller than most of the boys, the upside was that I could wear practically anything.

And the second I walked into work, I knew I'd hit it again — everyone was smiling at me, and a couple of the more senior marketing people even gave me a thumbs-up. Even the snooty girl at the Starbucks who usually didn't bother to so much as say hello to me told me that she thought I looked cute. Then it happened: No sooner had I returned to work, then right in front of everyone, including Emma Beth, I kind of tripped, and half fell, half toppled, over my right ankle, spilling half a tray of coffee.

"Tripped over your PJs?" Emma Beth said as I turned the color of a ripe raspberry.

"Don't worry about it," one of the assistant designers said as I limped out of the room. "Everyone here thinks your look is just great." Other people said other nice things. But all I could think of was what a big, stupid loser I was — thinking that I could prove myself at Libby Fine when, just like Mom and Dad had said, I wasn't much of anything at all other than a fifteen-year-old who liked clothes. I wasn't even smart, not like my parents were, or like Ben.

I felt worse and worse as the day went on, until, as I was leaving, Emma Bitch turned to me and said, "At least interns can't get fired." Instantly, it was like a bomb was about to go off inside me, shattering my skin to bits.

I couldn't stand it. The bomb was going to go off! My skin was already crawling, and I was hot and then cold, but mainly, I was exploding, exploding inside and turning into little bits of hideous garbage.

That's when it happened: In a store window, I noticed a fantastic pair of eggplant-purple boots, and just knew that, somehow, I had to have them. Next thing I knew, they were on my feet, and I was whipping out my cash card, flooded with relief.

It's a bit of a long story, but here-a-goes: I'm a swimmer, and built kind of big, especially in the butt and legs. What am I saying? My butt isn't "kind of big." It's huge, a country all of its own, and I hate it. Because I'm a swimmer, it's out there for all to see all the time, except not really, because mainly when I'm in my Speedo I'm also in the water, with my bottom half hidden. And the rest of the time, I wear pants or shorts with big blouses that cover up my back end. So there are a lot of styles I can't wear, even though I'd love to. Such as white jeans. Not in a million years would I expose my rear end to such humiliation as to be viewed by the countless minions at school in all its enormous enormity.

"But, honey," my mother says, "first of all, you have a beautiful figure. And second of all, your rear end is your engine. You've got a beautiful swimmer's body, strong and muscular. Most girls would kill to look like you."

But that was just my mother being nice, because first off, she's a very nice mommy, and second off, my dad split on us when I was too little to even remember him, so it's just me and Mom, with Hank, our smelly mutt. I talk to my so-called father maybe twice a year and hardly ever see him at all, and he never even remembers my birthday, so it's like I may as well not have a dad at all. But even though he's a jerk, my mother feels guilty about my not having a father, and is constantly making all these little sacrifices so I can have things that we can't afford. Which is where the white jeans come in: I made the mistake of mentioning that I loved white jeans, and the next thing I know, Mommy was like: "I'll get you some for your birthday!" And I was like: "Mommy, do you know how much jeans cost?" And she was like: "There are thousands of jeans at the Gap." And I was like: "You don't get it, Mommy. Because the only jeans that might look even halfway decent on me aren't at the Gap." And she was like: "But jeans are jeans." Then I had to explain that, sure, back in the day, maybe, jeans were jeans. But now? The only jeans that actually look good on me are designer jeans, which we can't afford, which is why most of my pants are from discount stores, and no matter what, I have to cover up my backside with a big blouse or T-shirt, and since I spend half my life in the pool, it doesn't really matter anyway.

"Then we'll get you a nice pair," she said.

"Earth to Mommy? Just look at me. In white jeans, people would think I was the great white whale."

Mommy is skinny, with skinny legs and arms and reddish-brownish hair that she wears as short as a boy's, and my father, Burton, is skinny and very tall. Hello? God? Because with these two as parents, where did I come from? My father must have wondered the same thing, too, because, as I said, he left us to move to Los Angeles when I was about a year old, and he doesn't even come to see his own father, my poppy, who lives in an old-age home in Queens and can barely remember who Burton *is*. (Join the crowd, Poppy!) Poppy is the sweetest thing you can even imagine, flirting with his caretakers and giving me candy when he thinks no one's looking. Sometimes he gets confused and calls me "Patty," which is the name of one of his caretakers, but usually he calls me "Precious Pumpkin," or "Angel," or "Sweetest." Mommy and I visit him almost every week, and every time I see him, I want to ask him how Burton turned out to be such a loser. He doesn't even help with child support. Mommy supports us by giving piano lessons.

"No, really," she said, straightening up against the wall the way she does when her back hurts. Her beautiful walnut-colored Steinway, in our dining room, is the one thing she kept when Burton skedaddled out of our lives. "I'm going to get you some fabulous white jeans. You need new clothes anyway. At the rate you're growing, you'll be as tall as Burton."

"Oh, goody. I can just be one giant freak of gigantism," I said. "They can put me in the circus."

"Are you kidding?" Mommy said. "What I'd do for some of your height. And anyway, I've decided. For your birthday, I'm going to buy you some white jeans, and there's nothing you can say to change my mind."

"How about we have to eat?"

"Don't be dramatic. We're not rich, but I make enough."

But she doesn't, not really. Which was another reason I'm so into swimming. I'm good at it — good enough that I could maybe get a scholarship for college. My coaches have always encouraged me, and our new coach — Coach Fruit, which isn't his real name but we call him that because he's always telling us to eat bananas and apples — keeps telling me that I'm a natural and if I work hard, I could probably get scholarship money, even at USC, where he himself lettered AND, EVEN MORE AMAZING, almost made the Olympic team. He has red hair and freckles but is tall and built like a swimmer with wide shoulders and kind of long arms: like a giant Dennis the Menace. I totally love him. We all do. But it isn't, like, *love* love, obviously. For one thing, he's at least thirty, maybe older. Also, he has a girlfriend, Bella, and she's so gorgeous it's not even funny and you can tell by the way he looks at her that he's, like, totally in love with her.

"You really think I could swim for USC?" I said.

"You've got what it takes to swim just about anywhere."

"Yeah, right," I said, thinking about how much college costs and how broke Mommy and I were.

"Why are you so skeptical?"

I thought about it for a minute, until finally I just blurted it out. "It's just Mommy and me. And we're not exactly what you'd call rich."

"One more reason why I'm going to have to work you hard," Coach Fruit said, which made me blush inside my body. Because for one thing, I probably shouldn't have told him that. It was private business. But also because of the way he was looking at me, straight through my eyeballs, like he could see my brain.

I was thinking about that, about how I'd spilled our financial situation to Coach Fruit, when Mommy, arching her neck, said: "It's not your job to worry about our finances. And anyway, I just picked up two new students. A brother and a sister. They're going to start coming once a week for a full hour, which really adds up."

"Oh, wow. Now we'll be able to buy a yacht."

"Oh, come on, Polly! Indulge your mother."

"But, Mommy," I finally said, "can we afford it?"

That's when she teared up. "Oh, honey! If I can't take my precious daughter shopping for her birthday, what kind of mother am I?"

So that's how I ended up in Mommy's ancient junky Ford Fiesta, driving to the Riverside Mall on one of those humid, warm, rainy days in late July that make you want to stay in bed for the rest of your life watching TV.

"I just wish you could see how really beautiful you are, just the way you are," Mommy said as she maneuvered the groaning car through traffic on Route 46. "It's this awful media that equates being thin with being attractive, when it's just not true." I've heard this lecture before. "I mean," Mommy continued as I gazed out the gauzy window at the blur of auto supply warehouses and giant discount stores and pizza parlors floating by, their colors blurring together in the wet sheen on the glass, "when you look at history, even as recently as the nineteen sixties, bigger women were considered the more beautiful. Marilyn Monroe. Elizabeth

Taylor. Neither of those women was really thin. And then, when you go back to any time before the twentieth century — I mean, if you don't believe me, go to the Met some time to look at the Rubens and the Titians. The more flesh, the better."

"Fine, only guess what, Mommy? I don't live in, like, the Middle Ages."

"How was practice this morning?" she said, changing subjects.

"Okay," I said, hedging. I'd broken my own record in the five hundred freestyle.

"How's the new coach working out?"

"He thinks we should be ready to win State tomorrow. If we even get into State this year, which is, like, who knows."

"He pushes you?"

"Yeah, I guess."

I don't know why I didn't tell her that Coach Fruit was amazing, or that he thought I could one day be seriously competitive. But for some reason, I felt like I had to hold back, leave a little of my life in reserve, just for me.

"I used to love to go shopping with your grandmother," Mommy suddenly said in this dreamy voice she gets when she talks about her own mother, who died when Mommy was still in college. "I'll never forget the first time she took me to Marshall Field's. I thought I was in heaven. I still remember what she bought me that day, too: a blue zip-up sweater with a hood, and these fabulous, sort of Art Deco plastic bangles. Only they didn't look like plastic. They looked like ivory."

"I know, Mommy. You've told me before."

"I have?" she said, pulling into the mall's parking lot with an expression on her face like she'd never seen so many cars before.

"Okay, then. Where to start? Macy's? Lord and Taylor?"

I guess I should be grateful that my mother likes to take me shopping and wants me to look pretty, and I am, but sometimes it's like she's *too* attentive, too into what I look like and how I'm doing. Which, I know, is so much better than, for example, my friend Robin's mom. I mean, poor Robin. The last time I saw her, she was practically in tears, and even though Robin's smart and pretty and really a nice girl, too, she thinks she's stupid, which is just not true, plus she thinks everything's her fault, which is also not true. Even though I don't see her much anymore, I feel bad for her. I mean, her mother is just a bitch. Versus my own mother, who can actually be *too* nice.

So naturally, every time I came out of the dressing room, Mommy said something like, "You look great in those!" Even though I didn't.

"I look like a hippo!" I said. Or: "I'm just too big to wear white jeans. I look like a lump of mashed potatoes."

It was right around middle school, when I started sprouting a figure, that Robin, who until then had been my best friend, started hanging out more with Becka, who was also part of our group of friends, just not my *closest* closest. They never really dropped me, as in: We're in, you're out. Even now, all three of us are friendly, saying hello in the halls and even, sometimes, having lunch or meeting for coffee or ice cream. But in middle school, it became obvious that they were both slated for cooldom, and I was so not. For one thing, both of them were beautiful — and thin. Plus, they both had a lot more money than I had. They had Frye boots and wore their jeans tight and skinny, drooping off their hips, clinging to their legs, tucked into their boots or into high-top sneakers. They even had boyfriends. I'd see them laughing together, drinking cherry soda, whispering. Whereas I just got big — big all over — and tall.

I started swimming at the Y.

It's hard to explain, but once I found my speed, I wasn't me, Polly, at all. I wasn't even a girl. I forgot that my mother had to teach piano lessons to spoiled brats in order to pay the rent, that my father had left us when I was a baby, that Poppy was stuck in an old-age home in Queens where the only people who ever visited him were me and Mommy, and that my butt was ginormous. I was fast. I was very fast. Faster, even, than most of the boys. It was like I could fly.

So I didn't even mind it all that much, Becka and Robin going off to be their own little club of two, without me. I changed groups, too, except in my own case, I didn't really have a group. I hung out with the other swimmers, but it wasn't like we were all best friends. Plus, because I was an athlete, I knew tons of boys. People thought I was, like, so popular. But it was more like I knew everyone and tried to be nice to everyone but at the same time didn't really fit in anywhere, with any particular group, or even with one single other person.

Even though I was crazy-busy with swimming, a part of me

really missed being best friends with Robin, especially in the summer, when half of West Falls went away and it was like living in a ghost town. But Robin was going into the city every day. The one time I saw her, at Starbucks, she was wearing swishy loose silky pants with a skinny top that showed off her collarbones and made her look like someone so glamorous and creative that I didn't even know her at all, and with her long beautiful hair pulled back into two tight braids, her face looked like a deer's, with high cheekbones and large liquid brown eyes.

It was at a store called Shake Your Groove Thing that I finally found them — *the* jeans. First, they fit. Second, they didn't make me look too fat.

When I came out of the dressing room, Mommy looked me up and down and told me to get a second pair, too, only in blue. "You'll need them once it gets cold again, for school."

"Do you know how much these cost?"

"It's your birthday present."

"They're one hundred and fifty seven dollars!" I said. "And tax!"

"This is something I want to do for you."

"We're going to starve to death! How can you afford all this?"

"Oh, honey," she said. "Am I really such a bad provider?"

"It's not that," I tried to explain, but it was no use — Mommy would get sadder and sadder, and feel guiltier and guiltier, and then she'd start telling me long stories about how much fun she used to have with her own mother, how much they laughed, how her mom would take her shopping to the new Bloomie's that had just opened up in their town. Which is how I ended up not just with one pair of white jeans, but with a pair of white jeans and a pair of blue jeans, both high-end.

On the day of my actual birthday, Poppy called from his old-age home in Queens to sing the "Happy Birthday" song, like he always does. From somewhere just behind him, I could hear Patty, one of his favorite nurses (they were all his favorite nurses), telling him that he ought to go on *America's Got Talent*. Then she got on the phone and said: "Oh, my! I know your granddaddy's so proud of you." I got a bunch of "happy birthday, Polly" messages on my Facebook page, including one from Coach Fruit! A few of the other girls on the team gave me little presents (a pretty box, a book, funny flip-flops). Mommy made me a cake. But Burton, as usual, was silent.

It's always the big question. What to wear for the first day of school. I knew that both Becka and Robin were going to once again look like movie stars. But I woke up feeling like yuck. A few days earlier, some kid I'd never seen before had run toward me on the sidewalk, saying, "Hey, Mike! What's up?" When he got up to me and realized that I was a girl, he apologized, but I couldn't shake the memory. There was just no use: I looked like a boy. A boy with a huge butt. Plus, it was hot out, and school wasn't air-conditioned. It would be a broiler inside. I put on a pair of shorts and an oversized blouse. At least I'd be comfortable.

But when I appeared for breakfast, Mommy said: "You're not wearing that, are you?"

"Why? What's wrong with it?"

"Nothing — except that you should wear your white jeans. Don't you want to feel confident on your first day of school?"

Maybe she was right. I mean, I knew I looked like I always looked: invisible and big at the same time. So I back to my room to try again. But I just couldn't do it. Not on the first day of school!

"Oh, honey," Mommy said as I gathered up my stuff to go to school. "I just wish you knew how pretty you are."

"Thanks."

"Well!" she said. "Have a great first day of sophomore year."

As it turned out, I *did* have a good first day. For once, my teachers didn't seem either bored or mean, and in chemistry a junior boy who was one of the best runners on the cross-country team asked me to be his lab partner. Robin came up to me and gave me a big hug, and even Becka, who I wasn't really friends with anymore, made a point of coming over and talking to me, asking me how my summer was, stuff like that. My old teachers waved at me as I passed by in the hallways, and Coach Fruit gave me two thumbs up, and I suddenly felt sorry for the freshmen, who looked so small and geeky and confused.

Then I went into the bathroom and saw this new girl — I'd noticed her in chemistry — and she was wearing the coolest dress I'd ever seen. She told me it was made of paper, and the first thing I thought was: *This is going to drive Becka crazy!* I wanted to ask her all about her dress and if she was new — because even though usually I'm on the shy side I was feeling like maybe sophomore year would be good after all — but then I noticed her staring at my bottom. My big, huge derriere.

"Well," she said, "later."

That's all it took. My heart sank. I looked at myself again, and saw what she saw: a girl who wasn't fooling anyone, with the biggest rear end in the world!

"Later," I said as the girl in the paper dress breezed out through the thick wooden door.

The rest of the day I had a stomachache. I mean, what had I been thinking? Like I was going to *ever* wear those white jeans that Mommy had bought for me? And then — what about the money! Mommy had spent more than three hundred dollars!

By the time it was time for swimming practice, my stomach hurt so much that I felt like I was going to be sick! It was important to show up for practice every day, but the first day of school was even more important, and I knew that if I sat practice out it would look bad and might even jeopardize my place in the upcoming season lineups. I didn't know what to do! But my stomach decided for me. It was gurgling and churning so much that I felt like I'd swallowed a piranha. Finally I had no choice, and decided that I had to tell Coach Fruit that I simply didn't feel well.

"I'm really, really sorry," I said.

But instead of getting angry at me or giving me the usual coach lecture about being part of a team and showing up for my teammates, Coach Fruit said: "You look so sad, Polly. Is there something you're not telling me? I mean, aside from your having a bad stomachache?"

Which is when my eyes filled up with tears. I was so embarrassed!

"What?" he said gently, and as the whole story tumbled through my mind — about how much Mommy and I were struggling financially and Burton had left us when I was only a baby, and how Mommy had taken me to buy new clothes that she can't afford, and how sad I was that Poppy had to live in an old-age home in Queens, and finally, how that new girl had looked at me in the bathroom like I was the star of Ugly Land — what popped out of me was: "How can I be a swimmer? I'm huge!"

He smiled. "You're strong."

"I'm a giant piece of blubber!"

"My girlfriend complains that she's too big, too," he said, laughing. "What is it with you women? You look like goddesses and all you can think is: *My thighs are too fat.* Or whatever."

"Bella thinks she's fat?"

"Can you believe it?"

"But she's so — thin."

"Yup," he said. "And great looking. Like you."

He was grinning from ear to ear now, doing a total Dennis the Menace, and suddenly I realized that, unlike Mommy, he wasn't saying all that nice stuff because he had to.

"You're a champ, kid," he said. "You just don't know it yet."

I was so startled that I just stood there like a fish, my mouth opening and closing. Then I smiled back. By the time I was halfway to the locker room to change into my Speedo, my stomachache was almost gone.

CHAPTER FIVE

Blanderella

• Ann •

M*e and my big*, huge blabbermouth mouth. I mean, it was funny for a second, but then that new girl blushed the color of my grandmother's favorite wine-red lipstick, and I knew that, once again, I'd gone too far.

She was wearing this awesome, and I mean *awesome*, paper dress. And what did I say? "If it gets too hot, you can just rip a couple of holes in it and — voilà — instant air-conditioning!"

Yes, I really said that. The girl got so red, I was worried she was going to die of heatstroke.

All I'd really wanted was to impress her — to make her think that I was even halfway as cool as she was. I mean: a paper dress! Any girl who can pull *that* off is a girl I want to know.

I'd love, and I mean LOVE, to wear something like that. But I never will. And that's because I'm what my mother calls "petite" and I call "I look like I'm twelve." Every time I've tried to wear clothes with a little flair, I look like a little girl playing dress-up.

I'm so small that I didn't even wear a bra until ninth grade! Mama says that, with a father as tall as mine is, I'm sure to grow, but in the meantime, I'm stuck with my jeans and T-shirts, my cords and pullovers, my denim skirts and button-downs. Not to mention that Mama has a thing about girls who dress, in her words, "like women of the street." By which she means in platform shoes, heels higher than an inch or two, miniskirts, bandage skirts, clingy tees, camisole tops, short-shorts, strapless or figure-hugging dresses, and any makeup other than a trace of lip gloss.

"It's plain disgusting, the way girls your age advertise their bodies like they're looking for customers," she says before launching into one of her typically endless stories about some teenager or another who she's trying to help: She's a social worker, and, as she puts it, she's "seen it all."

"College is where you're headed," she says. "College and maybe grad school, too. One way or another, though, you're going to have yourself a career. No detours for mess, no ma'am."

Hence my button-downs, my pleated skirts, my straight-leg Gap jeans, my cardigan sweaters, and my Mimi Chica dresses. You heard right. I still wear Mimi Chica flowered and printed junior dresses and skirts, even though no one else has since the year all the Jewish girls were having *bat mitvahs*. But Mama just *loves* Mimi. So much so that I'm surprised she didn't name me Mimi. Instead she named me after her own mother, Mama Lee. Mama Lee Livingston.

I love Mama Lee. She's the only one in the whole family who I can tell things to — true things that no one else knows, like how I want to be artist, and that even though I'm a mousecake, I love clothes so much that I want to launch a fashion blog. But the blog I'd do wouldn't be a typical teenage blog, with lots of "WOW" and/or "MUST HAVE" with uploaded pictures of clothes I like. I want to make it more artistic, and deeper, than that — more about how clothes are their own art form than mere fashion — except that I don't really like to write. As in: I hate it! I even told Mama Lee that since school started, I've been spending my afternoons in Ms. Anders's art room, learning figure drawing. "Well, that's just wonderful," she said. Versus Mama and Daddy, who pitched a fit last year when I signed up for Techniques in Painting, arguing that to fulfill my arts requirements, I should do computer design and journalism, like my perfect sister, Martha (aka Robot Girl), did. I mean, it's downright weird, how crazy they got about my taking an art class. The way they talked about it, you'd think it was dangerous, like experimenting with drugs or having a skydiving hobby. But when I asked them why they were both so freakanoid about my taking a basic high school art class, they both clammed up and changed the subject. And I know it's pathetic, but now I'm so scared that they'll find out about my extra time in the art room that I came up with this huge whopper of a ridiculous lie and told Mama that I was going to Debate Team meetings. I mean, really. Can you see *me* on Debate Team? I can't even open my mouth without putting my foot in it.

Robot Girl *had been* on Debate Team, culminating with her triumph as Debate Team captain. And now she goes to Princeton, goody-goody for her. But me? Ever since I'd launched that lie, a small, hard knot had appeared in my stomach and wouldn't go away.

"I'm so proud of you, making Debate Team sophomore year," Mama said over and over. "But the one thing that makes me proudest of all? It's that you and your sister are so close."

Were so close. I have a picture of the two of us on her bike, together, with me sitting on the seat, and Martha standing up, pedaling. We'd ride all over the neighborhood like that. Now she barely acknowledges my existence.

"It's like you're twins," Mama said.

"Except that I look like I'm in kindergarten."

"Your sister was the same at your age. Don't worry, you'll get your figure. Martha did, right? In the meantime, enjoy it! Think about poor Ashley. . . ."

Ashley is my second cousin. She sprung a figure when she was about eleven, and was taller than most of the boys, too. Her parents had to put her in private school because she was teased so much at her old public school. Mama brings her up every time I gripe about what I look like.

"Trust me, you're better off looking like you look. And some of these girls, honey? No self-worth at all. Poor Ashley dresses inappropriately, too, with so little self-respect. You don't want to look like that. Really."

Actually, I wouldn't mind. But, as I've already mentioned, what's the use? Except for my bangles, I'm like a walking, wall-to-wall beige carpet — just kind of there, in the background, inoffensive and unnoticeable. But even my bangles are proof of what a conformist I am: Each one of them was a gift from my parents for getting good grades. The most radical thing I've done recently, style-wise, was cut my hair very short, which I think gives me a slightly punk-radical-artist edginess — it used to be shoulder-length, worn straight, and parted on the side. I love my punk-short boy 'do, but Robot Girl says it makes me look like our first cousin Roger, who's her age and goes to college in California. So it's not like some random new girl wearing a totally funk-o-rama dress sits down with me and the Latins every day. They're the Latins because I know them from Latin class, except for two of them, who actually *are* on Debate Team, which in itself qualifies them for being Latins. The truth is, most of the girls I hang out with are not actually people I really am really friends with, not like I was with my old friends from elementary school and middle school — but the girl who was really my closest friend moved to Baltimore, and my second-closest switched into Catholic school, and the girls who'd been my friends when we were little had long since soared to the heights of popularity or jockhood or beauty-queen-bee-ness, so that by the time I got to high school I was on my own. And sure, I still saw them on occasion, but we'd drifted apart, leaving me with the Latins.

But that redheaded San Francisco girl? A *paper dress*. I mean, how great is that?

But I couldn't tell my parents about her, let alone about how I'd chased her off. The truth is, they were so ambitious for me, so certain that I was destined for academic greatness, that I could hardly tell them anything.

◇◇◇◇◇◇◇◇◇◇

A few days after my Huge Blabbermouth incident, I saw San Francisco girl again, this time in the hall. Or at least, I *thought* it was San Francisco girl. Same wild red hair. Same very pale, slightly freckled face. Same ridiculously blue eyes. Same "don't mess with me, dude" way of walking. Only she wasn't wearing a paper dress. She wasn't wearing any kind of dress. In fact, she wasn't really wearing anything interesting at all. What she was wearing was my own basic uniform of dullosity: jeans and a T-shirt, with flip-flops. No makeup. No fabulous metallic blue fingernail polish. No ropes of beads. *Nada.* I had to stare at her like five times and then stalk her to her next class before I was sure that it really was her, and then, finally, edging up on her right before the final class bell was about to ring, I said:

"Hey there, San Francisco! How's it going?"

She turned to look at me. "My name's Justine."

"Sorry," I said. "Justine. Like *Justin*, right? Only for girls?"

"Uh-huh."

"I knew this kid Justin once. He was a real dweeb."

She looked at me like my hair was on fire.

"Uh-huh," she said again.

"A total dork-out dweeb of dweebation," I added.

She must have thought I'd mainlined caffeine. "Well," she finally said. "My name isn't Justin. It's Justine."

"Just Justine!" I sang. "Just, just just — Justine!"

Then the bell rang and she went into her class, and I was late for mine and got a tardy.

What is *wrong* with me?

When I got home that afternoon around four, the first thing

I did was call Mama Lee. Here's what I said: "Can I come over to your house this weekend?"

"Prettier than ever," Mama Lee said, giving me a big hug. In the past few years, her cheekbones had become even more prominent, and her wide-spaced dark eyes even more wide-spaced. Her hair had gone entirely silver, and glowed, like it was backlit. And even though she had a slight limp from the stroke she'd had a few years earlier, her posture was erect and stately.

She was the most amazing person I'd ever known. She'd been the first in her family to finish high school; then she worked, doing whatever she could to save up enough money to go to secretarial school. And then, in 1951, she became the first black saleswoman ever to be hired at Bamberger's, which is where she met my grandfather, who worked on the loading dock. In old photographs, her long hair is pulled back into a smooth puff, and she wears pearls, cotton dresses with cinched-in waists or suits with padded shoulders, with smallish hats perched on her head.

"How's my baby girl?" she said as I inhaled the smell of her warm skin — part baby powder and part hand lotion.

"Okay, I guess."

She released me now to take a step back and look at me, like she always did when I came to visit. "Uh-huh, I see," she said. "Sophomore year, huh?"

"Yup."

"You're growing up fast! Tenth grade already. Imagine that!"

"It's no big deal," I said. "It's just high school."

"And you looking so fine!"

That was just so — so Mama Lee. She didn't even know how to be anything but my biggest fan, like she'd never even heard of being critical or demanding or cranky. She didn't know how to look dowdy, either — not even with the right half of her body listing a little. She was wearing a pair of navy slacks with big brass buttons and a white blouse, and her fingernails were painted red, like she was expecting some boy she had a crush on to come over instead of her dorky fifteen-year-old granddaughter.

"Baby," she said, "I'm so glad you came over today. Because I got some work you can help me with. Would that be all right?"

"No problem," I said. "Only . . ."

Only I didn't know where, or how, to start. With the fact that I loathed my junior-high-school-sized dresses? Or that I'd told my parents that I was on (gag) Debate Team? How about the fact that my parents didn't really have a clue who I was, seeing me as a smaller, younger version of Robot Girl, when in fact I was nothing like her and never could be? Or about my big blab-berthon mouth? My inability to push the STOP button? Or how about that new girl, Justine?

Finally I just said: "I'm just so stupid."

"What do you mean, baby?"

"Well, for starters," I stammered, "I talk way too much. I was trying to be funny, but instead I scared this new girl off at school. She was wearing a paper dress and I told her if she ripped it she'd have instant air-conditioning, and now every time she sees me she runs away like I've got the worst case of cooties ever. Plus, I have this stupid idea that I want to start a fashion blog, but who am I kidding? I have all these ideas, but I'm not a good writer. I mean, I'm just not. Plus, look what I look like. I look like I'm ten!"

She leaned back and laughed. "My, my, my," she said. "A paper dress? I remember those! They were a big hit, back in the sixties. I even had one, if you can believe that. Your grandfather thought I'd gone and lost my mind."

"I don't think it's very funny. I was such a total jerk! That girl will never talk to me again."

"It's a good thing you came over today, then, honey, because I have a few things I need your help with."

"Yeah, I know," I said. Every time I came over, Mama Lee had something for me to help her with, like reading something that was too small for her eyes, or explaining (again) how to use email.

"No, honey. No, you don't know." And she gestured for me to follow her up the stairs.

A minute later, I was rumbling around the storage space under the rafters, trying to locate Mama Lee's old trunk. It was so hot in there that by the time I found it, way in the back, I was soaked through with sweat.

But it was worth it.

Talk about finding a secret treasure chest! Inside were all of Mama Lee's beautiful clothes from when she was a young woman. There was a light-green poodle sweater; a fifties-style skirt with pleats; tailored black linen knee-length dresses; brightly flowered cotton dresses that buttoned up the front; cashmere sweater sets; and a deep-red dress with large white flowers and a pleated, flirty skirt. And accessories, too: hats, scarves, costume jewelry — strings of faux pearls, glass beads, rhinestone peacock pins. I was like: *No way.*

"Seeing that your mother and aunts never had the slightest interest in these, I was going to give them to the Goodwill," she was saying, "or to a thrift shop. Because, honey, they tell me that these old styles are in again. But instead, I think, so long as you're here, you should try them on. I wasn't but a bitty thing myself, you know. See if any of these old things suit you."

"For real?"

"What?" she said, laughing. "You think maybe your old Mama Lee might want to wear these herself? Do what I tell you, little girl. Go on now."

When I tell you that a miracle happened that day, I'm not even exaggerating: Almost all Mama Lee's old things fit me as if they'd been designed for my body, and what's more, in them, even with my short-short hair, there's no way anyone would think I was a boy. Every time I tried on a new outfit, Mama Lee shook her head back and forth like she couldn't believe her eyes, and when I came out wearing the one I loved most — the dark-red dress with the big white daisies — she murmured, "My, my, my."

"What?" I said.

"Take a look."

I stood in front of the mirror. And there I was, only it wasn't me at all, or at least not the me I was used to seeing. In Mama Lee's dress, I had . . . *curves*. True, they were small, but I had them.

Mama Lee looked at me, nodded, and said: "Honey baby, I was wearing that the day I met your grandfather. And now, just look at you. It's like I'm looking at my own young self."

"Really?"

"My, my, my," she said.

It's embarrassing to admit, but the first thing I did when I got home was put all my new old Mama Lee clothes at the very back of my closet. Good thing Mama wasn't home yet is all I can say. Because somehow I knew that if she ever knew about my new old wardrobe, she'd freak. So I hid it, dressing for school as I always did, in straight-legged jeans and cotton blouses, sitting at my usual lunch table, and going to my usual classes. Twice I saw Justine, but she must have caught sight of me, too, because both times, no sooner had I caught a glimpse of her than she was heading off in the opposite direction. When I saw her, I thought about my fashion blog: *There's a new look going around school, which I can only call . . . call what?* Even in my imagination, I couldn't write. I didn't have an ounce of courage, was the truth, and I'd never have the courage to wear one of Mama Lee's outfits to school. Not like Justine. Compared to her, I felt like stale bread.

As if she knew, Mama Lee called one night to ask me if I'd had a chance to wear any of her things yet. "I just can't!" I wailed. "Mama would kill me."

"How do you know if you never give her a chance?"

"I just know, is how I know."

"Aw, honey. You tell her that your old grandmother gave them to you on purpose, and wants you to enjoy them. You think your mother's a tiger, but underneath it, she's just a little old kitten."

Even after Mama Lee's pep talk, I probably wouldn't have ever screwed up the courage to put so much as one of her three-quarter-sleeve cardigans on, except that the next day, at school, the two most fashionable girls in our entire class came up to me at lunch and told me that they thought my short hair was cute. "You look like Halle Berry," one of them said. And, okay, it might not sound like a game changer to you, but when Becka Ramez and Robin Kohn-Chase tell you that you look like Halle Berry, it's kind of thrilling. Especially if, like me, you're kind of a nonentity, one of those nice girls who no one objects to but doesn't much notice, either.

The following morning, I did it: I put on Mama Lee's dark-red-with-white-flowers dress. Then I took it off. Then I put it back on. Then I took it off. Then I put it on one final time, and said a little prayer. When I went downstairs, Mama said: "Lord have mercy. Where on earth did you get that?"

"Mama Lee gave it to me." I could already feel the butterflies starting up in my stomach, the way they do when I know I'm going to be in trouble. "She said I was exactly her size."

"She did, did she?" Mama said. "And you're going to wear that?"

I nodded.

"To school?"

"That was the plan."

"Honey, you can't wear that to school."

"Why?"

"I don't really have time to explain it right now," she said, glancing at her watch. "And anyway, you're going to be late. Did you do that on purpose? Come down late so you wouldn't have enough time to change?"

"I overslept," I said, which wasn't strictly true. But I couldn't tell her that the real reason I was late was because I'd put on and taken off the dress so many times.

"Change it anyway," she said. "Or at least grab a sweater for it."

"I'll miss the bus!"

"I'm going to tan your grandmother's hide."

As I left the house, my heart was pounding wildly, but at the same time, I felt so pumped — and also so relieved — that I decided I'd just have to find Justine and apologize to her flat out. *Hi, Justine! Don't run away! Just quickly: I'm so sorry for all the stupid things I said to you! You probably think I'm a superjerk, but it's more like I'm just plain nervous, and stupid, too. And . . .*

Instead, as I rounded the corner from the 1-B wing to the 1-C wing, I ran smack up into the girl. Who was wearing the worst outfit ever. I mean, it was almost as if she'd gone from being Cool Daring Different Girl to I'm Ugly Don't Even Notice Me Girl. For one thing, her lovely reddish curls were all pulled back, tight, into this nasty little ponytail. As for her outfit, she was wearing baggy blue jeans topped with a man's button-down shirt, like a big old lump.

"Oops! Sorry!" I said as I literally careened straight into her, making her spill her books.

"No big."

"No, really," I said, trying to smile.

"Don't worry about it," she said, picking up her books and continuing down the hall, leaving me standing there, feeling stupid.

I ran after her. "I'm Ann," I said. "From a couple of weeks ago? I mean, from the first day of school? You sat with us. At lunch."

"I know who you are."

"I really am sorry," I said.

"And I really don't think it's any big deal," she said. "The halls are crowded."

"No," I said. "What I mean is . . ."

"What?"

"It was sort of an accident. I have them a lot."

"Whatever."

"I mean," I said, "what happened on the first day of school was."

"Oh," she said, blushing. Then: "Sorry, I shouldn't have sat with you guys. It's not like anyone asked me to. I just barged in." She looked like she was trying not to cry. I just stood there. Then I began, in my usual way, to blabber: "It's just that, it's not that I meant you shouldn't have sat with us. It was great you did. I mean. And that table? With the Latin Girls? That's what I call them, anyway. *The Latin Girls*. Sounds like the name of a band, you know? We're not even that tight. Not really. Not like my older sister, Martha, was with her little clique of robots and suck-ups. She goes to Princeton. She hung exclusively with the high school superstars, like you had to be the best at everything for them to even know your name, but we're not like that. We're more like: Rejects welcome here! Nerds, geeks, dweebs, wiener patrol, brainless jocks, albino science rats, ghetto wannabes, stoners, and loners — come one, come all!" I was sounding stupider and stupider. What was I saying? *OMG*. Plus, we weren't like that. We were just . . . we were just a loose group of girls who didn't know who else to sit with.

Justine was staring at me with her big round cornflower-blue eyes. "And me, I'm supposed to go to Princeton, too, if you can believe that — what a joke, ha ha on me. Because, you know, here we are in West Falls, land of the Good Public Schools, and we moved here for the schools, yada yada. Like, my father, he works in the city? It's a long commute for him; he complains about it all the time. But then, you know, we came along, and so here we are. Toodley-too! As for Princeton, I mean, what I really want to do is blog. As in: blog for the blogosphere of blogation."

"Got it," the girl said. She probably thought I was on drugs.

"And that's what I mean!" I said, even though even I didn't know what I meant. I didn't have a clue. It was like a small, insistent insect had entered my brain, and every time it flapped its wings, something even more random and stupid came flying out of my mouth.

Justine just stood there, looking like she was trapped in the loony bin. Then the first bell rang.

"Gotta go."

"Justine?" I yelped.

"Yeah."

"I talk too much and say stupid things. When I get nervous. Like now."

"Yeah, I guess so."

"And another thing. Your dress — your paper dress. I really did think it was cool. I did. I mean it. I was, like, jealous of you. Because you looked so great. Versus me . . ."

"Really?" she said, and though she didn't actually smile, her eyes curled up a little, you know, at the edges. Then she said: "What do you mean, versus you? Look at you. Where did you get *that*? It's awesome."

"Really?"

"Totally awesome," she said.

Then the second bell rang and we both made little waving motions, smiled little smiles, and, turning, ran to our classes.

CHAPTER SIX

The Day of Dread and Pancakes

• Justine •

In October, my mother did the stupidest stupid thing ever. Which was:

Made a date to go out with Becka — and Becka's mother. For Sunday brunch.

"Mom," I said. "The girl barely even acknowledges my existence. And when she does, she calls me 'Um.' "

" 'Um'?" Mom said.

"Trust me, she's not nice. She doesn't want to be friends with me. If anything, she hates my guts."

"I'm sure she doesn't hate your guts," Mom said. "And anyway, her mother is so nice. She totally thinks that it would be a good idea to get you two girls together. She said that Becka spends far too much time alone and that she could really use some new friends."

"Becka?" I said. "I don't think so. "

"Give it time," Mom said, which is what Mom always says when she doesn't want to deal with anything approaching reality.

Such as the fact that since we'd moved to New Jersey, my father spent even more time than before at the office. "Whenever he starts a new job, he's like that," Mom would say. "Just give it time."

"And anyway," Mom continued now, "it's not just going to be the four of us. There's another girl, and her mother, and someone else, too, who have been invited. Meryl thought it would be nice. . . ."

"Who's *Meryl*?"

"Becka's mother. And she said —"

"Forget it, Mom! I'm not going! Are you crazy? I'll answer that. Yes, you are."

"Meryl thinks it's a great idea. She says that Becka wants to graduate in three years and isn't taking enough hang-out time. It sounds like she's very bright."

"You've flipped, Mom! Did her mother also mention that Becka treats me like toe lint!"

"Actually . . ."

"Not happening, Mom. Because, seriously, you've become one of those hover mothers. You should never have given up your dancing. I'm not even exaggerating. This is insane! You need something to do! GET A LIFE!"

Which is when my mother started crying. Truth. As in: tears springing up in her eyes and trailing down her cheek. "It's not easy for me, either," she said. "Moving around so much. And you might not know it, but I'm concerned about you, too. Those awful clothes you were wearing, like you were trying to disappear."

"Yeah, well, as you can see, I'm over it." I was, too. Because ever since Ann had nearly tackled me in the hallway, I'd gone back to my natural awesomeness, such as what I was wearing that minute, which was, get this: pedal pushers with a Minnie Mouse sweater.

"And you don't have friends!" Mom continued. "Not one! I hate to see you so lonely. We got here in July — and it's almost Thanksgiving."

"It's not almost Thanksgiving," I said. It wasn't. It wasn't even Halloween. But at least it wasn't summer anymore. Because if anyone had told me that summer in New Jersey was like being inside someone's hot, wet mouth, I would have stowed away in a container ship heading for Hong Kong. But now the trees were yellow, orange, and red, and when I came home from school in the afternoons, I found Skizz stretched out on the window seat in my puke-pink bedroom, taking a sunbath.

"Plus," I said, "I do have a friend. I have Ann."

"Who's Ann?" Mom said, blowing her nose.

"My friend."

It was true, too, and Ann was awesome. On the other hand, Mom was so desperate for me to make friends that I'd been reluctant to say one thing about her. So it didn't surprise me when Mom said: "Why don't you invite her over for dinner some night so I can meet her? Is her family nice? What line of work are they in?"

"I don't know," I said. "But I do know that I don't need you making friends for me! God! I'm not going to that stupid brunch. How old do you think I am, seven?"

"Do it for me, then. Because you're not the only one starting all over again in a new place. I could use a few friends, too, you know."

"Way to turn on the guilt trip," I said, but by then Mom was blowing her nose so loudly that I'm not sure she heard me. Everything about her seemed so *sodden*. It was hard to believe that she'd ever been a dancer. So as usual, when it came to something Mom wanted me to do for her, I felt as if I had no choice in the matter. Especially since Dad had just announced that he might have to go to Germany on business during Thanksgiving, and then left on another business trip, this time for almost a week, and Mom didn't say anything about it at all except for: "You know how your father is. Work, work, work!" with that little pasted-on smile she wears when she's deadly pissed off. But at night, when she thought I was asleep, I could hear her crying. Even Eliza, when I Skyped with her about it, admitted that I wouldn't be able to get out of the brunch.

"A total butt-bite," she said. "But, Justine, it's your *mom*."

"Exactly," I said. Then I said: "I hate him."

"Who?"

"My father. He doesn't care about me or Mom. All he cares about is his career."

You know that weird silence that sometimes happens on phone calls that makes you feel like maybe you said something so wrong that you can never be right about anything again? That's what happened. Eliza didn't reply. And I felt this great black deep hole open up inside me.

"Just make sure you like what you wear," Eliza finally said.

"I swear to God," I said, "I'm going to break out in hives."

Even though I'd reclaimed my right to be awesomely spectacular and beyond extraordinary in all I wore, when it came to what I was going to wear for the Day of Dread and Pancakes, I didn't have a clue. It was Ann who, after inspecting every item in my closet, decided on my authentic Peter Max early seventies dress — balloon sleeves, a wide skirt, with a pattern of pink and turquoise and coral swirls, like the surface of the ocean during sunset. She also insisted that I top the whole outfit off with her grandmother's awesomely cool turquoise Lucite choker.

"I can't take your grandmother's necklace!" I said.

"Yes, you can. You have to. First, because it pulls the whole look together. And also, it would be like: *I've got style by the mile and you best not mess with me, because I got Ann in my corner.*"

"Yeah, really," I said. "You could take her down with one punch."

"My first blog entry? You know, the one I told you I'm going to write? It's going to be about you," she said, waving her arms around so her bangles chimed.

"Right," I said, knowing full well that the chances of Ann actually writing her so-called blog were minimal. The girl hated to write and procrastinated like crazy every time she had to write a paper, calling me and whining and begging me to help her find the right words, which was pretty funny, given how much she liked to talk.

Stroking my Peter Max dress like it was a puppy, she said: "I'm going to call my first entry: 'Maxing Out.' Get it?"

"Great."

"It'll be all about your Peter Max groove."

"Sure it will."

Like I said, Ann was great — but it had taken me a while to invite her over to Homely Acres. I'd been right about that, too. Because not five minutes earlier, when I'd introduced her to my mother, Mom had actually come right out and said: "I'm so glad that Justine is finally making friends."

"You don't want to look like you're trying too hard," Ann was now saying. "But you don't want to look like you're competing with her, either. But mainly, you just want to be as you as possible. *Comprende?*"

I *comprended*, all right. But just because I had my outfit figured out didn't mean that I wasn't still seriously and absolutely freaked out by the outrageously world-class stupid thing my mother did.

Every other kid in school seemed to know about it, too. Even the loud-mouthed jerk in English who'd made remarks about my paper dress seemed to know. *Ben.* That was his name. He was so skinny that he looked like a cartoon. "I hear you're having a big breakfast with the In Crowd next week," is how he put it, and when I asked him what he was talking about, he just grinned this huge, stupid grin and said: "I have my sources." Meantime, Becka no longer so much as glanced my way.

"Obviously, the girl has issues," Ann said.

Issues or not, she freaked me out. Freaked. Me. Out. And I'm not all that easily intimidated. Even Weird John, who was getting increasingly more useless, spending most of his time in class drawing things in his notebook that he wouldn't let me see, didn't get to me. Even when he purposefully exploded something in a test tube, or sat on my lap, or called me "Mizz Frizz," or took out his own eyeliner and insisted on doing my eyes.

But with Becka, I was a quivering worm. So when Mom got me up on Sunday morning with a cheery "Wake up, sleepyhead!" it was all I could do not to heave. The best I could do was believe in my outfit — that rock concert of colors that hugged my not-very-small waist in such a way that it looked like I had one, with platform shoes, and Ann's grandmother's choker, because as it turned out, she was right. As I clasped the necklace around my neck, I felt a kind of reassurance, a promise that, no matter what might come, Ann and I would be able to laugh about it afterward.

"I'm telling you, Mom," I said as we drove to the place where we were meeting them for breakfast because even though we lived across the street from each other there was no way we were going to drive in the same car because, duh, Becka considered me to be lower than pond scum and never in a million years would have agreed to be trapped in the same vehicle as me, "this is not going to be fun."

"Just cool it, would you? How do you know if you never try? Meryl told me that Becka wanted to go."

"Right."

It was one of those places with on-purpose-beat-up heavy wooden tables, where they put the entire menu on a blackboard. Becka and her mother, along with Huge Smile All-Varsity Girl — the same one who'd given me the evil eye in the bathroom on the first day of school and who sat, with her big-athlete-on-campus lab partner, in the front row in chemistry class — and *her* mother, were also there. As was Becka's sidekick, Fabulous-in-Lingerie Girl. Becka was looking her usual amazing, with skinny jeans and low-heeled black leather boots, a plain white blouse topped by what looked to be a real Chanel jacket, and that astonishingly beautiful Hermès scarf, swirls of pink and gray and green, that she'd been wearing the first time I met her. She didn't even look up. Not even when all three mothers started making noises about "letting the girls sit together," and promptly rearranged themselves so they were at the far end and the four of us "teens" were at the wedged-in end of the table. I ended up sitting directly across from Becka and Becka's sidekick, and next to Huge Smile All-Varsity Girl, who was wearing the kind of perfect blue jeans that pretty, popular girls from coast to coast wear, with an oversized sweater. Her hair was pulled back into a high ponytail. Her skin was as smooth as soap. I held my breath, waiting for the extreme awfulness.

But, amazingly — as in, flip me out with a feather — Big White Smile Girl immediately said: "Wow! I love your dress! Where did you get it?"

"Do you mean it?" I stammered.

"It's, like — fabulous. Really."

"Yeah," Sidekick added. She looked great, too, in a silky top that showed off her collarbones, and jeans, she looked like she could have been in a perfume ad. "It looks awesome on you. It sets off your hair."

I blushed, thinking about how my head probably looked like an exploded red dandelion.

"No, really. I love your style. Where do you buy your clothes?"

So I ended up telling her — telling *them* — about how, when I lived in San Francisco, I started getting into shopping at secondhand stores, and Big White Smile said that she wished she could pull off the look but was too big to wear anything but fairly straight-up American sportswear with a preppy accent, and I said that I'd kill to be tall and pretty like she was, and she said: "Yeah, but have you taken a look at my huge butt?"

"You?" I said. "A huge butt? You've got to be kidding me."

"If only. Don't you remember? We met, like, on the first day of school. In the bathroom, actually." She was blushing a little. "You were, like —"

"I know," I said, fingering Ann's grandmother's Lucite choker for extra protection. "My paper dress. I was trying to clean it."

"Yeah. I loved that dress, too. It was awesome! But — I don't know. It sounds stupid. But I could tell that you thought I had a huge butt. I mean, it wasn't your fault. It wasn't like you said anything."

"But I thought that *you* thought I looked like a freak of death."

"No way!"

Which was when Becka, at last, spoke. "Polly's always thought she was too big," she said. "When the truth, and everyone knows, is that she's strong. Which is why she's such a great athlete. Right, Pol?"

We both just looked at her. Arching her neck, Becka was like a swan among ducks.

Polly said, "That's what my mother says. But I don't know. I hate it!"

From the mom end of the table, Polly's mother leaned in and said: "Tell her, girls. Because you know what? This child of mine is so self-conscious that she won't even wear the white jeans she got for her birthday."

"What?" Sidekick said. "But you'd look awesome in white jeans."

"You totally would," Becka said.

"That's such a pretty scarf!" Polly then said, turning to Becka, and I could tell she was doing her best to be nice and to try to get the conversation going at something like a normal speed and temperature. Again I ran my hand around Ann's turquoise Lucite beads, feeling their smoothness, like a reassurance that there was hope. "You always have the best stuff."

"I got it last summer," Becka said after a while, "in Paris. A friend gave it to me." She fingered her scarf. Then, turning to me, she said: "But what I'd like to know? What I'd like to know is: What's with your beads? Going for the dog-collar look? As in: *bark, bark*?"

"They're my friend's," I said stupidly. "She lent them to me. I love them." By now the whole table had gone silent.

"I was only joking," Becka said. "Joking? Like I didn't mean anything by it? Like ha ha? Lighten up."

No one, including my bigmouthed mom, knew what to say. So we all just sat there in silence for an eternity or two until finally the waiter came to take our orders. Finally the conversation limped back, and my mother, using her fakest happy voice, said: "You know what's so great about getting you girls together? All four of you are so into clothes. You have so much in common."

"Mom," I said, "that doesn't mean anything except that we're in high school."

"Really," Becka agreed, while next to me, I noticed Polly blushing, and instantly felt bad because it was obvious that I'd hurt her feelings.

When the food came, I could barely touch it, and even though Polly kept trying to get the conversation back on track, with Sidekick Girl attempting to help her, by the time I got back to my Puke-Pink Palace, I was too angry — at my mother, at myself, at Becka, at everyone — to do anything other than fume. Even my reflection in the mirror was fuming. Finally, I went online to check my email and Facebook. Eliza was like: "SO?????!!!!!" I had about a hundred messages from Ann. There were a few other random emails, too. There were also two messages from Dad, I didn't even know where he was — San Francisco? (He still had some business there.) Detroit? Baltimore? In the first subject box, it said, "Hi, Pooky," and went on to read, "Miss you. How's school? How's Mommy? Love you. Dad." In the second subject box, it said: "For my sweetest." That was funny, because Dad never called me "sweetest." The message read: "Darling Sweetest — just to let you know that my last meeting will wrap up around eleven this morning, meaning that I should be able to catch an early afternoon plane to JFK and be in the city for dinner. Make a reservation? Billy." *Billy?* — that was a good one. He hated being called "Bill," let alone "Billy." Mom, as well as everyone else we knew, called him "William." I read the email about a dozen times before I understood that he'd sent it to the wrong email address — that it was meant for someone else. I could barely move, but just sat there, in front of my lit-up computer screen, staring at the message until there was a knock at the door and Mom popped her head in. "Actually," she said, a little half smile on her face, "I thought that Becka was really quite nice."

In early October, a miracle happened. And when I say it was a miracle, I'm not exaggerating. Aunt Libby called and said: "How would you like to come to Paris with me over Christmas?"

"No way," I said.

"Yes way. It'll be my birthday present to you. Aren't you going to be sixteen soon? That's a big year."

"You want *me* to go with you?"

"Do you know how lonely it is to be single in Paris over the holidays? But it's the best time for me to go, when things are quiet in New York. So what do you say? Want to join me?"

Talk about a no-brainer. Unfortunately, Meryl didn't see it that way. Hunched over her computer, she glanced up for about two seconds, shook her head, and said: "Look, honey, can we discuss this later? I've got a deadline."

"You always have a deadline."

"It's for my next book," she said. "It's important."

"*This* is important to me!"

"I need to discuss this with your father."

"What do you mean, discuss?"

"Discuss the issues."

"*Issues*? What issues? I'd be going with Aunt Libby!"

Instead of answering me, though, she returned to her computer and was so engrossed in whatever she was working on that she didn't so much as glance up when I said: "I hope your computer explodes."

It killed me, having to wait for Daddo to come home from work so I could tell him. So I didn't. Instead, I called his office and when his receptionist answered I told her that I had to talk to him right away. A minute later, he was on the phone, saying, "What's up, my sweet girl? Is everything okay?"

Of course I told him, right away, that things were fine at home and that there was nothing to worry about. Then I told him about Aunt Libby's offer and Meryl's twisted response, and he sighed and said: "Okay, honey. I understand. Let me deal with this one, okay?"

I knew something was up when, that night, Meryl came into my room with two glasses of cherry soda and sat on the end of my bed. But seriously? The cherry soda routine was getting old. As if she was going to coax me into telling her the truth, which was that I was in love. Because I knew exactly what she'd say: *Oh, I remember my first crush, too!* But my feelings for Arnaud were more than a crush, more than a schoolgirl's passing whim. As the weeks had dragged by, I'd come to understand that I couldn't be apart from him without something inside me dying.

"Honey?" Meryl said. "It's been a while since we really talked."

For a second, all I wanted to do was crawl into her lap and just spill everything, but as she handed me the cherry soda, I came to my senses. "Anything going on that I need to know about? I just hate to see you looking so sad."

"But I *am* sad, Meryl," I started to say. "I feel so — so bored. At school, everything is drama, drama, drama all the time, and I'm just not like that."

"High school can be tough all right," she said. "Which is why your dad and I agreed that you can go to Paris."

"You mean it?"

"Yes, but with conditions."

It was an old trick of hers — she'd take me to the movies only if I gave Lucy a bath, or she'd let me have a sleepover at Robin's only if I folded the laundry. I wondered if she had any clue that I was no longer in elementary school.

"What kind of conditions?"

"I want you to do something for me."

"Great. Blackmail. What is it this time?"

"I want you to come out to brunch."

"Meaning?"

"You need to open yourself up to new friendships. I mean it, darling. I know how hard it is, being your age, wanting things, feeling all that inchoate yearning for something better, something more exciting than going to classes and doing homework." I wanted to barf. Finally she spat it out. "We're going to have brunch with Polly and her mother."

"Uh-huh."

"And Robin . . . You sure you don't want some soda?"

"No."

"And someone else, too."

"Let me guess: You've invited Ann Marcus, with whom, let me remind you, I haven't been friends since first grade."

"Not Ann. Justine. Justine and her mother. I invited them both and they're coming."

Perfect. Just perfect.

"The girl is a freak. There's just something about her, Meryl, the way she looks at me with her little doggie eyes, like she wants to bite me with her little doggie teeth."

"That's what I mean when I say that I'm worried about you. Your attitude isn't helping you. I've met Justine, and frankly, I like her. She's funny. She's smart. I happen to think she's cute. And Judy is a doll. . . ."

"*Judy?*"

"Judy Gandler — Justine's mother. She's terrific. Really. And she's concerned, too, only, of course, about Justine. She says that Justine's plain old lonely. That she doesn't really hang out with anyone at all."

"Her problem, Meryl. Not mine. And of course she's lonely: She's a freak! No one wants to be friends with her, not just me. Why are you shoving her onto me like this? I can't stand the girl."

I went anyway. I mean, what was my choice? Plus, at least Polly and Robin were going to be there, because even though Polly and I hadn't been friends since middle school, she was cool, and Robin had been my best friend since forever. But the brunch was so horrible, with both Polly and Robin ganging up on me all because I made, okay, I admit it, this really stupid joke about Um's necklace, which was supposed to be funny but just came out weird. Plus, could I help it if the girl reminded me of a cocker spaniel? Just because I said her choker necklace was like a dog's collar, everyone acted like I'd called the girl an ugly loser from the bowels of hellacious hell. As I sat at that table, I felt more alone than ever.

Even Robin didn't get me anymore. The next day, as we were walking home from school together, I said: "I can't believe Meryl rigged up that stupid brunch in the first place. I mean, is she kidding me? Thank God you and Polly were there, is all I can say. But can you believe what that girl Um was wearing? What a weirdo. You're so much nicer than I am, though, telling her how great she looked and all when you didn't mean it. I'm just bad at those kinds of white lies."

But Robin was like: "But I *did* like her outfit. I thought she looked really cute." As for me, I'd worn my favorite Free People skinny-cut jeans, which I'd tucked into my favorite pair of boots — so called "riding boots" even though they weren't for riding — made of black leather, which I'd bought at Macy's of all places, and also, of course, my Hermès scarf, plus this sweet little knockoff Chanel-style jacket, and no one had made any kind of big deal over *my* fashion choices. That wasn't even the point, though, because I really didn't care. Now it was cold and misty with rain, and over my jeans and sweater I wore the raincoat that I'd forgotten to bring to Paris. And I know: A raincoat is only a raincoat, right? Wrong. Because this raincoat, my Donna Karan,

was a fashion statement in and of itself, long and elegant and tailored, made of black cotton sateen, with a pleated back gathered
together with a bow, square shoulders, and a tapered waist. Thank
God I had it, too, because it was another horrible, cold, damp day.
"Plus," Robin said, "I like that she tries different things."

"You would," I said.

"What's that supposed to mean?"

"Just that you like that kind of thing. Mixing things up.
Right?" It was true, too. Ever since working at Aunt Libby's last
summer, Robin had been into wearing two or three necklaces
together, mixing silver with gold, say. Or topping a beat-up jean
jacket with a delicate scarf. Today she was wearing brown
corduroy shorts over black tights, topped with an off-white
scoop-necked long-sleeved winter undershirt with small buttons, her long hair pulled into a long, tight braid, and her feet in
dark-purple suede boots. She was so out-there she was about to
topple off the cliff, but managed to pull it off anyway. It was
hard to believe that she was related to her twin brother, let alone
her totally spastic cousin, John. "You look great, by the way."

"Thanks."

"I have to tell you something else," I said.

"What?"

"Don't kill me, okay?"

"What did you do?"

"*Nothing.* It's what I'm *going* to do: Aunt Libby's taking me
to Paris with her in December."

She just stared, her eyes growing the size of quarters. "Oh
my God!" she finally said, dancing a little on her toes. "You're so

lucky. Paris! I'd kill to go to Paris with Libby Fine. I'd kill just to have that raincoat." It was true, too. Ever since I'd first gotten it, Robin had lusted after my Donna Karan.

"She's taking me for my sixteenth birthday."

"Oh my God. You're going to Paris with Libby Fine! You are the luckiest girl *ever*."

"It *will* be amazing," I agreed. "Especially since . . ."

"Since what?"

Until then, I hadn't told anyone about Arnaud. Except for the girl I'd roomed with in Paris, who didn't count, no one knew a thing. I took a deep breath. Then I said: "There's someone there I want to see."

"You mean a boy?"

That was so Robin. She still hadn't gotten over the boy she'd dated two summers ago at sleepaway camp in the Berkshires!

"Arnaud isn't a boy," I said. "He's — he's a university student. He's studying philosophy and might go to NYU for grad school."

"OMG!" Robin said. "How old is he?"

"Twenty."

"No way," Robin said, her mouth dropping open. "That's, like, *old*."

"Do you want me to tell you or not?"

"Tell me."

"But first you have to promise not to tell a soul. I mean it, Robin. Not one word. To *anyone*. Okay?"

"Okay."

"Promise?"

"Yes."

So I told her the story. I mean, not every detail, but the gist. *Including* the part about how badly Arnaud had wanted to go further than I had, how kissing him, as thrilling as it was, had become a kind of tug-of-war between his wandering hands and my buttons. Then I said: "I'm thinking that, this time — well, I think I'm ready to do it, to go all the way."

"You're thinking of doing *what*?"

"Why not? I'm almost sixteen."

"So?"

"And he loves me."

"Did he say so?"

"Well," I fudged, "not exactly. But he's *French*. It's different there. They're more sophisticated. More . . ." I finally settled on the word. "More subtle. Anyway, it's not a big deal."

"But it *is* a big deal," Robin said. "It's a huge deal. He's old, Robin. A lot older than we are. And he lives in Paris! Have you ever thought that maybe he'd just be using you?"

"You don't believe me, do you?"

"He's in college, Becka. I mean — that's a lot older than us. And how do you know he doesn't have a girlfriend — a real girlfriend, I mean, in Paris?"

"But he loves me."

"How do you know?"

"I just do," I said.

"Do you have even one single piece of proof?"

Which is when I realized that I did. In fact, I had two: the raincoat and the beautiful, expensive Hermès scarf. "Actually," I said, "I do. It's wrapped around my throat."

"OMG," Robin said. "And your parents have no clue?"

"What are you? Ten?"

"But, Becka! Are you sure?"

"What makes you such an expert?" I said. "You've never even had a boyfriend, you spend all your time babysitting, and —"

"I have had a boyfriend. Andy Clarke!"

"Andy Clarke was in fifth grade."

"And Louis Miller, from camp."

"Robin, that was summer camp. You weren't even in high school. Just think about . . ."

"About *what*?" She was turning pink, fluttering her eyelashes in this way she does when she's nervous. I was going to point out that she'd worn pajamas all summer but decided to start again: "Look, Robin. You're the only one who knows. Only, Robin?"

"What?"

"Seriously. Don't tell anyone, okay? This is, like — my whole life."

"Okay," she promised.

Back at home, Danny was downstairs, banging on his drums, and Meryl was out walking Lucy. I decided to write to Arnaud immediately, to tell him about my upcoming trip to Paris — and also about how I'd changed my mind about how I wanted to be with him. But as soon as I logged on to my email account, I saw it: an email from "intheknow@gmail.com" — someone I'd never heard of. I was about to delete it when I saw the heading: "An article by Meryl Sanders, PhD, excerpted from *Growing Pains Magazine.*"

> Teenage Tears and Fears
> No one ever claimed that the adolescent years were easy — for either the adolescent herself or her mother. But few of us, myself included, are prepared for the mood swings, tantrums, arguments, and downright hostility that can burst into hurricane strength as your little girl bursts into young womanhood. Take my own daughter. She spends her entire life on the phone, blabbing, and when she's not blabbing, she's obsessing about clothes. . . ."

I couldn't stomach it. I closed my laptop down and screamed. I screamed so hard my throat began to hurt. I screamed so hard that Danny stopped playing the drums and came upstairs to see what was wrong.

"Get out of my face, you little brat!" I said, howling, as he stood in the door with his jaw hanging open, clutching his drumsticks as if he planned to beat me with them. "Go on! Scram! And close the door behind you!"

God! I just hated her! All I could think of was running away. But the fact of the matter was that I had nowhere to run to. Aunt Libby would let me stay at her apartment, but given that she and Meryl were best friends, I don't think she'd let me stay more than one night. Polly was always in the swimming pool — and even if she wasn't, her apartment was so small that it barely had room for *Polly*. I reached for the phone to call Daddo — but then I remembered that he'd gone to some medical conference somewhere. I called anyway and left a message, but even if Daddo called me back right away, I was still stuck. At home. With *Meryl*. In my mind, I scrolled through everyone I could think of, and in the end, the only person who was even a remote possibility, the only person who might be able to help, was Robin, and we'd just had a fight.

I called her anyway. "What is it?" she said when she heard my voice. "What happened?"

"I can't even tell you. I hate them!"

"What? Are your parents getting divorced or something?"

"No, my parents aren't getting a divorce! Why should they get a divorce? It's me who wants a divorce. From my mother."

She didn't say anything. I couldn't even hear her breathe. "She wrote another article about me," I finally said.

"I know."

"What do you mean, you know?"

"Some jerk is sending it all around. I just saw it."

It was even worse than I thought.

"Why didn't you say so if you already knew? Why didn't you call me to see if I was okay?"

"But, Becka . . ."

"You're supposed to be on my side on this, not sneaking around reading articles about me and then not saying anything."

I slammed down the phone, locked my door, and threw myself on the bed and cried and cried until at last Meryl came home, knocked on my door, and said: "Whatever it is, I'm here for you." WAS SHE FRIGGING JOKING?

"You wrote about me again! It was on the Internet!"

"No, I didn't," she said.

"Don't lie! You're ruining my life! I'm going to kill myself!"

"Don't joke about things like that, Becka!"

I don't know why, but the only thing I could think of to do was wrap myself up in Arnaud's old raincoat. It smelled like him. In some ways, it even *felt* like him. Then I remembered the promise he'd made me make him: *I'll return it to you someday.*

I logged on and wrote him a quick email: "I'm coming to Paris over the winter holidays. I can't wait to see you! Love, Becka." Amazingly, he wrote me back immediately: *"Enchanté!"*

In the middle of the night, it started to rain again. I could hear the water pounding on the roof. When I woke up, it was still raining, and everything looked smoky and gray. I wrote a second email to Arnaud: "I have something special for you, a surprise. I'll tell you when I see you." Then I emailed Robin: "If you want, you can have my Donna Karan." I meant it, too. It had suddenly gone from being my favorite ever to something that made me sick. I didn't want to wear anything from Meryl! I didn't want any of her stupid presents, or false promises, or glasses of cherry soda for as long as I lived!

Then I got dressed, grabbed a bagel, wrapped myself up in Arnaud's raincoat, and headed out into the drizzle. As the door slammed behind me, I could sense Meryl staring after me.

CHAPTER EIGHT

The Flying Dolphin

• Polly •

A few days after that awkward, and I mean AWKWARD, brunch, I finally decided to actually wear the white jeans that Mommy had given me for my birthday. Of course, Mommy was thrilled — she'd been bugging me to wear them ever since she'd bought them for me, and I'd been feeling incredibly guilty about *not* wearing them. But I guess between all the girls being so nice to me, and how much stronger I was getting in the swimming pool, I was beginning to feel more confident in general. It was getting chilly, so I wore them with a long-sleeved blue button-down blouse, giving me a superclean and sporty look, and when I looked at myself in the mirror, I actually liked what I saw. True, I was slightly worried that once I got to school, the entire student body would stare at my back side. Even so, for the first time ever, I put on red lipstick (I usually wear pink lip gloss or nothing), and when I got to school, the first person I saw was Robin, who came right up to me and said: "Girl, you look hot!" I *felt* like I looked good, too, like even though Mommy and I lived in a small apartment and were constantly struggling with money, we had class. So it didn't even bother me all that much when I found out that my lab partner had transferred into another chemistry lab, and because of the numbers, Mr. Green put me with Justine and John. Actually, I was happy about being lab partners with Justine, because, just for starters, she was smart. The problem was John. Freshman year he'd sat behind me in English, making nonstop commentary about the size of my shoulders and arms. In middle school he'd given me a chocolate Easter bunny with its paws and ears chewed off. In third grade he chased me around the playground, threatening to pull down my underpants. Even in kindergarten he'd tormented me, mainly by trying to pull the heads off my Barbies. Now he sat hunched over his notebook, scribbling furiously away, completely oblivious to what Mr. Green was saying, and only looking up long enough to say: "Oh, golly, it's Polly." Or: "Got a dolly, Polly?" Or my favorite: "You look like a collie, Polly."

"And 'john' is the thing that people go potty in," Justine countered.

"Put a sock in it, Mizz Frizz," he said.

But it was as practice was winding down that things really got amazing. Before I even got a chance to take off my cap and goggles, Coach Fruit asked me to stick around for another minute. When all the other kids had gone into the locker room, he told me that he wanted to work privately with me alone every day, after regular practice.

I was so startled I didn't know what to say other than "What?"

"After practice," he repeated. "I want to work with you, one-on-one."

"You want to work with me?" I sounded like a parrot.

"I'm thinking twenty minutes. I want to get you to your edge."

"My edge?" (Polly want a cracker?)

"So what do you think? Want to give it a try?"

I did, but suddenly, as I stood there dripping wet, the thought of my huge butt made me feel like I'd morphed into an elephant.

"I've already told you that you're talented — that you've got what it takes. But now that I've seen you in the water day after day, and seen you under pressure, competing in events, how you related to your teammates, well, I feel that I wouldn't be doing my job if I didn't try to get you where you should be."

"I thought I was already there," I said. "I mean, you really think I can do better?"

I meant it. In only a few weeks with Coach Fruit coaching us, my times had improved by three seconds, four seconds, even, in breaststroke, six seconds, which is, like, almost unheard-of. Not that my *finishing* times were unheard-of. My finishing times were good, but it wasn't like I was breaking records, or even Western High records. But I was managing to beat my own times a lot, especially in my strongest event, five-hundred-meter free-style. I loved freestyle. It felt like flying. I'd hit the water and, just like that, I was pure motion, pure movement, like the water was pushing me along.

"You can do even better."

"If you say so."

"I do." Right then, Coach Fruit grinned this grin that was so cute it was like he was some little kid who'd been caught sneaking cookies. It wasn't just his smile, either. *He* was cute, like, all over, with his Dennis the Menace blond hair and big grin, and did I mention that he had two huge dimples, too? I wondered how old he was. No wonder his girlfriend was always hanging around. I would, too, if I were dating him. Which, of course, I wasn't and never would, and it was ridiculous even having a thought like that cross my mind. In fact, no sooner had I thought it than Bella herself showed up, her car keys in her hand. "Ready to roll when you are," she said.

He gave her a "just one second" sign.

"Okay, then," he said, taking a step toward me. "We have a deal?" He was so close that I could feel his shadow covering me. Was he going to hug me? Push me in the water? The thought even crossed my mind that he was about to *kiss* me. But of course that was stupid, for all kinds of reason, including — especially — that Bella was waiting for him by the door. Instead, he gave me a little punch on my right shoulder, the kind that says: "Way to go."

I was so happy that I forgot about the kind of stupid, trivial things that usually drive me crazy, such as the fact that ever since Mommy had dragged me to that breakfast, I'd wanted to *say* something to Becka. Such as: What makes you think you're so great? I forgot that the last time Mommy and I visited Poppy in Queens, he kept calling me "Patty" and dribbled his chicken soup all down his front. I forgot that Burton had, once again, totally ignored my birthday. I forgot that I had a math test that I wasn't prepared for. I even forgot about my big butt!

"That's great about the extra coaching," Mommy said when I got home. "Your coach must really think you're good."

"All I know is that I'm so hungry I could eat Hank."

"Woof," Hank said.

"You know what?" Mommy said. "I think I'm going to email to your father tonight, to tell him. Don't you think he'd want to know?"

"Burton?" I said. "Burton doesn't even know I swim. Why would he care that I was getting extra coaching?"

"I don't know," Mommy said. "It's just that — well, he is your father. I'm sure he'd be pleased for you."

"I doubt it. He doesn't even visit Poppy. Why would he care about my swimming?"

She just gave me one of her sad little smiles. But the idea that Mommy thought he might actually give a flying fig about my getting extra coaching made me want to cry.

It's just that she tried so hard for me. I wished she wouldn't, but she did. Like that breakfast that she and Becka's mom cooked up? Poor Justine. I wanted to kill Becka. What was her problem? But afterward, Mommy was like: "I'm so glad we did that! Aren't you?"

Now she was bustling around the kitchen, telling me that one day I'd be swimming in the Olympics. And the next day, when I got home? On my pillow was a box. Inside it was a silver charm in the shape of a dolphin, dangling on a chain. When I put it on and saw myself in the mirror, the dolphin looked like it was actually swimming. Something about the way the light caught it made it seem like it had a life of its own, swimming in the shallows of my neck. When Mommy saw me she threw her arms around me, saying, "My own little dolphin. The most beautiful creature in the sea."

Usually, when Mommy surprised me with presents, I felt guilty about them. I loved my new jeans, but I *still* felt guilty about them. I felt a slight twinge of guilt about the dolphin, too, but no sooner had I hit the water after school on Friday then all my guilt disappeared. I'd never felt calmer in the water, more sure of myself, more powerful.

"I like your necklace," Coach Fruit said as I climbed up out of the pool after practice. I was breathing hard, exhausted and exhilarated and sopping wet.

"My mom gave it to me."

"A dolphin for a dolphin," Coach said, giving me one of his adorable grins.

"Looking good!" the beautiful Bella called from the stands. Compared to her, I felt like a giant dripping sponge. I wondered if she knew how perfect her life was. Even so, I'd had such a great day that I felt that somehow I was at a turning point, that my whole life, mine and Mommy's, was going to get easier. . . .

But when I got home, Mommy told me that Poppy had pneumonia. "He's pretty sick," Mommy said. "Patty's worried about him." Even though Poppy flirted with all his nurses, Patty was the one who spent the most time with him. She was a large pink woman who always wore a pin that said: AND YOU CAN CALL ME YOUR MAJESTY.

"How sick?"

"She said we better come visit him soon."

It's hard for me to talk about Poppy without crying, because, first of all, he was the closest thing I ever had to a father, and also, because he was *Poppy*, and I loved him. When he'd gotten too sick and old to live by himself anymore, Mommy and I had talked a lot about having him move in with us, but in the end we'd decided that we couldn't take care of him properly, and even though he could have had my room, he wouldn't even be able to get up and down the stairs. Then we thought about moving closer to him, to Queens, but that didn't seem like such a brilliant idea, either. In the end, it was Poppy himself who'd decided to move into the old-age home, which he called "Senility Camp" and where he had a whole group of nurses whom he flirted with nonstop.

"How soon?"

"I think we should go tomorrow," Mommy said.

We found Poppy was waiting for us with an oxygen mask covering his nose, and watery eyes that looked like melting icebergs. He was skinny and frail, with brown and red bruises on his skinny arms.

"My two favorite girls," he whispered.

I kissed him on the top of his bald, pink, bony head.

"How are you feeling, Poppy?"

"Lovely. Isn't it a glorious day for a picnic? What do you say?"

"Poppy, you're such a flirt," Mommy said, squeezing his hand.

It made me so sad, seeing him like that. But even with an oxygen mask on and struggling to breathe, Poppy radiated a kind of happy, gentle sweetness. When I was little, and he still lived in the third-floor apartment where Burton had grown up, he'd let me play dress-up with my grandmother's old things, and would then take me out for an ice-cream cone or a hamburger. And there we'd be, me in my grandmother's ancient hats and silk nightgowns, sitting across from Poppy, in his bow ties (he always wore bow ties) and blazers.

Then Poppy began to cough, and another of Poppy's nurses, Linda, came hurrying in to prop him up and adjust his oxygen mask.

We sat there for a little longer with him, until, around lunchtime, Poppy fell asleep. On the way out the door, Mommy made Linda promise that she'd call if Poppy took a turn for the worse.

It scared me, seeing him like that. Not because I thought that Poppy would last forever. Over the past few years he'd gone from sort of okay to really-not-so-okay, so I knew that it was only a matter of time until we got the saddest phone call of them all. It was more that, as we cruised past the rusting hulks of what had once been factories and through poor neighborhoods of old brick houses that looked bowed down by the force of the wind, I realized, as if for the first time, how truly alone Mommy and I were in the world, how little we had, outside of each other (and Hank), and how precarious life itself was. With Poppy gone, we'd be more alone than ever. If it weren't for my swimming, well, I'm not sure I would have been able to see much of a future for myself — for myself and for Mommy — at all.

There was something, or rather someone, or rather *two* someones waiting for us when we got home. Actually, they were waiting for Mommy. Sitting on the front stoop, with their dad, were a brother and a sister who looked so alike that if the girl didn't have longer hair I wouldn't have been able to tell them apart.

"Mrs. Brenner?" the father said, rising. "Hi. We spoke on the phone about my kids starting piano lessons with you?"

"Oh, no!" Mommy said, blushing all over. "I totally forgot! How late am I?"

"Oh, not so late," the man said. The dude was huge — as if once upon a time, before he'd gone to blubber, he'd been a high school basketball player. He glanced at his watch. "Not so late," he repeated.

"I am so sorry."

"Listen. It happens."

"I just don't know what to say!"

"Forget about it. Life, right?"

"I guess you could say so."

"You can say that again! Life! Oy. I could tell you stories!"

"Dad!" the boy said while Mommy's blush faded and then rebloomed.

"Sorry," the man said. "It seems like it's my job to embarrass my kids."

"Let's talk after the lesson, okay?" Mommy said. Which, I couldn't help but notice, they did. In the living room, which is just outside my room. Mainly they talked about setting up a regular schedule for lessons, but also, they touched on other stuff: raising children, and living in West Falls, and how many fancy coffee shops there were, and then, just like that, the dude said: "How about I take you out for a cup of joe sometime?"

"Do you even like that weirdo?" I asked her after the two kids and their hulking, huge dad had gone home.

"Oh, honey," she said, "it's been so long that a man asked me out that I couldn't even tell you!"

"Does that mean you're going to go out with him?"

She gave me a half smile, as if she herself didn't know.

"Mommy!"

"I don't know."

She looked so uncomfortable that I felt bad for her — like she was a little kid and I'd been mean to her.

CHAPTER NINE

The Return of the Robot

• Ann •

Justine and I were lying around her pink bedroom when Mama called me on my cell to say: "You've got to get home immediately! Your sister's here!"

I groaned out loud. Hearing me, Justine's cat, Skizz, pricked up his ears.

"What was that all about?" Justine said.

"Robot Girl's home for Thanksgiving. For a full week. I'm not going to make it."

I'd already told Justine about how RG was totally my parents' favorite, about her straight As and how every college in America had wanted her, and even how Daddy was already planning for her to go the same law school he'd gone to.

"Seriously," I said. "Do you know what it's like, with all my eight hundred relatives sitting around the table eating turkey and treating Robot Girl like she's a genius and I'm — I'm *brainless.* It's this huge, big event at our house. The food. The decorations.

And then all the cousins and aunts and uncles. I'm getting a headache just thinking about it."

One thing I liked about Justine was she never took me very seriously. But at the same time, I knew that she totally got whatever I told her. Now she shrugged and said: "Let her be the perfect college brownnoser. What do you care?" And I was going to protest when she added: "And you don't even want to go to Princeton, remember? You're so much cooler than that. I mean, like the outfit you've got on now. How cool is that? If I were your sister and saw you looking so punk-cool-fifties-awesome-fab, I'd be so blinded by your sublime radiance of fabulosity that I'd get on the next train back to college."

"Except that she totally erases me. Most of my relatives, when they think of me at all, think of me as second best." I meant it, too. When RB was around, I was invisible, no matter what I was wearing.

Instead of responding in words, Justine started playing around on her MacBook, hushing me every time I asked her what she was doing, and finally saying: "Look at this, you big dum-dum."

It was a black-and-white photo of a model wearing a dress with a wide, pleated skirt and a narrow, button-down bodice, with cap sleeves, obviously from yesteryear.

"So?"

"You look like *this*, chicken-brain."

"But this girl's white," I said.

"That's not the point. The point is, how can Robot Girl erase someone as out-there and funktabulous as you are?"

"Easy for you to say. You don't have an older sister."

"I wish I did. I mean, do you have any clue what it's like being an only child? It's just me here. Me and Skizz. And we probably won't have any kind of Thanksgiving at all, not with Dad out of town. Again. I don't even mind so much. But poor Mom. She's really upset."

"Me and my stupid big mouth," I said, realizing at once that I'd done it again. Because as I'd gotten to know her better, I'd realized that Justine didn't have the world's greatest home life. Not with moving around all the time, and her dad, whom I'd never even met, not once, never being home. At least my father *cared*.

"On the other hand," Justine said, "I do have the Beckster right across the street."

I could never tell Justine, but I secretly thought that Becka had the most fabulous fashion sense of just about anyone at school, like instead of being a high school sophomore like everyone else, she'd already been launched into some other, better, glamorous realm, where men and women did nothing all day but drink champagne and look incredible. I'd been in school with her since kindergarten, and she'd even had good fashion then, with pink velvet overalls that she wore with little lace-up boots, or corduroy dresses with butterflies on them. Looking back, it was clear that even then she'd been destined for high school cool. With her matching red bows and red Keds, and her mini cowboy boots worn with denim rompers, she'd been the most photogenic kid in all of West Falls, and had even appeared on the front page of the *West Falls Gazette*. (Wearing overalls and eating an apple.) No matter what, other kids copied her: Last year, she'd started wearing white jeans with sleeveless turtleneck summer pullovers, and suddenly, every girl in our grade had the same look. Then she got this amazing raincoat with velvet trim and a bow, and by the time March rolled around, six or seven other girls had something similar. Recently, though, she'd ditched that raincoat and started wearing another one, this kind of beat-up man's raincoat, and voilà! Kids were already copying her. Sometimes she wore it with a fat belt tied around her middle, and other times with a man's hat, or with silk scarves. No matter what or how, she looked amazing. So amazing that I wanted to blog about her amazing style — except, of course, that I still hadn't launched my blog. And also, Justine hated her. And *I* hated writing. I wouldn't even know how to start!

"You know that girl Polly?" Justine now said.

"Of course. Everyone knows Polly. She wins all those sports awards."

"She's my new lab partner."

"No more John?" In his own way, John, too, was famous in our school — but he was famous for looking like a person who was planning to grow up to be a drug addict, or maybe a serial killer.

"Unfortunately, no," she said as she stroked Skizz. "We've been tripled up. But you know what? The first time I met her? I was like: *Nice house, no one home.* Even worse, because I thought she was just plain rude. But she's not, not at all. She's really great."

"I guess," I said, "If you like people who can only talk about sports."

"She's not like that. She's interesting."

"If you say so."

"What's your problem with Polly?"

"She's just, you know, totally into the jock thing," I said, and even though I knew I was talking a load of nonsense, once the words were out of my mouth, I couldn't stop: The Blabber Machine had taken over again, and I was in its grip like a babbling monkey. "She used to be different, but now that she's the superjock of the world, it's like she's too important to so much as notice the great unwashed. Just wait. You'll see."

But I could tell when I looked at her that she didn't see — or at least she didn't see what I saw, which was that it would be just like Robot Girl all over again, when she decided she was too old and sophisticated to do things with me anymore. Polly was a practically a school legend. Who wouldn't choose her over me?

The closer I got to my house, the more my head felt like it was being squeezed by an orange juicer. Of course it was true, what Justine had said: At least I had a family, which was more than a lot of people could say. Even so, I just kept feeling yuckier and yuckier, as if RG's *robotness* had already pre-erased me. So what, you may ask, was the first thing Mama said when I let myself into the kitchen door? "Oh, there you are, honey. You know what I was thinking?"

"What?" I said as I took off my jacket and hung it on the peg in the hallway.

"I was thinking that, well, maybe Martha can give you some debate pointers while she's here."

Then RB herself appeared. And she said: "What on earth are you wearing?"

I looked down at myself. I was wearing a three-quarter-sleeve off-white button-down sweater with a rhinestone poodle pin and peg-leg jeans, an outfit I thought made me look a little like Mama Lee looked in old photographs.

"Your sister's gotten into Mama Lee's old wardrobe," Mama said, shaking her head like there was a fly buzzing in her face.

"I can see that," RB said, smirking. She herself was wearing a Princeton sweatshirt, jeans, and running shoes.

"It was like — like a miracle," I started to explain. "Martha, you wouldn't believe the things Mama Lee —"

But she literally turned her back on me, saying: "Statistics are going to kill me."

"You're in college now," Mama said. "It's supposed to be difficult."

"And everyone is such a genius. Half my class is made up of valedictorians. And the other half were presidents of their high schools."

"Goody, goody," I mumbled.

"And the other half," RG continued, "are multilingual. Or they're classical musicians. Or both! It's intimidating!"

"That's three halves." I snorted.

"You wouldn't be there if you couldn't handle it," Mama said.

"I guess."

"And, honey, you look great! I think college is good for you! Don't you think so, too, Ann?"

RG looked like she always looked — like me, but taller, prettier, and with an actual figure. But she *did* look good, happy, like she had a wonderful secret. Her skin was perfect, and her big eyes shone.

"She looks just — dandy!" I said.

"And you look just — weird!" RB shot right back.

"Girls!" Mama said. Then, turning back to RB, she said: "Did Ann tell you? She's following in your footsteps and doing Debate Team."

"No way," RG said.

"Yes way," I said right before turning to flee to my room.

Two days later, the holiday arrived, and by four in the afternoon, the doorbell was ringing. "Martha! Ann!" Mama called from the kitchen. "That's probably your grandmother! Would one of you get that?"

Except to help Mama with the preparations, I'd barely come out of my room at all that day, partly because — and I know it sounds dumb — but I just couldn't decide what to wear. True, thanks to Mama Lee, I had a whole new look, but it *was* Thanksgiving, so I didn't want to come down the stairs looking like I was going out to hit the clubs. (Yeah, right.) On the other hand, I just couldn't bear to put on one of last year's plain, tasteful, just-above-the-knee dresses, which didn't even fit me so well anymore. I'd tried on pretty much every conceivable outfit in my closet until finally I decided on this amazing green velvet dress with big buttons covered in dark-green satin, a matching dark-green satin belt, and Mama Lee's Lucite beads. I loved the dress not only because it fit me so well, but also because when I saw myself in it, it was as if I could almost see my future: as a person of note, like Mama Lee had been, like a person who could grow up to be something daring and wonderful, and not something staid and steady, like being a lawyer or an economist or some kind of business executive. Someone like Mama Lee had been: daring, and charming, and utterly magical. I couldn't wait to see her face when she saw me in it! But when I went downstairs to answer the doorbell, she was so busy talking to RG that she barely glanced my way.

"Just let me look at you!" I could hear Mama Lee saying. Taking a step back so Mama Lee could admire her, RG looked like a walking advertisement for someone who'd been aiming for law school ever since she could potty. Her hair, parted on the side, was curled into a perfect flip, and she wore black silk pants with a matching black jacket over a blue silk shirt. "You're all grown up," Mama Lee said. "My, my, my."

"My, my, my butt," I whispered under my breath.

"And looking so fine! College must be agreeing with you."

"It is. I love it."

When the doorbell started ringing again, Martha gave me this look like: *It's your turn, brat*. Within minutes, the house was filled with relatives saying hello and kissing and putting their coats in the coat closet and asking my father for legal advice (not really, it was more like a family joke) and making a big fuss over guess who.

"Isn't she just a picture?" Mama Lee said, beaming.

I couldn't stand it anymore. "Mama Lee!"

Finally she looked over at me and, seeing my dress, smiled a smile so big I felt like I could curl up in it and never come out. "Oh, I almost forgot to tell you," she said, "I brought you something. It's over there in that bag in the corner. See?" Glancing through the little crowd of relatives who'd gathered in the foyer, I saw a Macy's shopping bag next to the coat closet. "What is it?" I asked. But just then Mama came out of the kitchen, still wearing her apron, and telling everyone else to go to the dining room and find a seat, pulled me away, saying, "I'm having a little last-minute crisis and really need your help in the kitchen." It wasn't really a crisis, of course: It was some burned mashed potatoes. But it gave Mama time to scold me about my dress, telling me that Thanksgiving was no time look like I was playing dress-up. I loved my dress, though: I thought it was beautiful and elegant and mysterious. "But, Mama!" I began to protest, but she just hushed me and directed me to start ladling out the soup. By the time I'd finished helping Mama, there was only one place left at the table, between my eight-year-old cousin Scooter and a friend of my father's who was going through a divorce and didn't have anywhere else to go for Thanksgiving. Across from me were Mama's aunt Ruth, my cousin Ashley, and Dad's divorced friend's friend who was visiting him from, like, Poland or somewhere. Mama Lee and RG were sitting side by side at the far other end of the table.

"What a wonderful feast!" Dad's divorced friend said.

"Do you have a Wii?" Scooter said.

"No."

"We do. Ha ha! Get it?"

"How old are you, now, honey?" my mother's aunt asked, and when I told her that I was fifteen, she said: "You are? You look like you couldn't be a day over twelve."

"Well, I am," I said. "Fifteen."

"Well, shucks," she said. Then, turning to Ashley, who was wearing a white sweaterdress that made her look practically grown-up, she said: "And you! How many boyfriends do you have?"

"None," Ashley said, blushing.

"I can't believe that! Oh! They must all be chasing you! I feel sorry for them, I really do."

On the other end of the table, I heard RG saying that Princeton sends a greater percentage of its students to graduate school than any other college in the country. "I guess it's never too early to start thinking about your future," Daddy said. Scooter started kicking the table leg, my great-aunt told me that when she was my age she enjoyed nothing better than going ice-skating on the pond they had out back out where they all live, in central Jersey somewhere, and I, not knowing what else to say, said: "That's nice, I guess."

Then the conversation lulled and, in the ensuing silence, Dad's friend turned to me and said: "What about you, Ann? Do you want to go to Princeton, too?"

"As if," RG said.

"Actually," Daddy said, "Ann's still a little young to be thinking of it. She's a sophomore. Next year is the year it all starts up again."

"What kinds of things are you interested in, Ann?" Daddy's friend persisted. He wasn't that old but he was practically bald. His face and head were a pale pinkish red, and I could tell he was trying hard to be nice to me.

"Actually, I like fashion."

"Ann joined Debate Team this year," Mama cut in from her end of the table. "Her father and I are looking forward to her first debate. That is, if she ever gets around and telling us when it is!"

"Are you kidding?" RG interjected. "It's late November — almost time for Regionals."

"You never said anything about that, Ann," Mama said. Everyone was looking at me.

"Just because I don't like to brag!"

"But, honey . . ."

"What's Debate Team?" my great-aunt said. "You mean when you argue about current events? I think we used to call that the Public Speaking Club."

My stomach was beginning to churn, and even though it wasn't, my bladder suddenly felt like it was so full it would burst. "Just because I don't tell you about every little thing I do, just because I don't tell the world about all my brilliant accomplishments all the time," I said. "I mean, can we just drop it?"

"I think that's a very good idea," Daddy said. Everyone was looking at me as if I'd just announced I was pregnant with triplets. Even Mama Lee. And I just sat there, like a frozen lump of crud wrapped in the most beautiful dress in the world. I felt so bad that it wasn't until nearly two days later that I remembered about Mama Lee's present. It was still waiting for me, in the corner by the coat closet: a Macy's bag filled with old *Vogue* magazines.

CHAPTER TEN

What to Wear to Therapy

• Robin •

My mother did not take kindly to my new raincoat, even though, as I explained to her about a thousand times, Becka had insisted that if she didn't give it to me, she'd give it to the Red Cross.

"It's just not right," she said. "Such an expensive coat. Are you sure you're telling me the truth?"

I hadn't even wanted the coat. Or rather, though I loved the coat, I didn't want to take it the way Becka was giving it to me — thrusting it at me as if it smelled like a dead animal. I made her promise to take it back the minute she changed her mind. But my mother didn't want to hear any of that. Instead, she wanted to talk about my going into therapy.

"Therapy?" I said. "Are you kidding? But nothing's wrong with me."

"Except that you have a shopping addiction."

"You've flipped, Mom. Just because I ran up those charges on your credit card last summer doesn't mean I have an *addiction.*

First of all, it was a mistake. What's more, I paid you back every penny!"

I had, too. Every time I'd made money babysitting, I'd turned it over to Mom. It had wiped me out, but it was worth it to get her off my back.

"I don't think so," Mom said.

"What are you talking about?"

When my mother is angry at me, she doesn't yell. Instead, she speaks very slowly, her voice pitched low. She was talking that way now, enunciating every word as if it were made of ice.

"I want to show you something."

"What?" It was all I could do to keep my knees from trembling. We were in her third-floor office, with the wind pushing gusts of rain onto the roof and down the gutters.

"Come see," she said, gesturing with a tilt of her head to her computer. She made a few keystrokes and scrolled down. "You paid over two hundred dollars to a store called Here. On — let's see — August second."

I was confused. Because, yes, I had spent a lot of money on those fantastic boots, but it was *my* money, coming out of *my* bank account. *Three months ago.*

"You want to explain this to me?"

My mouth hung open, like I was at the dentist's. "I don't understand," I finally said.

"Well, I do," Mom said. "You tried to pay for something you bought with your debit card. But you didn't have enough money in your account to cover it. So I got stuck with the bill."

"What?"

"Because you're a minor, our accounts are connected."

"But, Mom!" I said.

"You have a problem. A spending problem. This is the second time you've gone into debt to me over expensive clothes that you've bought that you don't need. Honey, you really do need to see someone, to nip this problem in the bud."

"Nothing's wrong with me!"

"Except that you can't control your buying habits."

"You want to send me to a *shrink*?"

"What do you suggest?"

"Are you kidding?" I said. "You know who goes to shrinks? Weirdo kids who are flunking out. Or girls who *cut themselves*. Juvenile deliquents with anger management issues. Or Ben. *He's* the one who needs therapy, not me. He jumps on my back at school and thinks it's hilarious." He did, too. I wanted to kill him. "You can't do this to me, Mom! I get good grades. I babysit every other second. I'm *normal*!"

Without even blinking, she turned to look at me. It was the kind of expression your teacher makes right before she gives you a detention. She wore an off-white, slightly stained cable-knit sweater, and her red lipstick was the consistency of rubber. Had she *ever* been young?

"One way or another," Mom said, "you now owe me — let's see." She stopped to make a couple of calculations. "Two hundred and eighty-three dollars and twenty-one cents."

"But the boots weren't even that expensive. . . ."

"But you also spent money at, let's see — Starbucks. A place called Nails of Utopia. And . . . the Regal Bagel."

"But I paid you down to the penny. All that babysitting I did, Mom. Those brats nearly killed me. I work twice as hard as Ben, but you don't get on him about the stupid stuff he does. I just don't understand what you want from me!"

Raising her eyebrows, like I was the dumbest dum-dum in the world, she said: "First of all, this isn't about Ben."

"He jumps out of the janitor's closet at school and freaks people out!"

"And as for you, you have a choice. Go and talk to someone about it, or I'm going to close down your checking account completely, and you can live on your allowance money. I'll give you a couple of days to think it over."

"Mom!" I whimpered. But she'd already turned her attention back to whatever it was she was doing on her computer.

"I'm going to run away to Mexico," I told Becka the next day in school, only Becka, as usual, wasn't listening.

She was too busy staring at Justine and Ann, who were sitting with a bunch of other girls a few tables over. "Would you take a look at Um and Ann. The two of them, I mean — they look like extras from some ancient TV show."

"Didn't you and Ann used to be friends?"

"Yeah, when I was five."

"I think they look good," I said, glancing over at them. What I was sure of was that they were cracking each other up, like Becka and I used to do, and as I watched them, I felt a mixture of longing and envy floating up my throat.

"You would think that," Becka said. "Given how, er, original your own style choices have become."

I was wearing a pair of Ben's flannel PJ bottoms tucked into my purple boots and cinched with a wide belt, with a tight-fitting black sweater. Because what was my choice? The truth was, ever since my internship, I'd started seriously lusting after what I can only call, gag me with a spoon, the Emma Bitch look: classy and classic of the kind it takes money to buy. Meantime, as usual, Becka looked unbelievably incredibly ridiculously fantastic, her killer jeans tucked into the most gorgeous pair of low-heeled black leather boots, which I coveted and would have given my right arm to own — not that Becka would have ever thought that way, given that her parents bought her everything she wanted. Those boots! That gorgeous Donna Karan — a real one, too! The trip to Paris! The cashmere sweaters!

"What's your problem?" I finally sputtered.

"*My* problem? *You're* the one who needs to see a shrink."

I was so angry that I felt like hitting her, and opened my mouth to say something when Ben, with his impeccable timing, came over with our totally weird cousin, John — when I say he's weird I mean he's so weird that kids at school had started calling him Weird John — who, for some reason, Ben didn't mind, and a couple of his geeky, nerdy, gawky friends (hard to believe he had them, but he did) and said: "Just the girls we were looking for."

"We're doing a survey," John said, blinking his mascara-coated eyelashes. "For the newspaper."

"Yes?" Becka said regally.

"And we wanted to ask you," he continued, but Ben took it over again and said: "About clothing. As both of you are known for your high fashion, we wanted to know whether it is true that there's a high correlation between shopping activity and neurosis."

"I'm going to frigging kill you, Ben," I said as the whole bunch of them, howling with laughter, turned and walked out of the cafeteria.

Two days later, Mom came into my room while I was doing my homework, sat on the side of my bed, and said: "I know you don't want to see a therapist. So I'm going to make it easy for you. Go and talk to Meryl."

I just looked at her — at this stranger who had once been my mother. She was wearing, get this, pink corduroys and a brown pullover sweater. There were faint traces of lipstick in the tiny lines at the corners of her mouth. Her hair looked like it had been frosted with fireplace ash. She and Dad had just had another fight, this time because Mom had thrown out all the liquor in the house. They'd yelled so loudly that I thought the house would fall down, until finally Dad had left.

"Great! So just head off to a bar, why don't you?" Mom had screamed as he got into the car.

"And what if I do?" he screamed back. "Are you going to ground me?"

Now she said: "I really don't think you get how serious this is. Which is why I already called her. And Meryl — you've known her forever, honey. She'd be a great person to talk to."

"Becka's mom? And you've already talked to her? Mom, this is my business, and you're blabbing it to the world? Have you *lost your freaking mind*?"

"Don't speak to me like that," she said. "It's either that or you go to someone else. I already have the names of several good therapists."

"I'm sure you do."

"Listen: You can either talk to Meryl, whom you've known your whole life and is like another mother to you, or I'll make an appointment with someone else. Your choice."

"And what if I refuse, which I do?"

"I already told you. Your cash card goes in the garbage disposal."

"I swear to God!" I said.

"And you'll be working for me on weekends, too. There are a lot of things I could use some help with around here."

I *had* known Meryl practically my whole life. When I fell off the toolshed in Becka's backyard, landing on the rosebushes, it was Meryl who'd carried me into her house and wiped me down with a cold washcloth. When I had this huge crush on this boy named Sam Smith in sixth grade, and he was mean to me, it was Meryl who'd made me laugh about it. She'd even helped smooth things over with my mom so I could work at Libby Fine. But she had a way of looking at me, with her eyes just resting on me, like she could read all my thoughts, that always made me feel slightly weirded out. Becka called it her therapist look.

She had on her therapist look the afternoon Mom dropped me off at her downtown office. Opening the door, she said: "I just want you to know, Robin, that I don't consider your being here an appointment. But I did agree with your mom that perhaps there's something in your thinking that's tripping you up, and that maybe I could help you get to the bottom of it."

Nothing like knowing that my mother is telling Becka's mother every last thing about me to make me feel all warm and fuzzy inside.

"All I did," I said, settling myself down on one of the two ultramodern chairs she had, "was spend too much money on some boots. It was a mistake. I know it wasn't anyone's fault but my own. I mean, I know I love clothes. But I already told Mom that I'd pay her back."

"Okay," she said, settling herself onto the other chair. "Let's talk about that, shall we?"

"I already told you. It was a mistake."

"You just said you love clothes," she said.

I shrugged. Like she didn't already know that.

"So tell me about what you're wearing now."

I was wearing an ivory-colored silk pajama top with big white buttons over my favorite jeans, with the eggplant-colored boots that had gotten me into so much trouble, and my usual array of necklaces.

"Huh?"

"Your outfit."

"What's wrong with my outfit?"

"Nothing. I'd just like to hear what you have to say about it. About your choices."

"Sometimes," I said, looking at my lap, "I just want to be comfortable."

"Aren't you comfortable?"

"What?" I had no idea what she was getting at.

"To me, your clothes suggest more than the desire to be comfortable."

I shrugged.

"Look: As far as I'm concerned, the two of us, we're just talking. You always look terrific. You just do. You could wear a paper sack and you'd look good. But I have to say that your outfit is unusual."

I took a long, deep breath. "If what you're trying to say is that I'm some kind of fashionaholic, like my mother probably says I am, I'm not. I love clothes, but it's not like I'm obsessed about them or something."

"I see." She recrossed her legs. "Tell me, then. What's going on at home? Things okay with your twin brother?"

"Oh!" I finally got it. She wanted to know if I had an inferiority complex to Ben, which I didn't, not really. "Everything's okay," I said. "I mean, Ben drives me crazy. He's a much better student than I am. But he always has been. And everything else is normal."

"How about with Mom? Things okay? With Dad?"

I could tell right away that she didn't know about Dad. But then again, no one did. He did all his drinking at home, or, I guess, at bars. Out there in the world, he was a law professor:

People looked up to him, even envied him for his long vacations and picture-perfect family.

She shifted position. "How about things with Becka? You two getting along okay, like always?"

Here, I almost laughed, but didn't. I didn't want to hurt Meryl's feelings.

"Yeah."

"Frankly, I'm a little worried about her. She's gotten to be so secretive with me. So quiet. We used to be so close. She used to tell me everything."

"Well, you know how it goes. I mean, we're in high school now."

"She's become such a mystery to me." I didn't say anything. "Just to take one example. Every time it rains, she wears this beat-up old raincoat."

"I know," I said.

"You do?" Meryl leaned forward.

"I see her just about every day."

"Of course." She leaned back against the sofa again. Then: "But why would Becka wear something that makes her look homeless when she has that gorgeous Donna Karan I gave her for her birthday? She wanted that coat so badly that I finally gave in, and you should have seen the look on her face when she opened the box." Gazing out the window, as if talking to herself, she said: "She hasn't worn it in weeks."

"Actually," I finally said, "she gave it to me."

"What? Do you have any idea how expensive that coat was?"

"I'll give it back. Really, I will. No problem! I mean, I love it.

But it's hers. But she said that if I didn't take it she was going to give it to the Red Cross."

"*What?*"

What was I supposed to say? I'd never felt more uncomfortable in my entire life. Turning back to the window as if I weren't there, she said, "And why won't she tell me where she got that that awful coat?"

Why? Because she has this huge crush on this twenty-year-old, and she thinks she's so mature, and she's planning on having sex with him in Paris.

Turning suddenly back in my direction, Meryl directed her gaze at me and said: "Do you have a boyfriend?"

"Me? No. No way."

"Do you not like boys?"

"Sure. I guess."

"Do you ever feel, I don't know — like you're in a hurry to grow up? To look sexy or racy?"

"Not really."

"Okay, then. Tell me what you're wearing."

I looked down at myself again. "Jeans. A silk top. A jacket. Boots."

"Tell me about them: why you chose them, what they mean to you, whether you feel good in them."

This was getting weirder and weirder. "You know what? My mom hates my clothes. Okay? But Libby Fine loves my look. She told me so herself, last summer, when I was interning for her."

Sighing deeply, Meryl leaned forward and said: "Okay. Point taken. But in the meantime, honey, will you do me a favor? If

Becka's hanging out with the wrong kind of people, doing things she shouldn't be doing . . ."

"What kind of things?"

"Is she seeing someone?"

"Excuse me?"

Grabbing both my hands in hers, Meryl leaned in so close that I could feel her breath. "I know you're trying to protect her, Robin. But I can read the signs. I'm a trained psychologist — a specialist in adolescent behavior! And if there's one thing I know about, it's how teenage girls close ranks in an effort to protect one another. So I understand that you don't want to betray your friend in any way. Really, darling, I do. But you have to understand. I'm Becka's *mother*, and ever since she's gotten back from Paris, she's been acting stranger and stranger, more and more depressed and high-strung."

"I don't know anything about it," I said weakly.

"Is she taking drugs?"

"Oh God! No! I swear."

"Drinking?"

"Absolutely not."

"Okay, then. Who is he? Is he someone I know?"

"I don't know!"

"Is she dating someone she shouldn't be — a stoner? A grown man? One of her teachers? Because I know the territory here. I know how tempting the bad boys are when you're your age."

She was pleading now. I felt sorry for her, but I was also angry — too angry to feel anything other than a desperate need to leave.

An endless eternity later, Mom picked me up. It was raining. As she drove, I let my eyes slide out of focus, so the world was streaked with red-and-yellow taillight blurs. "So, was that helpful?" Mom finally said as she pulled her gray Toyota into our driveway.

"Why don't you ask Meryl?" I said in the most sarcastic voice I could muster. For some reason, as soon as I said it, I felt even worse, and I continued to feel awful most of the afternoon, too, until finally I went online and, for less than ten dollars, bought myself a cute bright-green clutch studded with pink rhinestones. I knew that if Mom found out about it, she'd get on my case. But, first of all, there was no way she was going to find out about it, because this time I was paying for it with PayPal. And second of all, what was ten bucks?

CHAPTER ELEVEN

The Great Blue Whale

• Polly •

I knew something was wrong when, halfway through team practice, Coach Fruit stopped me in mid–flip turn to say: "Your mom needs to talk to you." I looked up through the steamed half windows: Outside it had begun to snow.

"What's wrong?" I said.

"Here — use my cell phone." It was Bella, who'd come down from the stands.

"Do you think just maybe I could have handled this without your help?" I heard Coach saying to her as I dialed home.

"Poppy died," Mommy said, picking up on the first ring. "I know. I could have waited until practice was over. But — oh, honey!" She sounded like she'd swallowed a wad of wet tissue.

"Don't cry," I said, but as soon as the words were out of my mouth, I started crying, too. "I'll come home right away."

"No," she said. "I'm sorry. I shouldn't have even called you! You stay at practice. I'll see you afterward."

It was so weird, because as I pulled myself out of the pool, instead of being sad about Poppy, all I could think of was that Coach seemed mad at me. Instead of wearing his usual grin, he was scowling, and his neck was taut, as if his jaw hurt him. I tried not to think about it — either about Coach being angry with me or about Poppy. Instead, as I toweled myself off, I burst into tears. Poppy — gone! I just couldn't believe it. Or rather, I could. He'd been sick for a long time. But never being able to see him again? I couldn't bear it! I tried to think about swimming instead, but as I walked home, all I could think of was: Who will take care of Poppy now? And then I'd cry even harder, my tears falling on my woolen scarf (a hand-me-down from Becka, when Becka and I used to be friends) and making my cheeks even colder than they already were.

Mommy met me at the door with a hug. Bending down to put my head on her neck, I could feel her small bones and her heart beating against mine. "I just got off the phone with your father," she said, wiping her face with one hand and leading me to sit on the sofa with the other. "The funeral's on Friday."

"Not until Friday?" I said. "But today's Monday! What are they going to do, put Poppy in a freezer?"

"Your father needs time to get here."

Suddenly I wasn't thinking about Poppy at all, but instead, was furious — at my so-called father. "Mommy! Burton lives in L.A. He could be here by tonight if he wanted."

"Apparently he has some complications."

"I don't even know why he has to come."

She ignored me. "You may have to miss school. Practice, too."

"Who cares about stupid practice?" I screamed. But then, with a sudden pang, I remembered how angry Coach Fruit seemed to be. And with State coming up, it was important that I didn't lose momentum. The last thing in the world I wanted to do was disappoint him.

Mommy squeezed my hand. "You're a good girl."

"Poor Poppy!" I said, bursting into a fresh gush of tears. Then Mommy started crying, too, and the two of us just sat there, blowing our noses and sobbing until Hank came over and slobbered on us.

On the day of the funeral, we both dressed in dark colors — Mommy in the same black scoop-neck dress that she wore to her students' recitals, and me in a dark-blue sweaterdress that she went and bought for me online, insisting that I needed a good winter dress anyway and that she wanted me to look nice when I saw Burton. "But I don't care about Burton!" I said. "And what about the money?"

"For the last time, Polly," Mommy said, "I have enough. I do. And I *do* care about Burton."

"Well, you shouldn't," I said.

The dress was — how can I put it? A part of me felt like it made me look like a bag of flour squeezed into a dark-blue mitten. But another part of me felt like I'd never looked better than I did in that dress, that it had been made for me and me alone — and that just didn't seem right, not for Poppy's funeral, not when I'd never see him again.

It was depressing, driving through Astoria, where every storefront was decked out for Christmas, with blinking lights and giant blow-up Santa Clauses, but even more depressing was when we got to the funeral home, where Poppy was lying in an open casket at one end of a small room, wearing a scuffed-up gray suit and a pink tie, his face looking like it had been painted with shellac, and his hands folded over his stomach, as if he was taking a nap. I just stared at him, thinking: *Where'd he go?* And then I began to think that they were going to put him under the ground, where he'd be cold, and shut in, and all alone. . . .

"Oh, Poppy," I whispered.

Just then, there was a hand on my back, and I turned to see a man who said: "Polly! Look how grown-up you are!"

"Hi?" I said.

"It's me. Your dad!"

"Burton?"

The last time I'd seen him, he'd had thick hair and a square jaw. But this man was balding, with a patch of scalp at the back of his head, red, puffy skin, with a ring of sparse hair the color of black ink.

"Hi, Burton," Mommy said, proffering her cheek to be kissed.

"Liz," he said. "Thanks for coming."

As if Mommy wouldn't come. As if it hadn't been Mommy (with me along) who'd been looking after Poppy ever since Burton had skedaddled off to his fabulous, kid-free life in Los Angeles.

"You're not a little girl anymore, are you?" Burton continued, scanning me up and down as if I were something he was thinking about buying. I tugged at the hemline of my sweaterdress, suddenly becoming hyperaware of how it hugged my hips and clung to my thighs.

"I'm fifteen."

He whistled. "I guess you are, at that." I noticed that, in addition to his weird, pasted-on-looking, ink-black hair, his gums were weirdly red. "Poor old Dad, eh?"

Which was when I was jolted out of my discomfort with Burton and into remembering why I was there. Poppy, lying in his one suit, which was shiny with age and too big for him, there in that coffin. I wanted to throw my arms around him and cry on his neck, but I knew it wouldn't help. He'd still be dead.

"So, Liz," Burton now said, turning to my mother. "You're looking well."

"Thank you."

"Still teaching the piano?"

"You know I am."

He clasped his hands behind his back, rocking on his feet. "So she's become a serious swimmer?" I could hear him saying to Mommy.

"You should see her, Burton. She's a natural."

"I can see she's strong," he whistled. "Her arms and legs are huge. She must be bigger than most of the boys. And in that dress — like a great blue whale! What are you feeding her, anyway?"

I felt so stung that I wanted to cry. Instead, I turned to see Mommy's face turning pink the way it does when *she's* about to cry. Then I turned to Burton and said: "Why are you such a jerk?"

"Excuse me?"

"You're probably only here to see if Poppy left you any money!"

"Polly . . ." He started to explain. "I don't think you understand. All I meant was that you've gotten so tall, so tall and so strong."

"Why didn't you ever come and see Poppy? Your own father! Whatever. Okay. You went ahead and abandoned me and Mommy. But Poppy? He's been sick for years. What is *wrong* with you? Are you *gay*?" I was so worked up I could have continued for an hour, except right then the priest walked in. He was round and pink and wore round, shiny glasses. He blinked, cleared his throat, and said: "Shall we begin?"

Sitting herself in the front row, near Burton, Mommy gestured to me to sit beside her. But I couldn't — I just didn't want to go anywhere near that loser. Instead I sat in back, with Patty and Linda, Poppy's nice nurses from the old-age home.

I don't know why, but as soon as she saw Burton making a beeline for me after the funeral, Mommy pulled me away, saying: "I'm going to get you back home in time for you to make your swimming practice."

"You are?"

"We can just make it," she said

I didn't want to hang around Burton — that was for sure — but I didn't want to swim, either. I didn't want to do anything but sleep. I mean, it just felt weird, going to school to swim like it was just an ordinary day, like nothing unusual had happened. And even though Mommy assured me that Poppy would have wanted nothing more than to get me to swim practice, once I hit the pool, I couldn't catch my rhythm no matter what. I was breathing hard — too hard — and my arms and legs felt rubbery in the water. It got worse and worse. So much worse that Coach pulled me out of the water to tell me to take a hot shower, put my clothes on, and meet him in his office, and boy oh boy, did he sound angry.

I was pretty sure he was going to lecture me, but instead, when I got to his office, dry and dressed again in my dark-blue dress, all he said was: "You were really off out there."

"It was my grandfather's funeral today," I said, "and my so-called father was there."

"I see," he said, frowning.

"You're angry at me, aren't you?"

"Why should I be angry at you?"

"I don't know," I said, but that wasn't true, either. He was angry for all kinds of reasons, mainly to do with how, even after all the work he'd poured into me, I was letting him down. To keep from crying, I dug my fingernails into my hands, afraid to look up.

"Damn," he suddenly snapped.

Sighing loudly, the way Mommy sometimes does when she's frustrated with one of her students or tired, he suddenly burst out with: "If I seem angry, it's because I had a fight with Bella."

It was one of those awkward moments. I didn't know what to do, or say, or even whether I had permission to breathe. So I just sat there, staring at my hands until, a few moments later, he said: "Sorry. I shouldn't have told you that."

I still didn't know what to say. So I didn't say anything. Finally he broke the silence: "So tell me. What's going on? Why are you so off?"

"You already know. Poppy died."

"And?" His voice was so soft and so kind, I nearly melted.

"His funeral was awful. Including the priest, there were only nine people there."

"Sounds sad."

"Plus, my father said that I'm huge!" I suddenly burst out.

"Huge?"

"He said I had enormous legs and arms. He said I'm a whale!"

"In those words, exactly?"

"Actually, he said I'm a great blue whale."

Coach just looked at me.

"And then I asked him if he's gay!"

"Is he?"

"What do I care?"

Suddenly I was laughing. I was laughing so hard, I could feel the chair shaking under me. I was laughing so hard that I was crying, laughing and crying as I remembered when Poppy still lived in his own apartment and Mommy and I would go over there for what he called his "famous lamb chops for his lamb chops" and we'd eat dinner in his cramped kitchen, Poppy telling jokes he'd heard on late-night TV. "Whatever," I finally said, catching my breath enough to get up. Which is when it happened. Coach Fruit reached for me. Pulling me into his chest, he murmured: "You are not a great blue whale." I knew he meant it as a joke, something to keep the laughter going, but when I felt

my chest against his, with only my sweaterdress and his sweatshirt between me and him? I thought I was going to melt right
into the gray linoleum floor.

It was the weirdest thing ever. Because even though I couldn't
stop crying over Poppy, at the same time, my mind was whirling
with what had just happened in Coach Fruit's office. Wouldn't it
be funny, I thought as I walked home, if Mommy and I both got
boyfriends at the same time? Except, of course, that Coach Fruit
would never be my boyfriend. I mean, the whole idea was ridiculous. But it had been fun to laugh with Coach Fruit about my
so-called father, and the more I thought about it, the more I realized how glad I was that I'd confronted Burton: Somebody had
to! Coach Fruit had told me it was great that I had, not that that
meant anything boyfriendwise. And just because Mommy had
gone ahead and had coffee with that weirdo lummox whose kids
took lessons from her didn't mean that she was going to start
dating him, either. Especially since all she'd tell me afterward
was that he "seemed like a nice man."

But when I got home, there he was, sitting on our sofa, looking huge and uncomfortable, like he wasn't sure that the sofa
would hold him. It wasn't that he was fat or ungainly so much as
big all over, with huge feet encased in square black shoes, and
long fingers. "Hiya, we met before, on the steps?" he said. "I'm
Alfred." I gave him my standard "see you" wave and started
heading to my bedroom, but Alfred (*Alfred?*) kept talking.

"My kids are really getting into it."

"Good."

"Piano, that is. Your mom's a good teacher."

"Yup."

"Polly, right?"

"Yup."

"We met before. When you were with your mom, coming home."

"Yup."

"You're a swimmer?"

"That's right."

"Your mother told me. She's very proud of you."

"She does that."

"My kids really, really like her."

"I'm glad."

"Their mother and I are divorced."

"Sorry."

"They live with me."

What did this guy want from me, anyway? A cookie? I honestly didn't know what to do. I had homework, and even if I didn't, I made it a habit to never, never ever, get into a lot of chitchat with Mommy's students' parents.

"I like your dress," the man then said.

"Thank you."

"It's pretty," he said. "It looks good on you."

"Can I, er, get you a glass of water or something?"

"No, that's okay. "

"Well, then," I said, "nice meeting you again."

"Nice meeting you, too, Polly."

From my bedroom, I heard the strains of a very tentative Bach — one of the Anna Magdalena minuets that I used to play when I still played piano. Then silence. Then my mother's voice. "Oh, Alfred! Did you hear? Aren't they doing well? Wasn't that just beautiful?".

In my mind, I could practically hear Poppy saying: "What kind of name is *Alfred*?"

CHAPTER TWELVE

The Debate Dress

• Ann •

*M*ama *waited almost* a week, but when she was ready, boy, did *I* get a talking-to. "I want to discuss what happened at Thanksgiving," she said as I reached for the Cheerios and poured myself a bowl. She herself was sitting at the kitchen table as usual, drinking coffee, the *New York Times* spread in front of her.

"Can this wait? I have to get to school."

"No, it can't wait."

"I'll be late. I don't want to get a tardy."

It was a standoff. Because if there was one thing my mother couldn't tolerate, it was lateness of any kind, especially when it came to school, where every jiggle and jot on my record *mattered*. But the Cheerios gave me away. Even now, they were hissing and popping, the way they do when you've just poured milk on them.

"If you have time for breakfast, you have time to listen," she said.

"But I have to brush my teeth and clean up, too!"

She wasn't biting. "You and your sister used to be so close. And now you're at each other's throats. What's going on?"

"Why don't you ask *her*?" I said. But I knew it was useless, because, first of all, RG had already returned to Princeton, and second, because no matter what, in Mama's eyes, RG could do no wrong.

"What happened to my pretty, happy, sweet girl?" Mama said. "I just don't understand. All of a sudden, you've become someone I don't even know."

"What are you talking about?"

"Your hair. The way you dress. Half the time, I don't even know where you are, and the only friend you ever bring home is Justine."

"What's wrong with Justine?"

"Nothing, honey. I like Justine — and I like her mom, too. It's *you* I'm concerned with. You're wearing those ancient styles, for one thing. And you look like — well, I just don't know what you look like anymore!"

"I like my new clothes," I said.

"Do you really? Honey, have you seen yourself in the mirror this morning? Do you have any idea what you look like?"

"What's that supposed to mean?"

Actually, it was a big day for me, stylewise, because I was wearing something I hadn't dared wear before: a bright-green pencil dress with bolero sleeves, which hugged my body perfectly and smelled like crisp tissue paper.

"I remember exactly the day your grandmother first wore that dress," Mama said, a wistful look coming over her. "Oh, and how she pranced around in it like a teenager! She looked so much younger than she actually was that, do you know, my own boyfriends — not that I had very many of them — more often than not thought she was my older sister, and not my mother at all. She was so charming — well, they all just fell right in love with her is what they did. Especially since I was so serious all the time."

"You're still serious," I said.

"She was secretive like you are, too," Mama said a moment later as her voice faded to a whisper.

"I'm not secretive," I said, my temper suddenly rising up. "I'm busy. With school. With studying. With after-school activities. I thought that's what you wanted me to do."

"Do you have a boyfriend you're not telling me about?"

I didn't know whether to laugh or cry. The most I'd done was gone out with a bunch of boys and girls together, usually for ice cream. Me, with a boyfriend? Like, who would I date? Justine's lab partner, John the Weirdo? My cousin Scooter?

"You're kidding me, right?" I finally said, my mouth sneaking into a smile. "How much caffeine have you had this morning?"

"This isn't funny."

"I don't have a boyfriend."

"Then where are you every afternoon? Debate Team only meets twice a week."

"What are you talking about?"

"Martha told me that Debate Team only meets twice a week."

And just like that, I was busted. She'd find out about Ms. Anders's art room and my dreams of becoming an artist — and then I'd be in for something I couldn't even imagine, something approaching such total condemnation that I knew I couldn't take it. I'd be a pariah, is what I'd be. Excommunicated from my own family.

The lie flew out of my mouth so fast I didn't even know where it came from: "Mama, I didn't even want to tell you."

"Tell me what, young lady?"

"I wanted it to be a surprise."

"What? Spit it out."

"I'm going to be representing Western High in the Debate Team final rounds. In — in January. I've been going in for extra coaching."

Mama took one good long look at me, and then her entire face relaxed into a grin. "Oh, honey!" she said. "I'm just so proud of you! I can't wait to tell your father."

Throwing her arms around me, she nearly choked me as I wolfed down the last of my Cheerios. For a moment, I wished we could just stay that way, locked together, just me and her, forever.

"You are so done for," is what Justine said when, at lunch, I told her the whole story. "Not to mention that you're stupid."

"What am I going to do?"

"But at least you look amazing. Doesn't she look amazing?" she asked Polly, who for some reason had a different lunch period than usual and was sitting with us — with me and Justine and the Latins, wearing her usual clean-cut goddess style of, in this case, her white jeans with a big white sweater on top. It was no use my continuing to be jealous of her anymore, either. Honestly, she was too nice to be jealous of, one of those girls who never ever said anything even slightly mean about anyone, even obviously horrible people like the assistant principal, Mr. Ward, who had a habit of slamming kids up against the lockers.

"She does," Polly said. Then, turning to me: "You do. You look amazing."

"You have to help me!" I begged.

"How am I going to help you?" Justine said. "Listen, dummy: You haven't done anything wrong, remember? Other than that dumb lie, I mean. I can't even believe she believed you the first time. Debate Team? I mean, even though it's true that you talk all the time —"

"Thanks."

"Earth to Ann: All you're doing is drawing and painting, and you're doing it right here at school. Under *a teacher's supervision*. What can *I* do? Ask Ms. Anders. She's nice. She'll understand. Maybe *she* can help you."

It wasn't a bad idea. Ms. Anders always had time for me. She was only a few years out of art school herself, the young kind of teacher who always had more ideas for the classroom than she could use. Lately, she'd been helping me with my figure work. Still, the best she could do was soften the blow.

"I'm doomed," I said. "There's no way out. If my mother ever finds out that I've been lying to her . . ." Justine rolled her eyes, completely without sympathy. "In my house, you don't lie. You just don't. When I was little, I lied this one time and told her that I hadn't eaten the last cookie, and when she found out I had, man, was she angry!" I winced, just thinking about it — how disappointed she'd looked, how small and wrong I'd felt. "There's no way out," I repeated. Then I had an idea. A flashbulb-going-off-in-my-brain idea. The best idea I'd ever had, *ever*. "Unless . . ."

"Forget it."

"But you don't even know what I was going to say!"

"Fine. What?"

"Unless I launch the blog."

"What blog?"

"The fashion blog I've been thinking about doing."

"Excuse me? You're making, like, no sense."

Once again, I explained that for months I'd been thinking about doing a fashion blog for teens. That I'd been poring through Mama Lee's old *Vogue* magazines and studying the fashion drawings, and how, with one swoop of the pen, fashion illustrators captured a look with more dexterity and excitement than a camera could ever match.

"But I'm not a good writer," I said.

"So you've told me."

"That's why you have to help me launch the blog!" I said as I began to see how I could unscramble the mess I'd made for myself. Justine would do the writing; I'd do the art. We'd launch over Christmas — and I'd tell Mama that I'd made up the lie about Debate Team so I could surprise her with something even better: an original blog. I could even argue that the blog could help me get into college. "I've already done a dozen sketches, or more. I just need someone to help me write it! If we do it together, it'll go viral. First just here at school. But then teens everywhere will read it. I even have a name for it," I said, getting carried away with myself.

"*Ann Has Gone Crazy*?" Justine offered.

"So you'll help me?"

"Sounds cool to me," Polly said, getting up to go. "Later."

"What's your stupid idea for the stupid name of your stupid blog?" Justine said.

"*Fashion High*. And it would be all about the fashion trends right here. Right here at Western High."

I was getting excited now, seeing my illustrated blog unscroll in my mind's eye as perfectly as if it were a movie. I looked at Justine. Justine looked at me. "I'll think about it," she said.

It wasn't until right before vacation began that Justine told me that she'd do it — she'd do the blog. That night, and for the first time in weeks, as I sat down for dinner I didn't have a knot in my stomach. Justine said that the first post should be about Becka, which was just fine with me, as I'd been wanting to write about her fabulous style all along. At last, I thought, I'd be able to tell my mother the truth.

Mama was in a good mood, too. Apparently she'd managed to get a whole family of little kids into Head Start and had gotten home early. In general she didn't put the kind of hours in that Daddy did. Even so, there were times when she got kind of crazed, and we'd have to order out pizza or Chinese. Tonight, though, she'd made my favorite: roast chicken with green peas and mashed potatoes. "Smells good," Daddy said, giving me a little wink. Then Mama turned to me and said: "I have a little present I want to give you."

I was confused. "An early Christmas present?"

"This has nothing to do with Christmas," she said. And a minute later, she'd gotten up from the table, gone into the front hall closet, and returned with a shopping bag from Bloomingdale's. "Go ahead," she said, handing it to me. "Open it."

Inside was, and I'm so not making this up, a two-piece women's business suit — slacks and a jacket — made out of brown-and-white tweed.

"Mama?" I said.

"For *Finals*," she said. "Debate Finals. When I saw it, I just couldn't resist!"

"That's a lovely outfit," Daddy chimed in. "Classy."

"It'll never fit," I said.

"It's a size two. Petite."

"I don't know, Mama."

"When I saw it — well, I couldn't stop myself. The color is perfect for you. It has your name on it, darling. And for Finals, you want to look — I guess the word is 'professional.' "

Fingering the expensive fabric, I prayed that it looked awful on me. "Go ahead, try it on," Mama said.

"Now? "

"After dinner."

"I have homework."

"Indulge me," she said.

What could I do? After dinner, I went upstairs and tried the suit on. The lining was silk. The fabric was perfect. It fit me like a glove. It also made me look like an accountant, and I absolutely hated it.

"Look at you!" Mama said, bursting into my room before I had a chance to take it off and announce that it was too big for me. "You look like —" She was close to tears. "You look like a *champion*!"

"But, Mama!" I said.

"Just wait until your grandmother sees you in this! I can't stand it! I'm going to call Mama right now and tell her myself."

I found myself beginning to mouth the word "but" again and again, but as I heard her in the next room, talking to Mama Lee in a voice filled with happiness, I knew it was too late. I'd never be able to tell her the truth now!

The morning Aunt Libby and I arrived, Paris slid by our taxi windows in a gray-and-pearl-white mist. There was a frosting of snow on the ground, and even in the early morning, people were out strolling, carrying their morning baguettes, or walking their dogs. I felt that rush all over again — that rush of the whole world opening up to me, of endless possibility.

The only problem was that Arnaud was still in the mountains, skiing with his family. He'd written me an email saying that the minute he was back in town, he'd tell me. But in a way, the extra wait made things even more delicious, more glamorous, more intoxicating. I couldn't wait to see the expression on his face when I told him that I wanted what he'd been wanting all along. . . .

The taxi pulled up at our hotel and two men wearing white gloves helped us out. Inside, it was beautiful, with views of the Tuileries and yellow silk curtains framing the windows. Libby and I shared a room with two double beds, each of them covered with thick white spreads that smelled like violets.

"Okay, I'm heading to dreamland," Aunt Libby said. "Why don't we both try to sleep a little?"

"Sounds good."

As Libby settled in for her nap, I went to the bathroom, shutting the door behind me. As I texted Arnaud, my hands were practically shaking. "I'm here. And I can't wait to see you!" I wrote (in French). It was six thirty, Paris time, so I knew I'd have to wait until later to hear back from him. As I unpacked, putting my things on the padded, silky hangers in the closet, my mind starting whirling around what I'd wear to meet Arnaud, what outfit would go best with the Hermès scarf Arnaud had bought for me on the rue Mouffetard. Just fingering it, as I took it out of my suitcase and placed it in the bureau drawer, made me feel like, just maybe, I could be a native Parisian. After all, I *looked* like one. I'd packed his raincoat, too — to give back to him, as I'd promised. I hated the idea of giving it up, though: It was my one sure reminder of our time together. On the other hand, every time I'd worn it, Meryl had gone into psychotherapist mode.

"You really want to wear *that*?"

"Obviously."

"Why?"

"Because I do."

"That's not an answer."

"What's the problem? It's only a raincoat, Meryl. Unless you need more information so you can write another article about me. I've even got a title for you. You can call it 'The Daughter Doctor's Daughter Has a Raincoat.'"

"I'm *serious*," she said. "Why won't you tell me where you got it at least? And don't call me *Meryl*."

"I *have* told you, Meryl," I lied. "I bought it last summer in Paris. I forgot to pack a raincoat before I left. It was raining, and this old guy at a booth was selling it for, like, two Euros. It was better than getting soaked."

She eyed me. "Even if that were the case," she said, "why do you continue to wear it?"

"It's no big deal. It's a *raincoat*. Why do you care?"

"Because I already gave you a very beautiful and expensive raincoat, the same one you'd been obsessing over, and then you turned around and gave to Robin."

"I know, Meryl. But she just kept begging for it. It was one of those girl things."

I thought I'd won, but then, one horrible day in December when it was raining so hard that I came home soaked, Meryl said that she felt bad about how much we'd been fighting, and wanted to do something fun with me to make up. "How about a pedi?" she said. "Does that sound good?"

Actually, it did. But as soon as we'd relaxed into side-by-side pedicure chairs, our two sets of feet immersed in hot water and the two ladies scrubbing our calluses off, I could sense it coming — whatever it was.

"Honey," she said, reaching over to take my hand.

"I hate when you use that therapy tone with me. What is it?"

"I need you to tell me. Who is he?"

"Earth to Meryl. Who is who?"

"Raincoat Boy."

"*M'excuser?*"

"That thing," she said, pointing to Arnaud's raincoat, which I'd taken off and hung on the salon's coatrack. "Who is he?"

"You don't know what you're talking about, Mother."

"I think I do, though. And whether or not you tell me anything, I need you to listen, and listen well. Because this is important. As important as — well, as your entire future."

"Oh God," I groaned, realizing how expertly she'd set the trap. I mean, what could I say, sitting there surrounded by strangers at Nails of Utopia while a petite Vietnamese woman with beautiful black eyes scrubbed and buffed my feet as if her very life depended on it?

"You're fifteen," she started by saying.

"I'll be sixteen in about two minutes."

"You're fifteen, and a sophomore in high school, and at your age, it's natural — healthy, even — to have strong feelings about all sorts of things. After all, you're in the midst of one of the most exciting and wonderful changes that anyone ever experiences." Oh God, I thought — here we go again. The Adolescence Lecture. It was straight from the pages of her Daughter Doctor series. "But you're not stupid, Becka, and you must be aware that teenage girls are also prone to making decisions about their lives, about who their friends are, about the kind of person they want to become, and especially about their bodies, that can potentially have lifelong consequences."

I opened my mouth to protest, but she cut me off. "I know what you're thinking, Becka. I know exactly what you're thinking and how you're processing everything I'm saying. But if I, your mother, don't say it, who will? I don't know who Raincoat Boy is, and you may never tell me, but I do know that since you've come back from Paris you've changed — for the worse, I might add. You're moody. You snap at me, at your brother, even at Lucy."

"Yeah, right," I said. "Anyhow, Lucy smells."

"You close yourself in your room for hours at a time, just sitting there in front of your computer on Facebook, or texting."

"Or doing homework, Meryl. How can I get my assignments, which, by the way, are posted online, if I don't go online?"

"Or mooning over whoever this Raincoat Boy is."

Trapped, cornered, with no' way out. "You're in therapy overdrive *projection*." My using one of her own favorite words did it: Meryl winced. "What the hell is it you want from me?"

"I want my daughter back," she said.

It was a draw. Meryl sighed — but a week later, I was in Paris, and nothing mattered anymore except Arnaud.

I was too hyper to take a nap, or even to hang out, so I went out for a walk. A few blocks from the hotel, I came across a row of boutiques and cafés. Though it was still too early for most businesses to be open, there was an OUVERT POUR LES AFFAIRES sign in the window of a hair salon. Literally: a *sign*. I'm not superstitious about stuff like that, but I walked right in there, and when, an hour later, I walked out, I had a whole new, much more sophisticated look. The hairdresser had not only thinned some of the bulk out of my hair, but also had given me highlights. True, I had spent almost every Euro I had, but I knew it would be worth it when Arnaud saw me and realized that the girl he was looking at wasn't some kid he'd met over the summer, but his equal, his soul mate.

Aunt Libby was still napping when I got back to the hotel, but I knew that I'd never be able to fall asleep, not when my mind was whirling away with thoughts of Arnaud. It was almost nine. Why hadn't he texted me back yet? Then it was ten, then eleven, then twelve. I was practically jumping out of my own skin! Even going shopping with Aunt Libby didn't help much — even when she insisted on buying me a pair of sleek black pants with stirrup straps. It wasn't until we were back at the hotel and I got a chance to go online that I FINALLY got his email. "If only I'd known that you were coming so soon. I'm with my family, skiing in the Alps, but back in Paris on Friday, like every year. Perhaps we can meet then? I would love to see your beautiful face, my sweet American girl."

But I *had* told him that I was coming then . . . hadn't I? What if he wasn't even on a skiing trip, but making the whole thing up? What if Robin had been right and he was too old for me and had another girlfriend and was only playing with me? What if he'd somehow found out that I was still in high school? I'd die! In a panic, I emailed back immediately. "But when am I going to see you?" The answer came a few minutes later. "As soon as I return to Paris," he said, and as relief flooded through me, he sent me something else: a picture of himself, decked out in skiing clothes and standing on top of a mountain.

I felt so much better that every stranger I passed on the street, every glimpse into the window of a café, every baguette and croissant seemed to be winking at me, as if they understood and had agreed to keep my delicious secret. I wore pencil skirts with billowing cashmere tops; high boots over skinny jeans; a midcalf camel-hair coat. As for my Hermès scarf, I wore it Parisian-style, wrapped several times around my neck and tied in front in an elegant little bow.

"Ooh la la," Aunt Libby said, loading me up with designer jeans, blouses, and other things that she insisted she had to buy for me. "*Très très chic.*"

Finally the day came. I'd gotten an email earlier telling me when and where to meet Arnaud: one o'clock on the Pont Neuf. Could anything have been more romantic? I couldn't wait to see his face when I told him my secret — the secret that the two of us, and the two of us alone, would share. The only question that remained was: What was I going to wear?

Libby was out all day that day — the only day, as it turned out, during the entire week that she had no time to spend with me. Which suited me just fine, first, because she wouldn't get suspicious, and second, because of everything else! I told her that I wanted to go to the Louvre and then, if there was time, to visit Notre Dame.

I wore the most sophisticated and Parisian thing I could think of: black knit pants tucked into my black leather low-heeled boots, topped with a black cashmere sweater and, of course, the Hermès. On my ears I wore the simplest of simple gold hoops, but otherwise I wore no jewelry at all. I was going for sleek and sophisticated, and when I saw my reflection staring back at me in the hotel mirror, I knew that, had I wanted to, I could pass for a real Parisian. My black boots shone with polish; my pants fit me perfectly; the sweater was simplicity itself.

The Pont Neuf wasn't far from our hotel. As I walked toward it, it began to snow, fine crystalline snowflakes falling gently from the sky and landing on my hair and eyelashes. I carried a black Michael Kors purse in one hand, and in the other I had Arnaud's raincoat, which I'd wrapped in tissue paper and put in a Clare et Clarent shopping bag. It was getting colder and colder, my breath coming out in a burst of grayish steam. But I was so excited, I was warm. Plus I'd timed myself perfectly to be just a few minutes late. Even so, when I arrived on the bridge — right in the middle, where we'd agreed to meet — I saw that I'd gotten there first. Impossible, I thought, glancing at my watch and then looking around. On one sidewalk was a family of tourists, the dad backing up to take a picture of his wife and kids. On the other side was a middle-aged man walking very fast, a woman walking her dog, and a group of university students — or at least they looked like university students, kind of on-purpose shabby, but too old to be teenagers. They were joking around and smoking cigarettes, wearing heavy black winter coats or parkas, with hats and gloves. But no Arnaud. I checked my watch *and* my phone. It was five minutes past one. Then it was six minutes past one. Seven, eight, nine minutes past one! Finally, I positioned myself on the sidewalk, in the dead middle of the bridge. Which is when one of the students from across the bridge walked up to me and said: *"Ah, mon petit oiseau américaine est ici."* Then, also in French: "Everyone! Come meet Becka, my friend from America."

"Arnaud?"

"Come see Becka!" he yelled over to his friends a second time.

But I didn't want to meet everybody. I didn't want to meet anyone — anyone, that is, but Arnaud. Hadn't he realized that I'd been standing there waiting for him all that time? And who were all those people, and why were they there? Clutching the shopping bag with Arnaud's raincoat in it, I felt my entire body go heavy and light at the same time, as if I were both a blown-up balloon and burlap sack filled with sand.

"This is for you," I finally said, handing the bag to Arnaud as his friends watched.

"*Ah, oui. Un present?*"

"*Oui.*"

He unwrapped it. "*Mon impermeable?*"

From the far sidewalk, his friends started laughing, like the sight of his raincoat was the funniest thing in the world. A moment later, they'd joined us on the sidewalk, all of them, including Arnaud, seized with some hilarity that only they understood. Finally, Arnaud turned to me and asked if I was hungry, which I wasn't. I was the opposite of hungry. But one of Arnaud's friends said he knew of a good café in the Latin Quarter, and a minute later, after they'd all conferred with one another, I found myself following along, pretending that I couldn't have been more delighted.

"So good to see you!" Arnaud murmured when, at long last, we were sitting next to each other at a long table covered with a not-very-clean white cloth.

"I promised."

"What did you promise?"

"Don't you remember? I promised I'd bring your raincoat back to you."

"You did?"

He took both ends of my scarf in his hands, tugging on them in a way that brought my forehead closer to his. "Lovely," he murmured, as much to my scarf as to me, and in that moment, I felt myself relax into his kiss. Except he didn't kiss me. Instead, he turned to his friends to say: "Let's celebrate Becka's arrival with food and wine."

Everyone smiled at me — but it was the kind of smile you give to a toddler who's stubbed her toe. They talked to one another and to Arnaud, and even though my French was really pretty excellent, they hardly talked to me at all.

As I sat there feeling more and more lost and alone and humiliated, one of the girls looked directly at me and said: "I love your scarf. *Très chic*."

"*Merci*," I said, feeling slightly better.

"I used to have one like that," she continued, fingering her own scarf, a lovely pale blue dotted with silver stars. "I lost it last spring."

"I hate it when that happens," I said, but she didn't seem to notice that I'd spoken. Instead, she directed her attention to Arnaud. "I am so stupid."

"Are you, *mon cher*?"

"I must have left my Hermès at your apartment."

"I don't understand, Ellie."

"My Hermès," she said. "I lost it. In May, I think. Maybe in early June? I bet I left it at your apartment. . . ."

"Ah!" Arnaud finally said, blushing a little. Then: "Do you think so?"

"Let me see it."

Reluctantly, miserably, my face on fire, I undid the scarf — *my scarf, the one that Arnaud had given me* — and handed it across the table. As Ellie took it into her hands to examine it, she murmured, "It *is* my scarf. The exact same one, with the little heart-shaped stain on the back of it. Why didn't you tell me that I'd left it over at your house?"

"I didn't know," Arnaud said. "I just assumed . . ."

"That you could give it to your American friend?"

He raised his hands over his shoulders, palms up, in a "who, me?" gesture, protesting that he'd made an honest mistake. "Oh, shut up," the girl finally shot back. "Your friend can keep it. It really doesn't matter."

But it mattered to *me*. So much so that, when the waiter offered me wine, I instantly said yes — and even though I'd never had more than a sip or two of Meryl's wine during dinner before, now I drank it all down, practically in one long gulp, and then had a second. By the time I got to my third glass of wine, I was feeling much more relaxed — sociable, even.

By the time lunch was over, the whole world had shifted: Arnaud's friends told me how good my French was and how much they wanted to come to America, and one of the boys kept flirting with me. So when they invited me to go to some party on the other side of Paris with them, I said yes. After all, I thought, if I didn't go with them, I'd *never* have a chance to tell Arnaud about my decision: my decision about us.

As we walked to the Metro, I took him by the arm, saying: "I really need to talk to you."

"Ah, *oui*."

"I wanted to tell you something. Because I've been thinking — all this time, since I left Paris last summer, I've been thinking about something. Something serious."

"You are far too pretty to be so serious," he joked.

He was barely looking at me now, his attention scanning his friends as they clowned around a few steps ahead of us. "But, Arnaud!" I said. "Remember, last summer, how I wouldn't, you know, go all the way?"

"What is this?" he said, finally paying attention.

"The thing is," I said, "I'm back, and I've been thinking that maybe — maybe I was wrong."

"I'm sorry about the scarf," he then said. "Really. I am very stupid."

"But, Arnaud!" I said. "Did you even hear me? I'm ready to *do it*."

Which is when all his friends stopped dead in their tracks and, while they tried to stop giggling, I threw up. All over my gorgeous black riding boots. Weeping, I wiped my face with the only thing I had to wipe it with: my — Ellie's — Hermès scarf.

When I was done, Arnaud put me in a cab. The last thing I remember as the cab pulled away from the curb was the sight of Arnaud tossing his beat-up raincoat into a trash bin.

CHAPTER FOURTEEN

The Stain

• Robin •

Even after that last round of insanity when Mom made me go "talk to" Meryl, she insisted that when it came to shopping, I couldn't be trusted. Not only that, but she started harping on, again, about how the Temple nursery school was always looking for extra help. She even came right out and said that she could see me making a career working with small children! Not that there's anything wrong with that, except that I had no interest at all. NONE. I'd show her, though — I had to! Compared to Ben, I was already second best. Which was just so unfair in every way that it made my hair stand on end. Sure, he was supersmart, but so what? The kid had barely ever worked a day in his life (unless you count the two-hours-a-day job Dad got him over the summer shelving books in the library at Dad's law school). Meantime, I busted my butt babysitting *and* handling my internship. No one I knew worked as hard as I did! Becka's parents gave her everything she ever wanted, including that beautiful raincoat, which Mom kept insisting was a "symptom" of my "clothing addiction," and which I didn't even feel like wearing anymore, not after Meryl had freaked on me like that. And sure, I'd love to wear designer clothes like Becka did — Libby Fine dresses or Coco *anything*, or just have the ordinary nice stuff that everyone else had. But Mom was so cheap about clothes that she didn't even buy decent duds for herself, insisting that her ancient hippie styles from her grad-school years were just fine, and her awful tattered sweaters from ten years ago would never go out of style. Even Polly, who lived in a small apartment and never even had enough money to go out for lunch, had a mother who was happy to buy her cute, fashionable clothes.

But just before the holidays, I caught a break and was hired to work the preholiday crush at Daphne's Designer Digs. It was the answer to my prayers, with a real salary, plus commission for each sale I made, which meant that I'd be able to pay Mom off (again) *and* have plenty of left over to buy myself a present, too. Recently, in addition to dreaming about stocking up on some high-end classic-looking woolen slacks and jackets and sweaters, I'd started lusting after the same kind of low-heeled black boots that Becka had, and when I say lusting, I mean it.

The only hitch was that Daphne herself wasn't crazy about my look, at least not as it pertained to working at her store. "Don't you have anything a little more conservative?" she said, taking in my swishy bell-bottom pajama pants, which I'd paired with an oversized sweater and my suede eggplant boots. I gave her a stupid grin. There was nothing in the entire shop that I wouldn't have given my right arm for. "You seem like a good girl, and I'm impressed by how much babysitting you do," she said. "But I need you — I need all my girls — to look they're about to go out to dinner at the White House. Which means the classic, tailored look: tweeds, knitwear — think Ralph Lauren if you will, or Gucci or Carl Lagerfeld. Valentino. Classic. Classy. Clean."

Had she read my mind OR WHAT?

Daphne herself was wearing a gray knit Jones New York wrap dress, with pearls. She had short blond hair and wide-spaced green eyes framed by lashes thick with black mascara. Her face reminded me of a kitten's, small and delicate, with a pointy nose, but her hands were bossy and masculine, with square fingernails and big knuckles.

"But," I had to admit, "I just don't have any clothes like that."

"Tell you what. I'll rent you one of my own dresses — two of them, in fact. I keep a few in different sizes for just this kind of situation."

Rent? As in *pay her money*? But she must have seen the look on my face, because she immediately explained that, if I was even reasonably good at sales, I'd be making so many commissions that at the end of my almost-three "crush" weeks at Daphne's, not only would I be making the big bucks, more than enough to cover the rental fee, but that when I returned the dresses to her, she'd return the rental fee to me anyway — or at least most of it. She'd keep ten dollars for herself in order to cover the dry-cleaning bill.

"And, hon?" she said. "One more thing. Your hair."

"What about it?" I'd recently been wearing it in two or even three or four braids.

"Either wear it in a single braid, which would look gorgeous with those cheekbones of yours, or pull it back into a chignon."

"Okay."

"So we've got a deal?"

"Deal," I said, grinning. It would be like playing dress-up, only this time in real designer clothes.

A minute later, I was rummaging around in Daphne's "rental" closet. From which I emerged with two of the most exquisite outfits I'd ever worn: a knee-length dress of pale-pink cashmere, real Chanel, and a black pantsuit with a fitted bolero jacket with velvet cuffs. Both outfits transformed me, so much so that when I saw myself in the mirror, it was like looking at a princess.

How predictable was it that Mom wasn't happy with my news? "A clothing store? Isn't that kind of like an obese person working at an ice-cream parlor? Yes, you need to make money. But isn't it more important to learn how to control your urges?" And how predictable was it that Dad said, "Very, very subtle," and Mom replied, "I'm not trying to be subtle, I'm trying to keep my loved ones from being stupid," and Dad stormed off, slamming the door behind him?

"Yo! Ho! What that be all about, y'all?" It was Ben, with his usual impeccable timing, eating ice cream straight from the container.

"Oh, for God's sake! Put that in a bowl! And sit down! You have the manners of an ape."

"Eeee, eeee, eeee," Ben said, bending down and swinging his arms near his knees to indicate apehood.

"I got a job," I told him.

"Cool," he said. "Where?"

"Daphne's Designer Digs. You know — uptown, near the Starbucks."

"Sissy gonna be richy-rich," he sang as he lurched, in monkey-mode, back to the kitchen.

Daphne had told me that the weeks leading up to Christmas were so busy it was insane, and warned me that there would be no time for phone calls or even texting, but I didn't believe it until I saw it for myself. Women came from all over northern New Jersey to shop at her store, and most of them seemed frantic. But for some reason, I was able to calm most of them down, and more often than not find something for them that was just right. And despite the craziness of it all, I loved it! I loved knowing that, after all, I had a good eye, and could tell at a glance what would or would not work for this or that woman. And even if it meant losing a sale (and the commission that went with it), I was honest with the customers when something didn't work. Just a few days after I'd started, Daphne took me aside to tell me that she'd gotten some nice comments about me from her customers.

I was so busy, doing so well, and making so much money that I didn't even mind it when Ben, as a joke, ha ha, hid under my bed until I got in it, at which point he started making scary noises, like a man was choking to death under there. I was about twenty dollars short of paying off my debt to Mom entirely. And then I'd be free. Free of Mom's nagging. Free of debt. Maybe I'd even be free, I thought, of Becka.

It sounds horrible, but with Becka off in Paris with Libby (LUCKY HER!) I was a lot happier than I had been for a while. It was the same feeling of when you're sick but not enough to stay in bed, but when you finally feel better it's like the whole world feels brighter? That's how I felt. Even when, at work, some customer or another got cranky (which happened *all* the time) or Daphne got in a snit over something, I just sailed through it.

Then Becka came back from Paris.

It was Christmas Eve, my last day of work.

She called me in the morning, just as I was pulling on that divine soft pink dress. In it, I felt so professional and grown-up, like there wasn't much that could come at me that I wouldn't be able to handle. The first thing she said was: "I'm going to slit my wrists!"

"Don't even joke about that."

"I'm not joking!" she cried. "I have to see you. Now! I mean it, Robin. I'm like — oh, I can't even tell you!"

"I have to go to work."

"Cancel it."

"I can't. It's a real job. At Daphne's Designer. I'm supposed to be there in about ten minutes."

"When do you get off?"

"Not until nine. It's the last-minute rush."

"Come over then. Please. Meryl's driving me crazy and . . ." Her words got gobbled up in her sobs.

"Fine," I finally said. "I'll come after work. Just don't call me there, okay? I'm not allowed to get phone calls. I'm not allowed to so much as glance at my cell phone to see if there's a message. My boss is a slave driver."

Work was even crazier than usual that day. "Santa Claus panic," Daphne explained with a shrug. It was nonstop until around eight, when I finally had a moment to myself. Except a second later, an older woman came in saying that she needed something extra special because she'd just found out that her favorite grand-child was bringing his fiancée over to meet her on Christmas day, and I must have hauled out two dozen different outfits before she found one she liked. In the middle of all that, Daphne came storming across the store and said: "Your mother's on the phone, Robin. She said it's an emergency."

An emergency? All I could think of was that Dad had gotten into a car accident. Or fallen down the front steps. Anything could have happened. My heart raced.

"Oh my God," I said into the phone. "What's wrong?"

But it wasn't Mom on the phone. It was Becka. "I have to talk to you!"

From the corner of her eye, Daphne was observing me. "I'll see you later, Mom," I said. "Don't worry, I'm coming straight home after work. I'm glad everything's okay. You scared me!" Then I hung up.

"Robin?" Daphne said as I returned to my spot on the floor. "What was that all about?"

"Just that she wanted to tell me where she's going to hide the house key for me," I fibbed. "We just got our locks changed. And Mom and Dad are going out tonight."

"Is that so?" Daphne said, looking at me with her face in a clench like someone just gave her a wedgie. "You know," she said as I reddened, "I really like you, Robin. You're a good worker, and you have what it takes. Do you understand what I'm telling you?"

"I think I do," I said. That's when I realized how much I liked her, too.

"What on earth are you wearing?" was the first thing Becka said to me when I arrived at her house, letting myself in the back door because, just like at my house, the back door was always left unlocked. She'd propped herself up on the eight million pillows on her double bed, a copy of French *Vogue* on her knees, and a glass of cherry soda on her bedside table, like when she was little. It was this dumb thing she did with her mother — the cherry soda, I mean. Downstairs, Lucy was howling at an imaginary squirrel.

"A dress?" I said.

"A dress for a grandma?"

"Are you kidding me? I love this dress. It's *Chanel*. And you called me at *work*, Becka! You said you were my mother and begged me to come over and now I'm here and you're insulting me?" I was angry now, my voice rising as I felt my empty stomach gurgling for attention. Scowling, she raised her eyes heavenward, as if I were so utterly and abjectly immature that she wanted nothing to do with me. As usual, she was dressed perfectly — in black velvet leggings, with an oversized black sweater on top. Lying on the floor were her beautiful, perfect black boots — the exact kind that I wanted — and thrown over her chair were more new clothes, including some Libby Fine originals. Reaching over languidly, she took a sip of soda.

"You're right," she said, putting her glass back down with a dramatic thud. "I should never have called you in the first place. You've started hanging out with the biggest weirdos in school. How could a girl who spends all her time babysitting and going to high school sports events — rah, rah, team — possibly under-stand? Not with your experience — or perhaps I should say your lack of experience. I'd just be wasting my breath, trying to tell *you*."

I was so stupefied that I just stood there, gaping.

"And you're right about the Chanel dress, too," she said. "I mean, you might look like a grandmother in it, but at least you don't look like you're dressed for a sleepover party."

That's when I lost it.

"You don't need to tell me anything. Because I already know! You had me over here so you can tell me all about your fabulous French boyfriend, and how great it was going all the way with him. Of course, that makes you a grown woman now, which means that you just can't bear being around boring unsophisti-cated people like me anymore! You're going to tell me that I just don't measure up, and how boring it is here in the suburbs, and how you hate everyone, and can't wait to go to NYU, and how much smarter and more sophisticated you are, even though you've been acting so horrible that no one likes you anymore and —"

"And?" she said.

"And your own mother has asked me to spy on you!" It felt good to let go like that — to really let her have it.

"What? Meryl did what?"

"Oh, don't worry," I said. "I never told her a thing. Not about your boyfriend. Not about how you planned to go see him and Paris and . . ."

"And?"

"And everything else!" I said.

Which is when she began to sob. And when I say "sob," I mean *sob*. The tears gushed out of her eyes, her face turned pink, and she rocked back and forth, clutching her pillow, as if she were one of those autistic kids who are so locked into their own bodies that the only thing that makes them feel okay is rocking. She sobbed so hard that I thought she was going to choke.

"He barely had time for me at all!" she sobbed. "I spent every penny I had at a hair salon so I'd look good and then he met me with all of his friends around — and they laughed at me! And then — the scarf he gave me? It was his old girlfriend's. Then I threw up! I'll be stuck here forever, in high school. I'll never get out of West Falls, New Jersey!"

I didn't know what to do. On the one hand, all I wanted to do was go home, put on some flannel pajamas and a pair of slippers, and eat a bowl of cereal. Tomorrow was Christmas and I hadn't even had time to help decorate the tree. Plus, why should I stay when everything that came out of her mouth was snide? Then I remembered how the two of us would spread out on her bed, surround ourselves with pillows, and tell each other stories, and later, as we got older, how we'd look at *Seventeen* magazine together, and tell each other our deepest secrets. How we'd drink so much cherry soda that we had to take turns making pee. She was the only person who could ever make me laugh about Ben, the only friend who knew how stupid I felt compared to him, the girl who understood what it was like to love clothes as much as I did. In second grade, she'd beaten up a kid named Kevin who'd been trying to pull down my underwear during recess, and in eighth grade she'd told the boy who invited her to the Valentine's Day Dance that she wouldn't go with him unless he made his best friend ask me, too. She'd always been the strong one, the brave one, the leader. And now she was rocking back and forth on her bed, sobbing so hard that she was gulping for breath.

I sat down next to her and hugged her as hard as I could. She clutched me, bawling, her howls of misery rising higher and higher, until suddenly, there was a whooshing sound as her door slammed open and Lucy jumped up onto the bed in an agony of doggie love. Licking Becka's face and neck, her tail thumping wildly, Lucy danced around on the bed. It was only after Becka's sobs had crazily turned into uncontrollable laughter that I realized my entire back was wet, and turned to see that Lucy had spilled cherry soda all over everything — me, the bed, the floor, the pillows.

Only it smelled too strong to be cherry soda. And that's because it wasn't. It was red wine: I knew that smell as well as I knew anything, and it had left a stain the shape of New Jersey on Daphne's pale-pink dress.

"Oh my God," I said. "Look what you did."

"Now you're going to tell Meryl about the wine, too, aren't you?"

I just looked at her — drunk, sobbing, hysterical.

"I'll lose my job!"

"It's just a job," she said. "You'll get another."

"But I like it there."

"Working as a salesgirl?"

"Can you at least pay to get it dry-cleaned?"

"I don't have any money, Robin. Didn't you hear me! I spent every penny in Paris! On my stupid hair!"

At home, Dad was passed out on the sofa, and all the lights were out.

CHAPTER FIFTEEN

Blue Is the Color of My Daddy's Lies

• Justine •

Oh, joy. Christmas. As if our Dadless Thanksgiving hadn't been bad enough, with just me and Mom trying to look happy for each other while we gnawed on the smallest turkey Mom could find, a few days later my father announced that he had another business trip coming up — a long one. Even so, he said he was going to be home by Christmas Eve. He stood there in the living room, grinning, as if he expected applause. "Oh, honey, that's wonderful news!" my mother said, bouncing up to give him a quick kiss.

"I thought I might spend some time with my two favorite gals," he said.

My mood could not have been any worse. I hadn't told anyone about the "darling sweetest" email from Dad — not even Dad. In fact, I'd deleted the email permanently, first clicking "delete," and then "delete forever," to make sure it was gone. The last time I'd had the pleasure of running into Becka, she'd looked at me like I was something nasty stuck on the bottom of her shoe, made a face, and hissed: "Yeah, *right*." And even though it wasn't a big deal, that "Yeah, *right*" was stuck on automatic replay in my mind. Meantime, Mom went around the house humming some ancient hippie folk song from when she was in high school, and talking about making this Christmas the best Christmas ever. "A new Christmas in a brand-new place," she said as she bustled about, making angel-shaped cookies and spray-painting pinecones gold to hang on the tree. Outside, it was snowing like crazy, with big white fluffy drifts covering the curbs and the gardens, making everything fresh and dazzling and magical. I hadn't lived in a place that had snow since when we'd been in Germany, and didn't have anything to keep me warm but an old, lumpy, stained white ski parka that had been Mom's in college, which I'd last worn at Eliza's thirteenth-birthday ice-skating party in San Francisco. And one day, while I was standing at my locker pulling it on, Becka had walked by and said: "Love the marshmallow look, Umster." The next day, she'd actually barked at me. As in: Woof woof. As in: I'm a dog. She looked her usual better-than-everyone-else-on-the-planet, with her swishing thick long black hair cascading down her cashmere-encrusted back toward her designer-jean-covered backside. "Or maybe," she said, "that thing you're wearing is more like mashed potatoes." Then Ann started bugging me about helping her with her blog.

"Can Santa bring me a new coat this year?" I asked Mom one day after having been on the receiving end of yet another of Becka's witticisms, this one comparing my hideous parka to "a walking mattress."

Mom was standing in the corner of the living room, boxes of tinsel and decorations spread out around her on the floor. "Perfect timing," Mom said. "Get yourself a snack and then help me trim the tree!" I didn't know which annoyed me more — finding out that my father had a girlfriend, dealing with Becka, or having to pretend that I thought Mom was actually cheerful, when anyone with half a brain cell could tell she wasn't.

"The coat, Mom?"

"We'll see," she said, whistling.

Yeah, right.

What bugged me the most, though? It was that, once upon a time, before I'd been born, Mom had had an entirely different life, as a dancer, and had just given it up, like that, like it was nothing. But it wasn't nothing. I'd seen the pictures. In her black leotards, her straight, dark-brown hair pulled into a braid or a bun, she looked like some kind of forest creature. There are pictures of her in college with heavy black eyeliner on, leaping across a stage, and other pictures of her in various impossible dancer poses: balancing on one leg while she leans impossibly sideways; arching back to catch her toes in her hands while balancing on the remaining five. She used to tell me stories, too — about staying up all night rehearsing, or how she danced under the moonlight one summer in Michigan — and now and again, she'd get so carried away on the tide of her memories that she'd get up and start dancing around the room. She hadn't done anything like that, though, for years.

I went into the kitchen and made myself a snack.

"So I was thinking," she said when I returned to the living room to help her with the tree. "With Dad gone for a whole week, you and I should have a girls' day out. Let's go to the city, do some shopping, maybe see a matinee? What do you say?"

Already, West Falls had the same emptied-out feeling that it had had over the summer when we'd moved. The bitch across the street was in Paris, thank the Lord. Ann was about to go to Florida, and even Weird John had left town to spend the holiday with his grandparents in Baltimore. Of course, that didn't mean he didn't find a way to annoy me long-distance, sending me various obnoxious emails and text messages, including one that said: "I want you to be the mother of my children."

"Meryl's worried about Becka," Mom went on in her oblivious way. "She's in Paris, you know. She's too grown-up for her own good. Meryl says she's utterly miserable and that her daddy spoils her silly. Poor thing."

"Oh, right," I said. "Poor Becka. She has to go to Paris over vacation. She has a daddy who buys her everything she wants."

"Just because we can't go to Paris doesn't mean that we can't have a good time right here, though," Mom continued. "So what do you say to my proposal that we go shopping one day in New York?" She was wearing a white sweater with black-and-red smiling reindeer on it, and holding a couple of gold-painted pinecones, which she'd just finished stringing to hang on the tree. She looked ridiculous, like a giant elf from Santa's workshop. "Honey?"

But for some reason, instead of answering her, I came on out with it: "Why did you stop dancing?"

"What a question! And anyway, I've told you."

"All you ever said was that it had gotten too competitive and it wasn't fun anymore. But that doesn't explain anything."

"What do you mean?"

"I mean," I said, suddenly feeling my voice rise in my throat and the flush that I get when I'm angry. "That it's like when you and Dad got married, you just stopped doing — well, everything."

"I wanted to be a mother more than I wanted to be a dancer."

"But, Mom!" I could feel the tears — of frustration, mainly — backing up behind the bridge of my nose, but squeezed my eyes hard before they could get any farther. "You don't do anything at all! Even if you didn't want to be a dancer anymore, you could have taught dancing, or been a dance coach, like in high school, or worked with kids on plays. You could have done *something*." My mother's life as a dancer was shrouded in deep shadows and blurs, as if it had happened a hundred years ago, instead of just before I was born.

"I consider being your mother something," she said. "Especially with your dad working so hard all the time. And don't forget that we've moved around a lot. It's hard to launch a career when you move every three or four years."

"Well, that never stopped Dad —"

"That's true."

But I wasn't finished. "— from totally focusing on *his* career."

She sighed heavily. "I didn't really ever want to tell you this, Justine, but I think you're old enough now. The fact of the matter is that I wanted to have a big family — four kids, maybe even five. So when I stopped dancing, it was because, when I got pregnant with you, I naturally thought that you were just the beginning of my being a mother."

"And you could only have me?"

"Yes and no," she said.

"Fine. I'm too stupid to understand."

She wrung her hands, suddenly slumping and pale, as if she'd never heard of spray-painted pinecones and homemade Christmas cookies and chestnut-stuffed baked ham with a honey-orange glaze. (She'd been talking about it for days.) Suddenly she looked so serious — her big grin and animated eyebrows disappearing to reveal a face so blank and exhausted that it was as if she hadn't slept in weeks — that I wasn't sure I wanted to know. She told me anyway.

"It was hard for your father, having a baby at home. Hard because I was so tired all the time, taking care of you — you had colic and cried a lot — and, of course, he was trying to launch his career. He had such big dreams, honey. He *still* has such big dreams. Just a few more years, he'd tell me. Just a few more years, and then we'd settle down for good, in a big house somewhere, with a big backyard so I could have a flower garden, and there'd be plenty of room for a swing set or a sandbox, anything I wanted. But for now, he said, while we were still moving around so much, he didn't think it was fair to have more children."

"In other words," I said, "he didn't want me to begin with. I was an inconvenience. I got in the way of his plans."

"Oh, no, honey! No! Never say that! Your dad loves children. And more important, he loves you!"

"Then why don't you have more children?"

Mom wasn't even forty yet. Whereas Eliza's mother was forty-one when she'd had Eliza, and as far as I could tell, Becka's mother was already close to fifty.

But all she said was: "Oh, honey! It's complicated." When I didn't reply, she said: "So it's all set, then? We'll go shopping tomorrow?"

The next day, Mom and I pulled on nearly identical oversized-sweaters-over-jeans-with-boots outfits, like a couple of shapeless, dreary twins in the throes of gender blending, and set off for New York. I would have preferred to step out in something more funktabulous, but it was so cold and so slushy that instead I went for warm, and even so, I shivered in Mom's hideously ugly old parka. On the train, as I watched the New Jersey suburbs slide by in shades of brown and gray and smoke, I got this awful feeling that I was dressed like such a loser that something bad was going to happen to me. Like my hideous coat was going to attract nasty, Becka-like commentary. It was a stupid thought, though, and by the time we were at Bloomingdale's, I'd pushed it away. Mom had headed straight to the Menswear department.

"Honestly," she said, inspecting stacks of men's sweaters, "what do you get for someone who has everything?"

"Beats me," I said, feeling something squeeze my forehead

and fill my mind with sawdust. Something about the combined smells of wool, tissue paper, perfume, and heat made me feel a little dizzy. Not to mention that my hideous white parka seemed to be growing, tumorlike, in all directions.

"Do you like this pale-blue color?" Mom said. "It would match Daddy's eyes, don't you think?"

"I think I need a little air," I said.

"Honey?"

"I'll be right back."

As I headed across the vast first floor, I looked over, and thought I saw my father. Except that Dad was in Montreal, on business — and not bent over a glass case in Fine Jewelry. Maybe he had an identical twin that he'd never mentioned, because this guy, whoever he was, was an exact replica.

"Dad?" I said, approaching, but the man kept on looking at whatever it was he was looking at. Maybe it wasn't my father after all. Except it was. I took a step closer.

"Dad."

This time he looked up, a blush the color of overripe eggplant spreading from his neck up through the tips of his ears. A moment later, he was giggling, and the moment after that, he pulled me to his chest in the fakest hug I've ever received — and that's saying a lot — and saying: "Pooky! What a wonderful surprise to run into you here! What are you doing?"

"Er. Shopping? With *Mom*. I thought you were in Montreal."

He let go of me so quickly you would have thought I was covered with stinging needles. Glancing down, I noticed that Dad was looking at a heart-shaped necklace. An *expensive* heart-shaped necklace, studded with sparkling stones the color of the San Francisco Bay.

"Nice necklace," I said.

"It's a surprise," he stammered out. "For your mother. You think she'll like it?"

Yeah, right.

"She's probably wondering where I am."

"Oh! Your mother's here, too! That's right! You said so, didn't you?"

I just looked at him — the same old ignore-me father that I've always had: tall and slim, thick black hair streaked with gray, a cleft chin that my girlfriends told me was "cute," and those beautiful light-blue eyes that Mom had always said was the first thing she'd noticed about him. To me, though, they looked as cheap and hard as a pair of blue marbles.

"She's in Menswear," I said, gesturing at the other side of the store with my head.

"Oh!" he said, more brightly than ever. "Then this will be our little secret, right?" I felt sick. He put his hand to his mouth and made coughing sounds.

I must have gone bright red or something, because he quickly elaborated. "Don't tell her about the necklace, okay? I thought I'd get her something special this year. What do you think?"

"Nice."

"Do you think she'd like it?" he said again.

I shrugged. By now I was desperate to grab Mom and head for the hills. Also, my dizziness had returned.

"Gotta go," I said.

As I turned from him, he caught my hand and, squeezing it, said, "Keep my secret, okay? I want it to be a surprise."

The only surprise, however, was that I got to the sidewalk and fresh air in time to not throw up. It had begun to snow again, and as I looked up to let the snowflakes fall on my face, I knew I was going to cry. Standing there in front of Bloomingdale's as hordes of shoppers passed me going in and out, I was going to start bawling — and if there was one thing I refused to do, it was to cry.

Don't you dare, I told myself, *or she's going to win.*

Who's going to win?

Becka, that's who.

As my mind cleared, I had an idea. And not just any idea — *the* idea. Suddenly, standing there in the snow, I knew exactly what the first blog that Ann wanted me to help her with should be about: Becka's raincoat. As I thought about what I wanted to say, I began to feel better. So much better that by the time I found Mom (she was still looking at sweaters), the sawdust had completely left my head. At last, I thought, someone would show Becka that she couldn't get away with it.

It wasn't until after Mom had bought a couple of sweaters, a book, and a heavy glass paperweight for Dad that I saw it: a blue-gray coat, very retro, with a wide blue velvet collar, blue velvet cuffs, and oversized velvet-covered buttons. By now we were in a downtown neighborhood where, one summer once upon a time, Mom had taken dance classes.

"I'm sorry," I said, "but I have to try that on."

"In those days," Mom said, ignoring me completely, "I was so athletic that I could leap five feet into the air."

"The coat, Mom! The coat!" I was staring into the shop's large front window now, practically panting with covetousness.

"What coat?"

"That coat!" Grabbing my mother's hand, I dragged her behind me into the store. A minute later, I was buttoning it up before an old-fashioned freestanding framed mirror.

It had a light-blue lining, perfectly intact, fell just below my knees, and fit me as if it had been tailored to my exact proportions. Not a stitch was out of place. Not a button was loose.

"Mother," I said, "I need this coat."

But she flat-out refused to buy it for me. "Let me buy you something that we'll both love," she said. "Something classic, something will last."

"This *is* classic," I pointed out. "Classic midcentury."

"No," Mom said. "Not in a million years."

"I don't think you understand," I said. "This coat and I: It's like we were meant to meet. We were meant to be together! We're soul mates, Mom!"

Which is when, you guessed it, my mother began to cry. "That's what your father used to say to me," she sniffled into a pre-wadded-up Kleenex. "He called me his soul mate."

Talk about a slam dunk. After her tears, all I could say was: "Maybe it's time to go home, Mom."

Could it get any worse? Yes, it could. Because when I got home, there was an email waiting for me from my father. "Pooky poo," he wrote. "Remember to keep my promise, okay? I want your mom to be surprised."

Turns out, though, that Dad didn't give Mom the heart-shaped necklace. He didn't give her *any* necklace. What he gave her was two books and a pair of turquoise earrings. "Oh, honey!" she said. "Thank you! What wonderful gifts." Dad grinned sheepishly. Then Mom gave Dad her several dozen presents, and Skizz, who apparently was as grossed out by the scene as I was, threw up a couple of hair balls. When Mom handed me my present — a big box wrapped in gold and tied with a red ribbon — I didn't even want to open it. "From me and Dad," she said, even though it wasn't from Dad at all. Chances were, in fact, that he had no more idea what was inside it than I did.

"Open it, honey," Mom said.

I couldn't believe it. Inside was the coat. The one from New York that Mom had refused to buy. The blue-gray midcentury sizzler with the blue velvet cuffs and collar.

"Do you like it?" Mom asked anxiously.

"Oh, Mom!" I said. "I love it!"

I did, too. I loved it so much that it hurt.

But what hurt even more was when, on the last day of Christmas vacation, Dad knocked on my door, came into my room, sat on my bed, and said: "Thanks for keeping my secret, Pooky." I was doing the final finishing touches on the blog — Ann and I had finally figured out how to do it. "What's that you're doing?" he then said.

"Nothing. A blog."

"A blog?"

"Just this thing. For high school. You wouldn't be interested."

"Of course I'm interested," he said. "I'm interested in everything you do. You know that, don't you, Pooky?"

"Can you please not call me that?"

"That's another thing I like about you. You're straightforward. Always have been. Which is another reason why I always know I can count on you to come through. And that necklace, by the way? The one I was looking at that day in Bloomingdale's? It was way too expensive. But I think Mom liked the earrings. Don't you?"

Yeah. Right.

"Keep up the good work," he said.

CHAPTER SIXTEEN

The Varsity Jacket

• Polly •

About a week before State, I looked up and noticed that Bella wasn't in the stands. She wasn't in the stands the next day, or the next day after that, either.

"Where's Bella?" I finally asked Coach one afternoon after regular practice, when everyone else had gone into the locker rooms to change and I was paddling around the shallow end. "I haven't seen her for a while."

Coach Fruit, smiling a sad smile, said: "I know."

"What do you know?" I continued, in our bantering way.

"We broke up," he said.

I gulped air, wondering whether it was possible that they'd broken up, at least in part, because of all the extra time he'd been spending on coaching me. Confused, I said: "Oh, no. I'm really sorry, Coach. Really."

"The only thing you have to be sorry for," he answered, "is if you don't work on your flip turns."

I worked on my flip turns — and my rotation and recovery —

but had a hard time getting into it. I had a hard time concentrating on my homework that night, too, and it took me forever to fall asleep. In the morning Mom asked me if anything was wrong. Wrong? Even though I knew that Coach Fruit wasn't interested in me, not that way, I'd never felt happier. I felt so happy that I pulled on my white birthday jeans and a white turtleneck sweater without giving my backside a second thought, tied my hair back into a high-up ponytail, and stuffed my feet into the imitation Uggs that Mom had given me a year ago for Christmas.

"Coach Fruit and his girlfriend broke up," I said as I scooted onto my stool next to Justine in chemistry.

"OMG, I just *love* Coach Fruit. He's just, like, OMG, so cute!" John the Weird mimicked. He was wearing his usual grunge outfit of black and black, with black Converse, his black hair sticking up as if it had hair spray in it, which it did, which I knew because he kept a can in his backpack to spray us with whenever he decided we were what he called "annoying." His black eyes looked blacker than usual, too, and shone, as if he were using illegal substances, except that as far as I knew, he wasn't. The dude never hung out with the stoners or even the hipsters. But I must admit that his recent habit of wearing bright-green sparkly eye shadow gave him an unusual look.

"What?" he said.

"Why are you like that?"

"I don't know," he said, shrugging, and a second later, he flipped open his notebook and started scrawling in it as usual. Which meant what it always meant: Justine and I would do the work, and John would sign his name to our final product so he'd get credit, too.

"Seriously," Justine said. "You have such a crush on him."

"Well, maybe. Kind of."

"Kind of?"

"You have to admit, he's pretty hot."

"Coach Fruit?" Justine said, her right eyebrow arching into a semi—question mark above her eye. "Coach Fruit is *not* hot. He looks like Big Bird."

"But you don't think anyone's hot."

"I do, too," she said. "I think Weird John's hot."

"Shut up," he said. "And, Mizz Frizz?"

"Yes, Poop Head?"

"I think you suck, too."

"I thought you wanted to marry me."

"Joke," he said. "Get it? Ha ha."

"Anyway," Justine said. "Even if he *has* broken up with his girlfriend, he's still your coach, and you're still a kid. He'll never like you back."

"I know. That's the problem. But do you think that maybe . . ."

"No," she said. "I don't."

Class dragged on for forever. But when, at last, the bell rang, instead of slinking out as fast as he could, like usual, John came over and, opening his notebook, showed me a sketch — more like a cartoon, actually — of me kissing Coach Fruit. I knew because he'd written our names underneath, along with the words TRUE LOVE in heavy black ink.

"And just in case you're curious," he said, "I'm going to post this on my Facebook page tonight."

I didn't even stop to think that, just maybe, John didn't have Facebook, and even if he did, he was kidding. Instead I lunged for the notebook, screeching, "Give me that thing!"

"I don't think so," he sang, backing away from my reach.

But I was at least as big as he was, strong — and quick, too. It didn't take much for me to bound over, jump up, and snatch the notebook from his hands.

"Give it back!" he said, but I'd already climbed up onto a table — well out of his reach!

"Please?" He was almost begging now.

But it was too good an opportunity to torture him. Tearing out the drawing of me and Coach, I ripped it into tiny pieces. Then, to make sure he didn't have any other nasty tricks up his sleeve, I began to turn the pages of the notebook while he wailed, "No! No! It was only a joke! I wasn't going to post it on Facebook! Would you stop?"

I didn't get it. The kid was practically turning the same shade of green as his eye shadow. I mean, what was the big deal? But then I saw: Weird John's entire notebook was filled with drawings of Justine. Justine in profile, with her hair fanning out, like lace, behind her. Justine with her head thrown back, laughing. Justine's hands. (I recognized them from one of the big silver rings she wore.) Her eyes. No wonder the kid had a hard time keeping up in class. Beneath me, the dude had turned from green to pink. "Please don't tell anyone," he whimpered.

"Are you going to keep your mouth shut about Coach Fruit?"

"I guess."

"Then I guess we have a deal."

I should have been relieved; after all, for once I'd gotten the better of John, and not the other way around. But I didn't. Instead, I felt like a bully. Could it even be possible that all this time the kid had been obsessing about Justine? And she couldn't stand him! I almost felt sorry for the dude.

Both John and I kept our mouths shut, like we'd agreed, but that didn't mean that my mind stopped talking. And all it said was: "Coach Fruit! Coach Fruit!" The only problem was — well, everything. Plus, with the State championships coming up, he didn't seem to think of me in any way at all — except as he always had, as a strong swimmer.

I practically lived in that pool. All of us did. No matter what shampoo I used, I couldn't get the chlorine smell out of my hair. When I fell asleep, I dreamed about swimming. Either that, or about Coach Fruit! I was so obsessed that I even thought that maybe I'd get my mom to invite him over for dinner — after State, that is.

"Wait a sec, Polly," he said one afternoon after practice when everyone else had gone. "I've got something for you."

"Oh, let me guess," I teased. "A brand-new bottle of water?"

"No."

"A rubber band?"

"Even better."

A minute later, he'd ducked into his office and was returning with something tucked under his arm. "I'd actually given it to Bella," he started to explain, "but when we broke up, she gave it back to me. And I sure as hell can't wear it anymore. So here" — he handed it to me — "you take it."

I couldn't believe it. It was a beat-up high school letter jacket with a large white *S* on it.

"Springlakes High School." He whistled. "I practically lived in that jacket."

I finally managed to stammer out a thank-you. It was the best present I'd ever gotten. Ever. I couldn't even believe it. His letter jacket? From when he himself had been the reigning champ? And why, of all people, would he give it to *me*?

"Good luck tomorrow," he then said, squeezing my arm just below the shoulder. "And remember to get a good night's sleep!"

"He gave me his letter jacket from when he was a champion at Springlakes High School," I nearly screamed into the phone.

"Never heard of the place," Justine said.

"That's not the point, and you know it! He gave me his *letter jacket*. Don't you understand what that means?"

"Can't say I do," she said. "I mean, other than that you're his best swimmer. For real, you *are*. He believes in you, Polly. And that's great. But so what? Like he told you, he can't wear it anymore. He's, like, *old*."

"Didn't they have sports back where you used to live?"

"I guess so," she said. "But it's not like I paid any attention."

"Well, for your information, one of the biggest things a boy jock can do is give a girl his varsity jacket. It's the high school equivalent of being engaged."

"Except? Polly? Hello? Your coach isn't a high school boy. He's your *coach*. And you're in dreamland."

But I wasn't so sure I was. Lots of girls ended up dating older guys. I'd even heard one story about a senior at Western High School who'd moved to Philadelphia to live with her tenth-grade math teacher a few years ago. Robin had told me that even Becka was dating some older guy — some guy she'd met in Paris. My own mother had dated one of her professors in graduate school — before she'd met my father, that is.

"It's not unheard-of, you know," I finally said.

"Maybe not," she agreed. "But it should be."

"You're absolutely no help."

"I'll be in the stands tomorrow anyway. Me and Ann are coming. Unless you don't want us to?"

I hugged Coach's varsity jacket to my chest and told her that of course I wanted them to come.

"Merry jingle bells," she said.

It was going to be a long day. A *very* long day. Even with only four of us representing Western High, there was a lot of sitting around. As usual, I'd be swimming freestyle — both the two-hundred- and one-hundred-meter races. And as usual, I was all pumped up.

When my first event was called, I climbed onto the block as if it were my own private country. And just like that, the starting whistle was blown and I was in the water and then at the far end of the pool and back. I wasn't aware of anything other than the sound of the water rushing past my ears and the sense of my own strength. One lap, two, three, and finally, my heart bursting out of my chest, I was finished. I looked up. My time was good. And immediately, Coach was standing above me, telling me that I'd done well.

"The girl who won beat you by less than a second," he said. "And she's a senior — swimming next year for Rutgers."

"No way."

"You did awesome," he said.

I was pleased — and as I climbed up out of the pool, I looked up into the stands to see Mommy, Justine, Ann, and — blow me away — even Robin cheering for me. *Together.* Some guy I didn't recognize at first was cheering for me, too. My eyes were still a little bleary from the water, though, so I blinked and looked again. And I couldn't believe what I saw. It was Weird John. He was holding up a sign that said GOOD GOLLY GO POLLY!

"You got your fan club, I see," Coach Fruit said, coming over to stand beside me.

"Yeah. I guess."

"Well, you can count me in, too."

"Thanks, Coach."

"No, Polly," he said. "I really mean it. The way you swam out there —"

"I felt good."

"And other things, too — how much heart you show . . ." But again he stopped, letting his sentence dangle in the air, incomplete. Finally he just said, "Keep it up," and returned to sit with the other coaches.

It felt like a million years until my next event, but it was really no more than forty minutes until the one hundred meter, my strongest event, was called. This one called for a fast start, an all-out approach, and a strategy that called for slow breathing and constant, all-you've-got strokes. I'd actually done it once in under a minute, and I was hoping to do even better this time. The announcer announced the next event. I stretched, adjusted my goggles, and climbed onto the block. There was maybe ten seconds left until the last event was over and it would be our turn to start, when I glanced up into the stands again, thinking I'd wave to Mommy. But I couldn't even find Mommy, let alone wave to her. Instead, my eyes stopped to rest on this gorgeous blond woman wearing a white sweater over white jeans:

Bella.

"Swimmers get ready."

I crouched into racing position.

"Get ready, get set!"

She was blowing a kiss at Coach Fruit.

And the horn blasted, launching me up and over the block, until, boom, I hit the water. But instead of it opening up for me, like a Polly-shaped pocket, it slapped me at the top of my head, angry and hard. Already I was behind — I could sense the bubbles left behind by the girls in the lanes on either side of me — and as I struggled to catch up, to find my rhythm, to be the champion that Coach Fruit thought I was, I felt a sharp pain, like a knife sinking into my calf, and barely got to the far end of the pool before I had to stop in utter agony. "Oh my God, oh my God!" I said over and over again as I hauled myself, limping, out of the pool. I tried not to cry — not in front of all those people — but I did anyway. Thank God I was already soaked, or Coach Fruit — or worse, Mommy — would have noticed.

One of the refs told me to sit down, and as I sat, he worked my calf, massaging the cramp away. "Sorry, kid," he said. "It happens to the best of them." But all I could think of was how disappointed Coach would be in me — and how I'd not only gone and ruined my own chances of getting any kind of college scholarship money, but sunk the team's standing as well.

The last thing I wanted was to look up to see Coach Fruit coming over — but of course he did. As Justine would say: He was my coach, and that was his job. "The same thing has happened to me," he said, giving me a reassuring pat on the back. "It's all right, Polly. Really. I promise. It is."

But it wasn't all right at all. I was a fifteen-year-old kid who could swim, with a skinny mother who barely made enough money to pay the rent and a creepy father who could never love either one of us, and worst of all, I'd never see my Poppy again. In a few days it would be Christmas, and once again, Mommy will have scraped up every penny to buy me something nice. Even after I got up to walk back to the rest of the team, and everyone started clapping, I couldn't bear to look up into the stands.

CHAPTER SEVENTEEN

The Most Beautiful Boots in the World

• Robin •

On Christmas Eve, my parents had a fight over whether to make stuffing with or without roasted chestnuts. Dad wanted them because that's how his mother had made Christmas stuffing, and Mom said: "Guess what? I'm Jewish. You make the stuffing." To which he said: "You know I have a thousand exams to grade. Can't you do it this year?"

"*This* year? I do it *every* year."

"I help."

"No, you *say* you help, but you don't. You show up in time to make the salad dressing."

"For God's sake. What do you want with me? I have a job, you know."

There was a pause. Then: "Have you started drinking *already*? You just don't care about your family at all, do you?"

"Keep your voice down. The children . . ."

"As if they don't know! As if they don't already know that you prefer Scotch to them."

"Give me a break. I'm doing the best I can."

"Some best."

Christmas sucked. Ben came down with the flu and went around the house coughing and hacking up green gunk. Becka, my former best friend, flat-out refused to pay for the damage she'd done to Daphne's pink dress. The dry cleaner told me that he'd never be able to get the stain out completely. Mom and Dad gave me a pair of cheap-looking light-brown leather boots that I instantly hated. And I was terrified of what Daphne would say to me when I told her about the ruined dress.

A few days later, I found out.

"I'm sorry," Daphne said, her lashes heavy with mascara. "But don't look so downcast, hon. You just have to buy it back from me, and with your discount" — she bent over a calculator, and started adding up and subtracting figures — "you still come out ahead." Then she reached into her cash drawer and handed me some twenties and a five. It just covered the amount I owed Mom, plus enough to buy me a new bottle of nail polish or a double latte.

"That's all?" I said.

"Like I said, I'm sorry, hon. But I was clear with you about it. Otherwise, whenever I lent a dress out, I'd run the risk of a girl running off with it."

"But I didn't run off with it," I said. "I'd never —"

"I know you wouldn't, but no matter what, it's not the end of the world."

It was no use to explaining what had happened. She wouldn't care. And why would she? I was just some kid who helped out during the holiday rush.

Trying to hide my disappointment, I shrugged. "Okay. Thanks."

Just then my cell phone rang: Becka. What did she want? "Excuse me," I said as Daphne returned to her work.

"Oh my God," she said. "My mother is going around talking about me!"

"And?" I said impatiently.

"I don't know what to do! I'm going to kill her! Or myself! I mean it, Robin."

"What are you talking about?"

"Oh, for God's sake, just get over here. Please! If you were really my friend, you'd get over here right now!"

"But I'm at Daphne's Designer. I had to buy back that dress you ruined," I tried to explain.

"Listen, Robin. I know I screwed up, okay? And I feel bad about it. But what do you want me to do? I already said I'm sorry!"

"You did?"

"That's so like you, isn't it? Everything that happens is my fault."

"But it *is* your fault, Becka. And you never admitted it."

"You know what? If that's how you feel? Forget about every-thing. Forget we were ever friends! You can hang out with Um and all her freak friends for all I care!"

"Not everyone's parents give them everything they want! I worked hard for that money!" But Becka has already hung up.

"Hon?" Daphne said as I put my cell phone back in my purse. "You okay?"

"Okay?" I said. "Okay. No, I'm not okay! I'm extremely not okay." And there was something so sympathetic, so open and straightforward and plain old bullshit-free about the way that Daphne was looking at me that the whole story poured out — about how I got my summer internship only because Becka had interceded for me, how much I loved clothes, my parents' constant fighting, and finally, how Becka had gone and spilled wine on Daphne's pink cashmere dress.

"That *is* a whole lot of drama, ain't it?" Daphne said when I was done.

"I guess."

"And you say you want to go into fashion?"

"It's kind of a dream of mine," I said. "Too bad both my parents think I'm such a loser."

"My daughter's into fashion, too," she said. "I guess that's not such a surprise, though."

"I guess not."

"But, hon, I've got to ask you: If you're so into fashion, and I don't doubt you are, why are you going around wearing pajamas?"

I looked down at myself. I was wearing the same heavy knit bell-bottom pajama pants I'd worn for my interview, a long-sleeved T-shirt topped with a puffer vest, and a woolen scarf that I'd gotten for Christmas.

"It's not that you don't look cute," Daphne said. "You could wear a sack and still look cute. But I still have to wonder why a girl with your pizzazz is wearing PJs. When you first came in here to ask for a job, my first thought was: Where are this girl's parents?"

"*What?*"

"Don't be like that, sweetie. I understand. I mean, when I was your age, I was into all kinds of out-there fashion — hippie platform shoes, peasant blouses, you name it. But not once did I wear a nightie anywhere except to bed."

I was on the verge of tears. But how could I explain it to Daphne — or to anyone — that in some sense, I *didn't* have parents. Or at least not the kind I'd once had, the kind who bothered to make sure that I was tucked into bed at night, and had been read a story, and had warm clothes to wear in winter.

"Tell you what, though," Daphne said. "At least you've got yourself one classy dress. Maybe you can have it dyed black, and then, when you have an occasion, you'll knock 'em dead."

It was a nice idea: me, in elegant suits or simple, shirtwaist dresses, in ankle pants with excellent high heels or out-there bubble dresses with lace and silk. But it was only an idea. On my budget, I could barely get dressed at all. My one comfort was that at least I'd made enough to pay Mom back.

As I turned to go, Ben texted me, saying:

> You made it to the big time, sis! You're in a blog! And Becka's gon go nuts when she finds out about it!

I was going to text him right back, but right then my eyes fell on a new shipment of boots that Daphne hadn't completely unpacked yet. And I saw them: the boots of my dreams, the exact same ones Becka had. "Would I be able to get discount on these?" I asked Daphne. To which she said: "I don't see why not." When I walked out of Daphne's, I had seventeen dollars left, and the most beautiful boots in the world.

◇◇◇◇◇◇◇◇◇

I'm embarrassed to admit it, but I couldn't wait to get home so I could log on and see the blog that Ben was all worked up about. *If* I could sneak past Mom and Dad and run upstairs to my room before anyone noticed that I was carrying a shopping bag.

For once, I was in luck. Mom's car wasn't in the driveway, which probably meant that she already returning unwanted presents. Inside, Dad was slumped over, asleep in his favorite chair in front of the fireplace. Ben was in the TV room, watching a football game.

But as I tiptoed past Dad, Ben started hollering and cursing and screaming, "Off-limits, morons!" And Dad woke up.

"What do you have there?" he said, indicating the shopping bag I was carrying.

"Nothing," I said. "I went to Daphne's to pick up my pay-check. And she gave me some . . ." I had to think fast. "Some fruit!"

"Did she?" Dad said from deep down in his throat, like there was a snake coiled in there that made it hard to get the words out.

"Apples!" I said as I headed past him toward the foot of the stairs.

"Apples, huh?" Now he was standing up, and his words were slurred. Meantime, from the next room, Ben was screaming: "No! No! Say it ain't so, Joe! You guys are killing me! KILLING ME!"

"I like apples," he said, more clearly this time. "I'd like to eat an apple just about now." He was giving me this look that just about paralyzed me, but right when I thought I'd be busted, he slumped into his chair again, and said: "Where's your mother?"

"I don't know."

"You don't know where your mother is?"

"PLEASE DEAR GOD DON'T LET THIS BE HAPPENING. RUN, YOU IDIOT, RUN!"

"Sorry!"

"That's what I say, too," he said. "*Sorry*. But does that change anything?"

"Sorry, Dad, but I don't know what you're talking about."

"That's what your mother says," he said, slurring his words again. "That she doesn't understand what I'm talking about. Even though I'm a professor of law. Hundreds of students understand what I say, write down what I say, and in fact hang on my every word, but she can't understand me."

"Sorry," I said again.

"So let me ask you this," he said. "Do you, my only daughter, understand me? Do you? Do you?"

"I guess?"

"Just answer the question! If I'd talked to my dad the way you talk to me, he would have shut me up but good."

"But I didn't say anything!"

"You're being fresh!"

"What's your problem?"

Suddenly I realized that I'd heard those words before. Coming from my own mouth. But this time, Ben was too slow to come in and rescue me. This time, my twin brother burst into the living room a few seconds *after* Dad had hauled off and hit me, sending me and my beautiful, expensive black leather boots sprawling.

CHAPTER EIGHTEEN

Raincoat, Raincoat, Go Away
• Becka •

I could barely face going back to school. Everyone was talking about what they did over Christmas vacation. I dreaded being asked. But the subject didn't even come up. Instead, people just kind of . . . *stared* at me. It was so weird. But it wasn't until I overheard some girls talking about a blog called *Fashion High* that I got on my iPhone and Googled it, and there it was: a blog about me — about me and Arnaud's raincoat!

Here's what it said:

> Welcome to the inaugural issue of Fashion High,
> a blog for and by fashionistas — those of us who
> can't fall asleep at night without seeing the latest
> ballet flats and designer jeans dancing across our
> dreams.
>
> Where to start? Because here at Western
> High, we are every type, from preppy princesses

to hipsters to retro hippies to hip-hop queens to flat-out fabulous.

But one girl — and one look — stands out and above all others.

We speak, of course, of The Raincoat. We've taken note of it — and we know you have, too. The Raincoat is tall and raven-haired, and, like a raven, she flaps her wings from high in the sky. Her large, beat-up men's raincoat flapping behind her like wings, she soars through the halls, trailing in her wake dozens of smaller ravens — would-be ravens who, over the rainy months of November and December, suddenly starting flocking to her call, to show up wearing large men's raincoats of their own. All of them, that is, except her friend, herself a fashionista of the first order, but whose own inclinations have tilted her toward a look that combines nightwear with in-the-know in a way that dares the fashion gods themselves to do better.

The rumor is that The Raincoat spends time in Paris. Is that where she acquired her fashion sense? Is that where she acquired her raincoat?

Sure, she has the look. Is she fabulous or what? But is it really a look anyone wants to emulate? Is it really a look that anyone else CAN emulate?

What will she bring back from Paris this
time? *Fashion High* can't wait for its next trend.
What do you think? *Fashion High* requests
your feedback!

Plus, it had drawings — lots of them, in pen-and-ink. They
made me look like — well, like a raven! Or maybe like a bag
lady, like someone who'd just escaped from the nuthouse!

Did everyone really hate me that much? Or maybe everyone
didn't hate me. Maybe only the blog writer hated me. Was I that
horrible? Couldn't they just understand that I was miserable?

And I was more miserable now.

I had to find out who had written it, and make her —
them — take it down. Why couldn't people just understand?
Even Robin didn't understand me anymore. Even she thought I
was just, well, a bitch! But I wasn't really. Not deep down. Not
in that place where I used to love Meryl, and she used to love me
back, and everything was simple and easy and free. I just didn't
know how to be friends with anyone anymore! Maybe, after all,
it was me who was a freak — and not them. Maybe that's why
Arnaud treated me the way he had: because he knew, too!

When, as I headed toward my first class, I heard a bunch of
girls giggling behind my back, I felt myself going hot and cold
all over. Worse, when I turned around to stare them down, they
scurried away. *Ignore them*, I told myself. Maybe they were just
jealous. After all, they'd have a right to be, especially because
what I was wearing that day, for the first day of school after the
winter break, was as entirely an incredible outfit as any I'd ever

put on. It was a gray woolen Libby Fine minidress, topped with a Libby bolero jacket, and my black boots. I'd tied my hair back into one long braid, and as I walked, I could feel it swishing back and forth along my spine. I could also tell that people were *looking at me*! Ignoring everyone, I walked on.

But just as I was coming out of the bathroom, I saw Robin hurrying up to me. "I need to talk to you!"

"I thought we weren't friends anymore."

"There's something I have to tell you."

"That you're a whiny crybaby?"

"Okay. Just forget it, then."

"Fine."

"Fine."

But there was something in her voice, some catch, like backed-up tears, that stopped me. Plus, she looked weird, like she'd been playing makeup with her mother's cosmetics and had forgotten to wash it off. And just like that, I figured it out: She knew who had written the blog.

"You know, don't you?"

"Know what?"

"Who wrote the blog."

She looked at me as though I was from Mars. "Huh?"

"Tell me, Robin. I mean it. Who wrote that stupid blog?"

"First, if you didn't notice, I'm in it, too. And second, I have no idea!"

"Who. Wrote. It." By now I was so upset that my voice was shaking, I was so angry. "Tell me, Robin. Because if there's something I need to know . . ."

As the words flew out of my mouth, Robin seemed to shrink a little inside herself, as if she were protecting herself from a blow. Which is when, in a flash, I figured the whole thing out: Robin felt guilty. She'd already gone blabbing to Meryl about Arnaud, which was how Meryl knew about "Raincoat Boy" to begin with. Then Meryl had gone blabbing to Um's mother. And now Um knew all about the raincoat — and everything else, too! It was so obvious, I wanted to scream. But I didn't. Instead, I took Robin by both shoulders and shook her.

"You!" I said.

"What?"

"You told my mother about me."

"No, I didn't."

"You did! I can tell by your face." It was true, too. Robin's face was going pink around the edges, and her eyes, coated with way too much makeup, were like spinning black discs. As if mascara could cover up what she'd done! "You told Meryl everything. And she gossiped with her new friend from across the street. Who turned around and told Um!"

"But I already told you! I don't have a clue who wrote it! And I didn't tell your mother anything! Not even after everything!"

"Everything? Everything like what? Like I gave you that Donna Karan that you're so obsessed with? Like I helped you get a job last summer with Aunt Libby?"

"And like you got drunk and spilled red wine on a dress that doesn't even belong to me? And didn't even offer to pay for the dry cleaning? How about that?"

"Meaning what, Robin? On the worst day of my life, I spilled wine by mistake, so you felt free to go blabbing to my know-it-all mother about Arnaud?"

"On the worst day of your life? How about my life? You're not the only one with problems, you know! You don't care about anyone but yourself!"

"At least I don't go tattling all over town, telling other people's secrets!"

"But I told you! I didn't say a word! Not to your mother — not to anyone."

"I'm going to find out who did this," I said. "And kill them."

"But wait!" Robin was trailing behind me now as I stalked down the halls, looking for someone, anyone, who could tell me. Polly! Polly would know — she was lab partners with the freak. But I couldn't find her. Then the bell rang, and I saw her hurrying to class. But she was inside before I got a chance to catch up with her, and when the final bell sounded, I was alone in the hall.

I'd never felt so trapped. Even after what had happened in Paris I didn't feel as trapped as I did now. Because at least in Paris, I could go back to the hotel and cry, and when Libby came back, I could tell her — well, not everything, but enough so that she'd give me a giant hug and then take me out for some shopping therapy. But now, as I walked down the hall heading toward English, I could tell that it was going to be a lot worse than I had thought it would be, because just about everyone — including the freshmen — was staring at me. Heads literally turned to look at me when I walked into class. Third period, with Um in it, was particularly horrendous. After fourth period, this senior girl who I'd never even seen before came up to me and said: "Hey, where's your raincoat?"

I was just about ready to flip out when, at last, I ran into Polly, who, when I asked her point-blank, turned a little red around her eyes, and then told me that she wasn't actually one hundred percent sure, but that she'd heard some talk. . . .

Which was all the evidence I needed. I was going to kill that Um, and then I'd unmask all of them, starting with Robin!

In the corner of the cafeteria, sitting with her usual gang of misfits and weirdos, was the biggest misfit weirdo of them all. A moment later, I was standing over her, saying, "Just so you know, you are pathetic. You and your little crew of rejects and uglies."

That's when I noticed that Ann was there, too — Ann, who'd been my best friend in kindergarten. I don't know why I hadn't noticed her before, especially because she was the only black girl at the table. Her green eyes were as big as lollipops. Her cropped soft sweater was the color of a green lollipop, too. Around her neck was the same turquoise choker that Um had been wearing at that awful brunch Meryl had dragged me to . . . and as that memory flooded over me, I felt even more trapped, even more desperate and furious — at EVERYONE!

Then something truly awful happened: I burst into tears! There — right in front of those awful, immature, geeky girls! They sat there frozen, every one of them, until Ann got up and started to come toward me.

"Get away!"

All eyes were on me as I turned and, taking my time, walked through the cafeteria, down the hall, to my locker, and finally, out the door.

The only one at home was Lucy, who jumped on me when I let myself in. I'd skipped lunch, but I wasn't hungry. Even Daddo wouldn't be able to help me with this one. Somehow, I knew that the only solution was to get out of there — not just out of the house, but out of West Falls. Then I saw the books stacked neatly on the kitchen table: *The Daughter Doctor Does the Teenage Tango*, by Meryl Sanders, PhD.

Her new book. Opening it randomly, this is what I read:

> When exactly do our darling daughters leave behind their innocent charm to become, by turns, boy-crazy, sibling-hating, competitive, moody, premenstrual, angry, self-defeating, or any combination therein? In my own house, I watched, sometimes with horror, as my first child, once a beautiful, sweet, cooperative little girl who delighted in playing dress-up, playing house, and collecting dandelions, turned into a veritable monster of hormonal chaos. . . .

An hour later, I'd hauled every single copy of that book I could find to a Dumpster a few doors up from us, where one of the neighbors was putting an addition on their house. Then I crawled into bed. I dreamed I was trying to climb a flight of stairs, but it was as if my legs were made of concrete, and I could barely take even one step without being exhausted and frustrated. Then I dreamed that I was in the middle of a war zone, with bombs exploding everywhere: *Boom! Boom! Boom!* I was so afraid that I woke up. Which is when I realized that the bombs I was hearing were real — and coming from down the hall. The Little Jerk was in his room, banging on his drums.

Before I even had time to think about it, I went downstairs and grabbed one of his baseball bats. The next thing I know, I was swinging it — smash, smash, crash, crash! "No! No!" Danny was yelling, but I barely heard him — or rather, his cries made me even angrier. I'd show him, the Little Jerk! How dare he ruin my peace of mind like that, interrupting my studies and my privacy with his incessant banging? When I felt him jump on my back, I flipped him around, and just like that, he fell, with a thud, onto the floor.

Returning to my own room, I caught sight of my own reflection — tall, dark, slim, with long dark hair and perfect clothes. Except for my face, which was blotched with red, I was perfect. Perfect in every way. So perfect that grown men stared at me and my own mother tried to keep me back. So perfect that it hurt. So perfect that the only thing I could do was destroy that perfection permanently. Smashing my fist into the glass, I watched as my perfect image shattered into dozens of fragments and fell on the floor. Though my hand was bleeding from a hundred different cuts, for the first time in almost a year, I felt no pain at all.

CHAPTER NINETEEN

The History of the Red Dress
with the White Flowers

• Ann •

It never occurred to me that Becka would freak out. But there she was, standing over Justine, screaming so hard that her eyes bulged and her face turned red, screaming so hard that, in the end, I felt like every kid in school was staring at us — at me and Justine, that is. Because even though we hadn't signed our names to the blog, rumors were already spreading that we'd written it. Becka herself figured it out! I don't know how she did, either; Justine and I had sworn not to tell anyone at school about it, and the only person who may have had some idea was Polly, but she'd been so wrapped up in her swimming Finals that she could think of nothing else.

"Uh-oh," I said to Justine after Becka was finally gone. "I guess she read it."

"Guess so."

"She's gone bonkers."

"Honestly? Serves her right," Justine said, stabbing the air with a knife.

"But, Justine!" I said. "She's really upset. We shouldn't have done what we did."

"It was your idea, remember? Remember how you begged me to write it?"

"Yeah, but it was your idea to write about Becka's raincoat. Oh God. I feel bad."

"You're kidding me, right?"

"But, Justine. She was *freaking*."

"And you know what? We didn't even say anything mean! What's her major maladjustment, anyway? That girl's a terrifying toad. Anyway, she had it coming to her."

I just sat there, my mouth hanging open like I was at the dentist's, as Justine stood up, gathered her things, and stalked out of the cafeteria. *Great*, I thought. *Just what I need. More drama.* As if the drama of Christmas week in Florida with my family hadn't been bad enough.

To wit: We flew to Florida and took a taxi to our hotel. As usual, my sister and I were in the same room. The minute the door closed behind us, she turned to me and said: "Mama told me that she got you something special to wear for Debate Finals."

"True."

"And that she just can't wait to see you up there."

"Yup."

"And that you're so into it that you spend all your free time practicing."

"I guess."

"And that she's so proud of you."

"As she should be."

Finally, with a slam of the closet, Martha turned to me and said: "And just what do you think you're up to, anyway?"

"Meaning?"

"Oh, for God's sake, little sister. Do you not remember that I was, in fact, on Debate Team? And that I did, in fact, go to Finals?"

"How could anyone forget? You're still bragging about it."

"Look, it's better to tell me than to face them."

"What? Tell you what?"

"Are you doing drugs?"

"Yeah. Right."

"Because if you are — and I'm serious about this, Ann — just don't. But, for God's sake, if you are, you have to tell me! You have to tell someone! People ruin their lives with that stuff."

"Really? Because no one's ever told me that before."

"Here's something else no one's ever told you: You are truly an idiot."

"And you are truly a control-freak goody-two-shoes suck-up with a superiority complex who thinks she's the boss of the world!"

Which was when something truly weird happened. My sister sat down on the bed, her shoulders slumping, and said: "Ann, we don't have to be enemies, you know."

"We don't?" I snickered.

"Look, you might not know this, but you're Mama's favorite, and always have been. So why do you compete with me all the time?"

"Don't you have it backward? First, it's you who's always putting me down, and second, I'm barely even a shadow of your shadow."

She continued to sit there. Then she squeezed her eyes shut. "You really don't get it, do you?"

"What don't I get?"

"Look, I took a class this semester, in psychology, and there I was, me, written up on the blackboard: the perfect firstborn kid who only wanted to please my parents."

"Exactly. You've given them bragging rights from now until doomsday. All they talk about is their daughter who goes to *Princeton*."

"Yeah, and now I'm stuck. I mean, what if I were to tell you that I'm not even sure I want to stay at Princeton?"

"*What?*"

"Do you have any clue how much pressure there is there?" There wasn't a single crease on her perfectly pressed pink button-down blouse.

"Your choice."

"Everyone is already gunning for law or medical school."

"Including *you*."

"I don't know, Ann," she said.

"Guess there's a first time for everything," I shot right back.

She started unpacking, taking one pastel-colored blouse after the other out of her suitcase, along with her white capris and polo shirts, her espadrilles and boat shoes. Her voice remained quiet when she said: "Look, I know you're not on Debate Team, Ann. You'd hate Debate Team. Even *I* hated Debate Team. The only reason I did it was because Mama and Daddy thought it would help me get into college."

By now I was unpacking, too: the fabulous red dress with

the white flowers from Mama Lee, a pair of her polka-dot capris, a fabulous white sleeveless blouse with a midriff tie — all that great bonanza of bounty.

"You may not know it, but it's you, not me, who has it good. First of all, just look at you, with your pixie thing going, your arty friends, your creativity."

"Which makes me what? A giant loser."

"No! It makes you *original*. I've seen your sketchbooks, Ann. You leave them all over the place."

"I do?"

"Duh. You think it's easy being your sister?"

For the first time in my life, I was speechless.

"I don't see why not," I finally said.

"Anyway," she said with a little shrug of her Lacoste-covered shoulders, "you can tell me what you're up to, or you can face the music when Daddy and Mama go to Debate Finals only to find out that you've played them. You may be able to fool Mama, but don't try it on me. You couldn't debate your way out of a wet paper bag."

"What's that supposed to mean? That I'm stupid?" Sincerity or no sincerity, I was angry at her all over again.

"It means that you don't care about stuff like that — and why should you? If I had even an ounce of creativity, the last thing in the world I'd want to do is Debate Team." She let out a long sigh. "Not to mention that you talk so much, and so fast, that no one can keep up with you!"

"You just love to put me down, don't you?"

"You really don't get it, do you?" she said again. "I've tried to cover your butt with this stupid debate lie of yours for as long as I can, but it's about to blow up in your face, and you don't even know it."

"Way to condescend to me again," I said.

That's when she burst into tears. "Why can't you, for once in your life, just be *nice* to me?"

And with that, I felt awful. As in: really, really awful. Like I'd been mean to a five-year-old, or lit a dog's tail on fire.

Which is when I just kind of melted, and told her about the blog that Justine and I were about to unveil, and how, when Mama and Daddy finally saw it, they'd be so proud of me that they'd be able to forget all about Debate Team.

When I was finally done explaining, she looked me dead on and said: "Let me get this straight. You concocted this entire stupid story about being on Debate Team because you're afraid of telling Mama that you've been spending your afternoons in the *art room*? Why would she care? What are you, crazy?"

"But that's just the thing!" I wailed. "She does care. Every time I mention art, she freezes and gives me this *look* like she's going to get sick."

"Oh, come on."

"But it's true! I'm supposed to be *you*."

"What do I have to do, slap you so you'll wake up? It's easy for me, getting good grades. But you're the one who's just so cute and funny, and cracks everyone up all the time, and looks like Mama Lee — unlike me, who looks like Daddy! — and on top of all of that, you're totally Mama Lee's favorite, so much so that she even gave you all her beautiful clothes! As if I didn't even exist!"

"But I thought you hated Mama Lee's — my — clothes."

"I love them," she said.

Then she said: "But I couldn't wear them anyway. I'm too big. But you would have thought that, just maybe, she would have let me have a hat or something. A pair of gloves, or a ring. Instead, you got everything."

"Do you want some of mine?" I finally said.

"No. She gave them to you, not to me."

I felt so sad that I almost hugged her. Instead, I said: "But that still doesn't explain anything at all about why Mama is so weird about my doing anything even a little bit artistic, including in the way I dress!"

We'd come to a deadlock. Then my sister came out with the biggest whopper of all: "I was never, ever supposed to tell anyone this."

"What?"

"It's about Mama. About Mama and Mama Lee."

Then she told me.

"When Mama was younger, she was secretly engaged to someone else — I mean, someone who wasn't Daddy."

"*What?*"

"He was an artist. And a lot older than she was. A whole lot older. In fact, he was an old boyfriend of Mama Lee's. He used to come over to the house. That's how Mama met him."

"Mama dated an old boyfriend of Mama Lee's? How is that even possible?"

I wasn't sure I wanted to hear the answer, but Martha continued. "Mama Lee didn't know a thing about it, but Mama had started posing for him. For his paintings. She'd go to his studio, or wherever, after school. But she told Mama Lee she was doing something else, a school club, and with Mama Lee working, she didn't even think to check up on her."

"I don't like where this is heading. . . ."

"First he painted her sitting in a chair, just gazing off into the distance."

I bit my lip.

"Then he did a bunch of sketches."

My stomach began to make noises.

"And then he did another portrait, this one just of her face."

I was getting impatient: "So?"

"Finally, he did his famous painting of her. And when I say famous, I mean it. It's in a museum somewhere, even."

"Yeah, right."

"It is. I swear, Ann, I'm not making this up. You can Google it if you don't believe me."

"Believe what?"

"The famous painting of Mama. It's called *Black Beauty in Red and White Floral*."

"Huh?"

"That red dress. With the white flowers. The one Mama Lee gave you."

"What about it?"

"Mama's wearing it in that painting. She took it from Mama Lee's closet and posed in it. She thought she was going to marry that man. But he was still half in love with Mama Lee!"

"I think I'm going to lose my lunch."

"The painting was in some gallery somewhere and Mama Lee found out about it and pitched a fit and then the whole story came out and she broke the two of them up but good."

It was like someone had punched me in the stomach. I could barely think my own thoughts. Finally I said, "Mama told you this whole long story?"

"Yeah, and she made me promise not to tell anyone! She said even Daddy didn't know all the details. And now I've gone and told you, and if she ever finds out, man, is she going to be angry."

Suddenly my sister looked very, very tired, very old and worn-out and without hope. "Just don't tell her you know," she pleaded.

"But I still don't get it!" I yelped. "Just because Mama wore that one dress for the painting and, well, *whatever*, doesn't explain why she insists that I have to dress like the world's biggest conformist and act like someone who's never had an original thought or original impulse in her entire life."

"Like me, you mean?" Martha said. Which is when I felt myself flushing hot and deep, and for the first time since I'd first met Justine, I wished I could, just for once, keep my big mouth shut forever.

For once, I had to admit it: Martha was right. Even so, I just couldn't do it. I couldn't tell Mama the truth. Not even when we got back from Florida and I went over to Justine's for one final edit of our blog. Not even when Mama Lee called me to tell me that Mama had invited her to the Debate Finals and that Mama was "just brimming over with pride." Not even when I went ahead and Googled *Black Beauty in Red and White Floral* and saw the painting with my own eyes: my beautiful young mother, wearing my — Mama Lee's — favorite fabulous dress, the red one with the tight waist, cap sleeves, and big white flowers.

And now Justine was angry at me, Becka was furious at me, and the entire high school was talking about the drama that had happened at lunch. I sprang a headache, and then a stomach-ache, and by the time the final bell rang I felt like I was going to vomit. All I wanted to do was go home, undress, curl up into my bed, and sleep. But when I got home, Mama, who was usually working at that hour, was waiting for me. She didn't look too happy, either. This is what she said: "I just got off the phone with Justine's mother."

Now, in itself, that wasn't that weird. Justine's mom and Mama had started talking soon after Justine and I had become friends. What *was* weird was: first, that she'd bothered to tell me she'd spoken to Justine's mom on the phone, and second, that she was home in the first place.

I took a tentative step or two across the kitchen floor, heading, I hoped, to the hallway that would lead me to the stairs that would allow me to escape to my room.

"She wanted me to know that something Justine wrote — something on Facebook or something like that — went viral. Something about Becka. And that Becka's so upset that she broke something — something about drums, and then a mirror."

She looked at me as if I'd just started the third world war.

"The upshot is that Becka's in the hospital."

"Oh my God."

"You probably already know that Justine's mom — Judy — and Meryl Sanders are friendly, even if the girls aren't."

I nodded.

"Judy's at the hospital right now."

"Mama," I said, "are you saying that the girl tried to kill herself?"

"I don't really know. Judy didn't know, either. What I do know is that Justine had something to do with it."

"What? Who told you *that*?"

"Why? What do you know about it?"

"Just that Becka flipped out in lunch today," I fudged. "She screamed at Justine and me. She was, like — out of control."

"That sounds familiar."

"What do you mean?"

"Ann," she said, "I think it's time we had a little talk, don't you?"

"What? Why?"

"How about we start with Debate Team." The way she said it, it wasn't a question.

Martha had squealed. I wanted to pound her brains in.

"Sit," Mama commanded.

"Your sister is very worried about you," she continued after I'd taken my usual seat at the kitchen table. "Very. She's thinking of taking the semester off."

"Not for my sake, she isn't."

"Even so, she may not go back to Princeton next semester."

"Kill me now."

"You aren't on Debate Team, Ann. Explain yourself."

"First I have to kill her."

"Your sister has nothing to do with your choices, Ann. You and you alone chose to lie. You and you alone have chosen to hide your activities from me. You and you alone have decided to prance around in your grandmother's ridiculous outfits, like — like I don't know what! Like you're trying to draw attention to yourself. As if you don't get enough love and attention at home! Oh, you're so much like Mama Lee that you may as well be her clone. But it's over, do you understand?" Finally she just gave me *the look*, her big brown eyes and steady gaze holding mine until I had to look away.

"What do you *want* from me?"

"How about the truth?"

"I haven't done anything wrong! I swear!"

There was a silence. A long, long silence. Finally, Mama broke it. "I'm not sure I have reason to trust you. But I will hear you out. You can thank your sister, by the way, for assuring me that, though you've been sneaking around, you're not fooling around with drugs or boys. So if it isn't drugs, and it isn't a boy-friend, and I think by now we can be pretty sure that you're not spending your time with the Debate Team — what is it? What are you hiding?"

"Mama," I finally said, "there's something you don't know about me."

"Are you trying to tell me that you think you're a lesbian? Because, honey, if you're gay — you're a little young to know if you are or not, but if you are, that's okay. Your dad and I love you no matter what."

"But, Mama, that's not it!" I said. I didn't know whether to laugh or cry. Finally, with my eyes squeezed closed, I said: "It's that — I want to be an artist."

She looked at me as if I were speaking Chinese.

"That's where I've been in the afternoons. In the art room at school. Working with Ms. Anders, my art teacher."

"That's what this is all about? Frankly, I find that hard to believe."

"But it's true! That's what I've been doing! I've been learning to — well, mainly to draw."

"You've been learning to draw," she said in a voice that let me know she'd just about run out of patience.

"Well, I like painting, too. Actually, I love it, Mama. I love painting. I love just — just everything about it, the feel of the brushes in my hands, and the smell of the paints, and how sometimes my hands know what they're doing, like they've got a mind of their own."

"I see," she said coldly.

"You hate me now, don't you?"

"Hate you? Honey, how could I ever hate you? I love you with my entire heart." Mama's voice was trembling now, and there were tears in her eyes. Then her voice hardened. "But I must tell you that I'm both concerned and furious. Which is why I have to find some way to punish your butt so badly that you'll never, never ever, pull this kind of idiocy again."

"Mama?"

"For lying. For pretending. For dishonesty of every kind. For your abominable disregard for me. And for your behavior to your sister. "

"But, Mama!"

"And as for art — there's just no future there for you, Ann. Unless you're willing to live on nothing for the rest of your life." She shook her head. "Honey! Listen to me loud and clear: Art is all right for rich kids. But for people like us? We can't afford to go fooling around with that kind of nonsense. And nonsense it is. I learned the hard way. You don't have to."

"But, Mama!" I wailed. "Daddy's a lawyer! And you have a good career, too. We have plenty of money!"

"Do you have any clue what it's like out there, Ann?"

I looked down at my feet.

"Exactly. So I'd suggest that, instead of defending yourself, you think long and hard about what I just said. Especially about Becka."

"What's she got to do with anything?"

"Why don't you tell me?"

"Me?"

"Yes," she said. "You."

"Oh my God," I said, utterly panicked as the stories my brain was already spinning came to the surface of my consciousness — how the art I was doing was really making posters for the Debate Team, and how it was obvious that Becka had come to school drunk — but just before I launched into a whole new set of lies, I heard a siren in the distance, thought about Becka being in the hospital, and decided that I had to tell Mama the truth instead.

So I did.

No sooner had I walked in the door when Mom came hurrying out to greet me, but instead of her usual overhug, she took me by the shoulders and, her voice elevated, said: "What do you know about Becka?"

"That she's the world's biggest bitch?" I still hadn't quite gotten over what a hissy fit she'd thrown in the cafeteria over the launch of *Fashion High*, particularly since Ann's sketches were totally flattering. My only question was how she'd figured out that I was connected to it.

"Did you have something to do with Becka — something that set her off?"

"Mom — the girl doesn't even talk to me except to insult me. You know that."

"Tell me the truth, Justine. I just got a call from Meryl. Becka's in the hospital."

"What did she do? Choke on her own nasty vapors?"

"No, she did not. She slit her wrists."

"What?"

"Right in front of her brother, too. Apparently he was the one who called 911."

"Mom, look: I don't know what Becka's mom told you, but slitting her wrists is not the girl's style."

"Honey, I was here when the ambulance pulled up. I heard the siren — and I went over there right away."

"You can't just mind your own business, can you?"

"For God's sake, Justine! This isn't about some stupid quarrel between you and Becka! Don't you *get it*? She's in the hospital right now — and it's where I'm going, too — because of something you wrote."

"What? Who told you that?"

"Meryl said something about some website, some blog. You and Ann — I knew you were up to something up there. I'm not an idiot, you know."

"Oh, really?" I then said. Suddenly, with Mom screaming in my face, I felt like a caged animal, hot and scared and desperate all at once. My heart was pounding. My palms were sweaty. Had Becka *really* slit her wrists? Over our blog? Because if she had . . . But as anger welled up inside me, I lost track of what I'd been thinking.

"You're not an idiot?" I said. "Are you kidding? Mom, you are, hands down, the biggest idiot ever. Not only have you followed Dad around from place to place, like some stupid, loyal dog, but you quit your entire dancing career for him. You quit having any kind of life at all!"

"This is a topic for another occasion," Mom said.

"I don't think so, Mom, because if you want to talk about idiots . . ."

"Not now, Justine. I mean it."

"Spending hours finding the perfect Christmas gift for him when he gives you some cheap earrings . . ."

"That's enough!"

"That he doesn't have a clue who either of us are . . ."

"I need to get to the hospital."

". . . only you're such an idiot that you think he actually loves you, that he actually cares, when in fact you're an even bigger idiot that Becka's mom, and Ann's mom, and all the other moms in the world put together, because you and you alone are the mom who doesn't even have a clue that she moved to New Jersey so her husband could be closer to his girlfriend!"

It was like she'd just been bitten by a poisonous snake. Or like a blizzard had just blanketed our entire living room with drifts of deep snow, bringing utter stillness, utter silence.

"What did you just say?" she finally said.

"Dad has a girlfriend. She lives in New York."

Swallowing hard, Mom said: "I'm going to the hospital now to see if there's anything I can do for Meryl. In the meantime, you're grounded. And I mean it, Justine. You're not even allowed into the backyard!"

I watched TV. I went onto Facebook. I called Ann, but she didn't answer. Then I called Polly, but she didn't answer, either. I even called Eliza, who was still, duh, in school. Then I had a pressing urge to call Robin, but didn't even know her last name, and anyway, what would I have said? *Am I a murderer?*

Because suddenly that's what I felt like, and I saw my future, too, locked up in some JV prison with a bunch of girls who did heroin and already had two or three children and carried knives just in case they needed to cut your face. The next moment, I was standing over the toilet, dizzy with dread, coughing up — well, nothing. I tried to puke, but all that came out was spit.

Skizz came up to me and rubbed against my ankles.

But I still found it hard to believe that Becka would try to kill herself — especially over our blog, which I read and reread and reread again, until I didn't even understand what it said. The next thing I knew, Dad called me. Here's what he said: "What the hell is going on, Pooky? Your mother left me a message saying that there's been some emergency."

"Like you could care," I said.

"What's that supposed to mean?"

What was it supposed to mean, anyhow? I didn't know — but suddenly, I didn't care, either. I didn't care about him. I didn't care about Mom. And I didn't even want to *think* about Becka!

"You could have at least bought Mom that necklace."

"What are you talking about?"

"The one you were looking at in Bloomingdale's when I ran into you there even though you said you were out of town on business. The one with all the diamonds."

"Sapphires," he corrected. "And I decided they were too much for your mom. You know she doesn't go in for fancy."

"Not like some people. How much of my future college tuition did you spend on that thing, anyway?"

"What? Pooky — you're talking in riddles."

"*I'm* talking in riddles?" I said. "Me? Your own little Pooky? Because let's face it, *Billy*, I'm not the only one who hasn't been real clear about things."

"That's it. Are you on drugs? I'm coming home right now!"

"I wouldn't if I were you."

"Listen here, young lady. You don't talk to me like that. Ever. Understood?"

"Not a good idea," I singsonged.

"I'll be home in thirty minutes, at the latest. And you're going to stay put. Do you hear me?"

"Loud and clear."

But instead of staying put — I mean, was he kidding? — I ran away. I didn't know where to run to, though, so it was a challenge. Clearly, Ann's house was off-limits, and anyway, we'd just had a big fight and I wasn't really sure I wanted to talk to her. I called Polly, but her mother said she wasn't home. And basically, except for the random girls I sat with at lunch, I didn't have any other friends who I considered actual, live, close, good, want-to-actually-hang-out-with-them friends. So I headed out the door and wandered aimlessly for a while, until, ta-da, I had a master brainstorm. I'd go to Weird John's house and just kind of hide out there until Mom was so worried about me that she'd forget that I was responsible for Becka's suicide attempt.

Except I didn't have the slightest idea where Weird John lived — if he lived anywhere in particular at all, that is. To the extent that I'd thought about it, I'd just assumed that he lived in a garbage dispenser, or perhaps in a log, with a bedroom decorated entirely in Death Cult and Astrovamps posters, with ripped black sheets covering the windows. No matter where he lived, I thought, there'd be bunches of smaller and larger Goths, and perhaps a dog corpse or two rotting on the front lawn.

I did what I swore I'd never do, and called him.

It turned out that he only lived about ten minutes away from me, and his house, if anything, was even more boring, in that Homely Acres way, than mine was. In other words, it was a standard-issue rectangular box, the exact proportions of your typical shoe box, with a row of windows on the second level, and picture windows on either side of the front door. The front mat featured a cheery WELCOME TO OUR HOME and, instead of a mailbox, the Weird family had a metal poodle balancing a mailbox on his poodle head. There were frilly white curtains in the windows and, when I rang the doorbell, it chimed tunefully, like a brass instrument.

Weird John appeared at the door, dressed in his usual at-least-two-days-old black, his belt studded with miniature spikes, like the pointy ends of thumbtacks, his eyes outlined in blue eyeliner, and a new earring, in the shape of a skeleton, dangling from his left earlobe. "So I understand that you've landed in deep doo-doo."

"Who told you that?"

"Everyone told me."

"Can you be slightly more specific?"

"And —"

"What?" I was following him down the stairs now, presumably to his lair, or whatever you call the place where someone with his, er, aesthetics and taste might sleep.

"I love you, Frizz."

"Shove it."

"I do."

"Shut up and tell me who told you."

"But I love you! I do!"

"Are you *trying* to be a jerk, or does it just come naturally to you?"

"I'll do anything to help you. Anything at all. Are the police after you?"

"Because I wrote a blog?"

"What? No. Because of what you did to her. To Becka."

"Why? What'd I do?"

"Don't try to deny it, Frizz. Not when half the school saw you go after her with that knife!"

"*What?*"

"After she went up to you in the cafeteria and you stabbed her in the arm."

"Earth. To. John. I didn't stab the girl. I didn't stab anyone. I don't have a knife. Where would I even get one, in the cafeteria? I didn't do anything at all. Except — write that stupid blog!"

"Are you saying . . ." he said as he swung open the door to what turned out to be a TV-slash-Ping-Pong-table room, but before he could finish his sentence, I was confronted by the sight of both Polly and — blow me with a feather — Robin, sitting together on the room's beat-up sofa, eating ice cream. For some reason Robin didn't look so good, but in the shadows of the basement room, I couldn't tell why. All I knew was that I was doubly embarrassed, first for being at Weird John's in the first place, and second for being in the same room as Becka's best friend, whom, on top of everything else, I'd just blogged about! But I didn't want to let on about how panicked I was. Instead, in an offhand way, I said:

"Excuse me? Now I'm totally confused. T-O-T-A-L-L-Y."

"It's okay," he said. "We'll save you."

"I don't need to be saved!" I screamed.

"Then what are you doing here?"

"I'm, I'm —" My mouth gaped open like a dead fish's.

"Exactly."

Suddenly I was miserable. Not the way I'd been miserable before, either, with a combination of frustration, fury, and fear. Now I was just plain old, flat-out, dumbed-down miserable. "Why are you two here?" I said to the girls.

Polly spoke first: "John called and said I needed to get here immediately. That we had to figure out how to save you. So here I am."

"But I don't need to be saved," I repeated. "I didn't do anything! Except write that stupid blog!"

"It wasn't that stupid," Robin said.

"Thanks," I said. "But why are you of all people here?"

"What do you mean?"

"You were in the blog, too. And isn't Becka, like, your best friend?"

"*Was*," the girl said miserably.

"Don't tell me that John called you, too."

She stared at me like I was a Martian from Mars, until, finally, and with a little quiver in her voice, she said: "My father got really angry. Then he hit me. So I'm hiding out here. Me and my mom and brother, too. You know. For safety. Because he was, like, out of control."

"*What?*"

"He hit me really hard. So we came here."

"Here?" Truly, I was more puzzled than ever.

"John's my cousin," she said.

That's when I noticed two things: first, that Robin had obviously been crying, and second, that her left eye was swollen and purple.

"Oh God!" I yelled. "I wish I'd never written the dumb thing, okay?"

It was bad enough, my hiding out in Weird John's Ping-Pong room, with half of Western High thinking I stabbed Becka, Becka herself in the hospital, my mother in a state of shock over Dad, and Dad about to get home to find that I'd defied his orders and disappeared. Plus, I'd written something so mean that Becka had gone and slit her own wrists, and Robin's dad must have found out about it, too, and hit her because of it. Only that didn't make sense. On the other hand, nothing else did, either.

Because in all my bad times, all the times that I was the new kid in school, or Dad didn't seem to have a clue who I was, or

Mom pretended that everything was hunky-dory when it wasn't, never — not once — had I been so miserable that I'd wanted to hurt myself. I'd never even threatened to hurt myself. I'd never even *cried*.

"I'll take care of you — I'll look after you — no matter what you've done," WJ said. "We all will, right?" Then he lunged for me, holding me so close to his chest that I could smell his full smell: deodorant and powder and hair gel and sweat, mixed with cigarette smoke and mint gum. It was my lowest, most humiliating, most shameful moment ever — trapped in Weird John's Ping-Pong room, with Weird John's arms around me, and Polly and Robin just staring at me, as if they, too, thought I'd gone and murdered the girl. Even worse, as John held me close, I relaxed into him. But the worst moment of all came when, all of a sudden, I started to cry.

CHAPTER TWENTY-ONE

The New Scarf

• Becka •

W_{hat} *I remember* best is my mother sitting by my bed in the hospital, holding my hand while doctors and nurses rushed back and forth, attending me. "But why?" she kept saying. "Why did you do such a thing to yourself?" Her face was the color of rain clouds, and there were small speckles of light brown under her eyes. "Why? My darling, why?"

I just turned away, letting the IV drip into me, the painkillers, the sleeping pills.

"Why?" I heard her say as I drifted into a beautiful, painless sleep.

Several hours later, when I woke up, the only thing I heard was the beeping of a machine by my side. There were green curtains pulled partly around my bed. Mom was sitting in the corner. Daddo was pacing.

"How do you feel?" he said.

"Tired."

"They gave you something to help you sleep," he said,

taking my bandaged palm very gently in his hands. He smelled like he always smelled: like antiseptic soap and mint tea. "Does it hurt?"

"Not much," I said.

"Good," he said, kissing me on my nose, like he had when I was a little girl. I closed my eyes.

When I opened them, he was gone. "He's taking a walk," Meryl said. Then: "What happened? For God's sake, Becka, tell me. Did something happen in Paris? Was it that blog?"

"You know about the blog?"

"Everyone knows about the blog. Those girls who did it — well, they've pretty much owned up. I'm fond of Judy Gandler — and I like Ann's mother, too. We used to carpool together! But don't worry. Your father and I will see to it that the girls will be severely punished."

For some reason, even from within the sawdust that my brain had become, I felt nothing but fury — but not at either Um or Ann. Instead, it was my mother I was angry at. So angry that I wanted to do to her what I'd done to Danny's drums. Except I couldn't. I felt so tired and so weak, my limbs heavy, like when once, a couple of years earlier, I'd fainted during field hockey practice. Suddenly I remembered another time I'd been sick — I think it was with bronchitis. I'd been little then, and in the middle of the night Meryl had carried me from my bed to the bathroom, where she'd rocked me on her lap as she blasted the shower to make steam.

"No," I said.

"What do you mean, 'no'?"

"I mean, that blog didn't have anything to do with it."

"What?" She was weeping now, not even bothering to wipe the tears away. "If it didn't have anything to do with that blog . . . I just don't understand."

But I did. There was no other place to go, no one to turn to but Meryl herself. I looked at the lowered ceiling, how the panels looked like they might fall in.

"Why did you try to kill yourself?"

"I didn't."

"Are you sure?"

I nodded, but even that hurt. Even if I hadn't bled to death, I was choking on my own anger. She didn't understand anything! Suicide? Me? But as usual, she had to stamp my behavior with a label that she'd gotten out of a book.

"Who, or what, made you do this to yourself?"

I took a deep breath. "You did," I said.

Then I fell asleep.

Even after they let me go home, the only thing I wanted to do was nap. My stitches itched, everyone at school was sure to be talking about me, and just about no one — other than Aunt Libby, that is — called. Danny wouldn't come near me, even at dinner, and when we passed in the hall, he made a little darting semicircle around me to make sure that there was space between us. Nor did it help when my parents announced that they were going to have to punish me for busting up Danny's drum set. They just hadn't yet figured out what the punishment would be.

"You're kidding, right?" I said.

"Sorry, kid," Daddo said.

"Dad's right," Meryl said.

"What are you going to do to me?" I said.

"We'll let you know," Daddo said.

"Oh, great."

Meryl kept apologizing all over the place for not being what she called "there" for me and, true to her Merylness, suggested that the two of us go into mother-daughter therapy, *together*, a suggestion that was so ridiculous I wanted to scream. She felt so bad that she was getting on my nerves, because somehow, and once again, she'd turned my misery into something that belonged to *her*.

It was when she once again started up with the cherry soda routine that I knocked that stupid glass out of her hand and screamed: "Can you stop already?"

"What do you mean?" she gasped.

"It's not about you, Meryl. It's about me."

"I know it is, darling — and I'm trying to help — to understand. . . ."

"But that's just it," I wailed. "I hate cherry soda!"

"You do?"

"That's what I mean. You're so caught up with you, you, you all the time — with your being my mother, the world's great expert on being a mother — that you don't even see what you've done!"

"I'm not following. I don't understand —"

"Your *books*!" The words came in jagged lumps out of my throat. "Your books — they're all about me! Your stupid cherry soda for the teenage soul. You've made a career writing about *me*! But it's not about me, is it? It's about you — you and your career. You and your being a better mother than everyone else. Only guess what, Mom? You're not a better mother. You're a terrible mother!"

She gasped like I'd punched her in the stomach. But I didn't care.

"Every kid in school knows it's me in your books. You even go on the radio to talk about me. It's like the only reason you had me was so you could be famous." My words came out with spit now.

"Famous? I'm not famous."

"But you want to be. So you've turned me into a subject. A character! And what you're doing — it's like, it's like you're *poisoning* me. I'm *real* — and you're supposed to be my mother, not someone who sneaks into my business and then uses me to get published!"

"But I've always shielded you — and guided you — and protected your privacy."

"You're kidding, right? Because guess what? You don't protect me. You expose me. And then you humiliate me. And then you pretend that you care."

Which was when I saw it happen: Right before me, she wilted. Wilted like a balloon animal and, her shoulders shaking, she walked out of the room and down the stairs.

A few days later, when I had to go back to school again, everyone acted like nothing had happened, either ignoring me completely or being superfriendly, like I was their best friend. I knew that everyone thought I'd tried to commit suicide, but I was too tired to go around setting the record straight. I was in no mood — for anything. All I wanted to do was get through my classes, do my homework, and read. Thank God I liked my room, is all I can say, because I spent most of my time there.

The last person I wanted to see was Um. But about a month after I got my stitches out, there she was, on the doorstep, with a small wrapped box that she handed to me, her face as red as her hair as she said, "I'm really sorry, Becka. I really am."

My first impulse was to slam the door on her face, but for some reason, something about the way she looked — like a dandelion that had been stepped on — made me feel sorry for her.

"Thanks," I forced myself to say.

"I really am sorry," she said. "About the blog. And about your — your accident."

She looked so miserable that, instead of slamming the door on her face like I felt like, I took a deep breath and said: "Why did you do it?"

She shrugged. "It's kind of a long story." Then, amazingly, the girl began to cry. And when I say cry, I mean sob, as in a gusher.

"I'm just really sorry!" she said again, her face and eyes turning as red as her curly hair.

"Okay, I get it!" I said. "Just, just . . ." I couldn't think of what to say. "Just stop crying. It wasn't your fault, okay? It really wasn't."

She looked at me the way she'd looked at me on that hot day last summer when I'd first met her: like I had two heads.

"I'm not an idiot," she announced.

"I know you're not," I said.

"Whatever." She looked away, and then she turned and trotted across the lawn.

"Did your mother make you give this to me?" I yelled in her direction, but she'd already reached her side of the street, and must not have heard me. I tried again: "Justine!" For half a second, she turned — but only slightly. Then she was inside.

That's when I noticed that there was a FOR SALE sign in front of her house.

They were moving again? No wonder the girl was a wreck. I'd kill myself if I had to move halfway through high school.

And not only that, but as I sat there with the box in my hand, I realized something that I'd kind of known all along: that blog about me was, in its own mean way, good, especially the pictures. Plus, it was a great idea. It was such a great idea that I should have thought of it myself. Of course, it would never go up again, not after everything that had happened.

Oh well, I thought as I went back up the stairs to my room. Nothing would change. I'd somehow get through the year, and then, if I was lucky, I'd find something not too boring to do over the summer, and then, eventually, I'd go to college, and maybe even have a boyfriend, and leave all the awfulness of the year behind me. After all, after the way I'd acted, who would want to be friends with me again? I didn't even blame them. Even *I* wouldn't hang out with me if I didn't have to. And as for my mother, she'd never really understand at all — not what she'd done to me or what I'd done to myself. My only hope was that, somehow or another, I'd grow up and be able to leave my old self far, far behind.

But just as I was thinking these thoughts and picturing the next two years sitting alone in the cafeteria and having kids avoid me in the halls, my cell phone starting ringing, and glancing down, I saw that it was Robin. I hadn't spoken to her in ages and didn't know why she was calling me now. She let me know soon enough, though. "I didn't have anything to do with that blog," she immediately said.

"I know."

"But you said I knew something about it. But I didn't."

"Sorry. I was angry that day. And anyway, I know it didn't have anything to do with you. Um just came over to say she was sorry, all right? She admitted everything. So don't worry about it." My voice was shaking when I talked, but I got it out anyway. Then I said it again: "Don't worry about it. Really. I know you had nothing to do with it."

There was a long pause, and then: "Justine came over?"

"*Justine?*"

"That's her name."

I swallowed hard. What had made me think it was cute to call the girl *Um*? "She handed me a box," I said.

"What's in it?"

"I don't know."

"Why don't you open it?"

"You think I should?" I said. "What if it's a stink bomb? Or a dead rat or something?"

"What?"

"I don't even blame that girl for hating me," I said.

"She doesn't hate you," Robin said. Then, very slowly, she said: "No one does."

My eyes were misting up so much that when, finally, I opened the box, I wasn't even sure that I saw what I saw. Because inside it wasn't a stink bomb or a dead cockroach or a bunch of old chewed-up chewing gum hardened into a twisted rictus, but rather, a silk scarf, gray with blue and green butterflies flying on it. The note read: "I hope you like this scarf."

"It's a scarf," I said.

"Is it pretty?"

"Yes," I said. "It's beautiful."

Are you sure you'll be okay here by yourself?" Mommy said, standing over me wearing a new, light-blue dress and the string of pearls that her own mother had given her for her twenty-first birthday. I'd never seen her look so pretty. Her nails were polished and her dark hair shone. I was halfway through a history paper that was due the next day, and it was just about killing me.

"I'm almost sixteen. Why wouldn't I be okay?"

"I just don't want you to be lonely."

"I know, Mommers. And guess what? I'm fine. I have to write this stupid paper. It's ruining my life."

"But you sure you'll be okay? If there's any problem, you'll call me on my cell phone, right?"

"Right."

"You have Alfred's cell number, too, right?"

"Yes, Mommy."

"And you're sure you're all right?"

"Happy birthday," I said. "And please go away now."

"But it's not my birthday."

"Whatever. Have fun with Weirdo Man."

Finally, she kissed me and left.

It *was* hard to believe, but shortly after Poppy's funeral, she'd started going out with Alfred for real. First there was that coffee, and then they had lunch, but by week number three it was dinner, from which she'd come back flushed and laughing. "You're kidding," I said when she'd told me how much fun she'd had. "*Alfred?*"

"You know what?" she said. "He's a very nice man."

"But, Mommy . . . *Alfred?*"

"But what, Polly? Who do you want me to date, your swimming coach?"

I guess I must have blanched, or blushed, or otherwise turned color, because as soon as she'd said it, she slapped her palm over her mouth, and said: "Oh, honey! I'm sorry! That was insensitive of me."

I'd never told Mommy about Coach Fruit — other than about what a great coach he was, I mean. But she did know that he'd given me his jacket. And she also knew that, after the first time I'd worn it, I'd stuck it in the back of my closet and never worn it again.

"I just don't see why you have to date such a loser," I finally said.

Now, through the open window, I could hear the two of them laughing and talking as Mommy followed Alfred to his waiting car. I got up and looked out. He was handing her a bouquet of flowers as he held the door open for her, and she was gazing up at him, her face like a petal in the moonlight.

At least the season was over, and I didn't have to see Coach Fruit again until swimming started up in the summer. But without swimming, I was bored and antsy. I missed the team. But mainly, I just felt incredibly stupid. Stupid and humiliated and dumb. But it turned out that when school started up after vacation, nobody remembered my crush on Coach Fruit, or my jacket, or even how poorly I'd done at State — not after that blog had hit and everyone became so distracted over the ensuing drama that even Weird John forgot to torment me. Even so, with Poppy dead, and my dream of getting a swimming scholarship gone, I felt like my world was falling apart.

But my world didn't fall apart. It just got boring. Boring and cold and dark. Both Justine and Ann were punished for, like, forever, so I didn't even have anyone to hang out with, not really, and with Robin going through her own mess at home, she wasn't all that available, either. The only person I knew who didn't seem to have the winter yucks was my mother, who went around the house singing. And just when I didn't think things could get any drearier, Burton called. This is what he said: "I need to talk to you, Polly."

"Okay," I said.

"I mean in person," he said. "When can I come out to see you?"

"I thought you lived in Los Angeles."

"I'm in New York," he said. "Clearing up a few things from Poppy's estate. And I need to see you. It's important."

"Let me ask Mommy," I said, looking out the window as the snow swirled blindly through the dark night. In the next room, she was playing a Beethoven sonata, I forget which one. In the kitchen, where I was working, Hank was asleep in the corner, dreaming about chasing cats, his paws trotting against the air.

"I've already talked to her," he said. "She's cool about it. I mean, I know I haven't been much of a father to you . . ."

"You can say that again."

"And you have no reason to feel anything for me, but . . ."

"I guess so."

"But this is important. Please?"

He took the train to West Falls the next day, meeting me at the Daily Brew because Mommy said that it would be more comfortable for both of us to be in a neutral, public spot. Also, she had students and didn't want any big scene while she was teaching. He looked even worse than he had at Poppy's funeral, his face a gray green, and his skin greasy, as if it was covered with a light sweat. His clothes were too big on him, too, his pants flopping a little around his ankles and his jacket drooping over his shoulders. To add to the homelessness effect, he carried a beat-up shopping bag. Truthfully, the only reason I'd agreed to meet him at all was because Mommy had looked so sad, and when she told me that it was important for me to go and talk to him, her voice had begun to quiver, like she was about to cry. Finally I'd said: "Fine!" and, Mommylike-to-the-max, she'd thrown her arms around me.

But that didn't mean that I wanted to be there. All I could think about was what a jerk he'd been to me and Mommy at Poppy's funeral. All I could think of was how much I — well, I hated him, is the truth. He sat down across from me, anyway, and calmly ordered a cappuccino for himself and, even though I'd said I didn't want anything, a hot chocolate for me. When our drinks came, he took a sip, looked into his coffee cup, and said, "Aren't you going to have your cocoa?"

"No."

He hung his head. Then he said: "I'm dying."

Just like that.

"What?"

"Your mother already knows," he said. "But she agreed to let me tell you myself."

"I don't understand. Do you have cancer?"

"Kind of. It's complicated, what I have."

I felt like a nonperson. Like a rock. Like a stick. Like I was suspended in midanimation: a drawing of a person, instead of an actual one.

"And believe it or not, you — you and your mother — are going to come into a little money."

"But I thought you were broke," I blurted out when, with a thud, my heart began to beat again. "You never even buy me birthday presents."

I was so confused that I could barely understand what he was telling me — he was dying? He was going to give me money? What was he doing here, with his gray face and floppy clothes? What was *wrong* with him? Why was he just sitting there, drinking cappuccino? Why had he ordered me a cup of hot chocolate even when I'd told him that I didn't want it?

"The money belonged to your grandfather," he said. "My father had more than he let on, and he left it all to me. Even the house in Queens. He'd been renting it out for years, and now it's worth something."

"I'm going to inherit his house in Queens? Mommy and I are going to have to move to *Queens*?"

For the first time ever, I saw Burton laugh — or rather, chuckle. A little semichuckle, that is, like a cross between a laugh and a cough. "I sold it already," he said. "And the money will be yours after I'm dead."

Finally it dawned on me: He was serious.

"What's wrong with you?"

"Meaning?"

"Are you really dying?" I could barely whisper the words out.

"I'm afraid so."

"What do you have?"

"Pretty much everything," he said.

Suddenly I was furious. So furious that I wanted to throw my hot chocolate right in his face. How dare he just show up out of the blue like this, just sit there, all calm and weird and greasy looking, and tell me that he was dying? What did I care? What did it have to do with me? I got up to leave.

But just as I was pushing myself away from the booth, he caught me by the wrist and, gripping hard, said, "Polly. Please. Sit."

But I didn't. I couldn't. Instead, I just stood there, frozen with rage. Then he took a deep breath and said: "I have AIDS."

"You're gay," I said.

But he wasn't. He was an addict. Or that's what he said: He said that he'd been hooked on heroin since before I was born and had gotten AIDS from a needle. He said that that's the reason my mother had kicked him out — because he was using. Ever since, he said, he'd spent most of his money on doctors and medicines. He'd never wanted to tell his father, though: He said that he'd been Poppy's pride and joy and just couldn't bear to let him know what he really was.

"Mommy kicked *you* out?" I said. "But I thought — I thought . . ."

"Never mind," he said. "None of it matters anymore."

I was still standing, frozen to the spot, when he reached down for his battered and creased shopping bag, and handed it to me. "For you," he said. "It was mine in high school. For basketball. I know it's hard to believe, but once upon a time, I was a great athlete. At least that was one thing I could give you — speed and strength. Oh well."

Inside was a varsity jacket with the letters MHS on it. It was maroon and ivory, a perfect vintage example of the type. "Thank you," I said.

"Why didn't you tell me?" I screamed at my mother the minute I got home. "All these years — and I thought Burton was merely a jerk. And, okay, maybe he is a jerk. He acts like a jerk. But, Mommy! He has AIDS. He's going to be dead soon."

"I know," she said. "That's why I told him it was okay to tell you."

"But *you* never told me, did you? You never mentioned the fact that he was a drug addict! Or that he was sick! Or *anything*!"

"I thought it would be worse for you that way," she said. "If anyone knew. If your friends knew — if the parents of my students knew. I needed to make a living, Polly! I needed to do what was best for you!"

"And so you lied about Burton?"

"I didn't lie."

"You didn't tell the truth, either."

She hung her head. "I did the best I could, honey. Please believe that. And after a while — it was just easier to let it go. He was out of our lives anyway. What good would it have done you to know who your father really was? To know who your *mother* really was?"

"But, Mommy! You didn't know he had AIDS. It wasn't your fault."

"But I knew he used drugs, honey. I knew it when I met him. And I knew it when I married him. And I married him anyway."

"Why?"

"I know you can't understand it, honey," she said, "but I was in love. He was older than I was, and handsome, and my own father was so cold, so distant — and your father believed in me. He believed in my talent as a musician. And he himself was wonderful. He could sit down at the piano and play so beautifully that you could have sworn there were angels singing." There were tears in her eyes, and she looked about twenty years younger than she'd looked before. "He was everything to me," she said. "He was magic."

"God," I said, feeling even more uncomfortable than I had been with Burton. Mommy — young and in love? I just couldn't picture it. I wanted to puke my brains out!

"Even though I still loved him, when he got sick, I just had to ask him to leave. What choice did I have?" She looked away. "I just didn't want him anywhere near you."

"And just like that, he left? He didn't even put up a struggle?"

"It was me, honey, not him. But you have to understand. I couldn't take care of a baby and look after a sick man — not when that man was HIV positive, and was still using, and God knows what he might bring home next."

"But he didn't want to?"

"To what?"

"Leave?"

Mommy hung her head. "He was so ashamed. Of his habit. He went through all his savings, and then all of mine. He had to sell his piano — a beautiful grand piano, not a baby grand like mine. His own father didn't know how sick he was. He never told him."

"I feel kind of nauseous."

"I'm sure you do," she said.

"I'm going to be sick."

"But you aren't sick, honey. You're the least sick person I've ever known."

"I'm sick in my head. I'm sick in my chest."

"You may feel that way now, but that's because you have a heart that feels. You're healthy and smart and kind and good, not to mention a terrific athlete and the prettiest girl I've ever laid eyes on."

I threw up anyway. I never wanted to talk to my mother again. I didn't care that my father was dying. But I wore his jacket to school anyway. It was the least I could do. I wore it with my white jeans, and a white turtleneck sweater, and my Ugg knockoffs, and, for the first time ever, I didn't care what other people thought about me. I liked my look just fine.

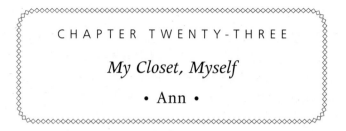

T*he weirdest part* of that whole long winter? *Fashion High* was a hit. A huge hit — even more successful than my fantasies for it had been. And after the news filtered through that Becka was going to be all right, even Mama could see that what we'd done hadn't been all that bad.

She grounded me anyway. For a month. She also made me promise to apologize to Martha, which grossed me out, *and* write a letter to Becka: a real letter, on paper, and not an email. "But what can I say to her?" I said. "The girl probably hates my guts anyway. What can I say that will make a difference?"

"How about 'I'm sorry'?"

So I sat down and wrote it. And wrote it. And wrote it again. Finally, on maybe the tenth time, I got it to where I didn't think it was dog poop. This is what I wrote:

Dear Becka,
I'm sorry about how hurt you were by our blog. I

now realize that blogging about you was more than selfish — it was cruel. I don't think of myself as being a cruel person, but that's what I was on the blog. I think deep down I'm jealous of you, which is partly why I did what I did — and that's not an excuse, just the truth. I mean, you always look so amazing, and you're so confident. Whereas I still look like I'm twelve years old, and when it comes to putting clothes on, I'm not sure I know what I'm doing. We used to be friends when we were little, and I hope maybe we can be friends again. I truly am sorry.
Ann

I still felt like one of yesterday's Tater Tots, though. A Tater Tot with a mean streak so mean that it goes viral on the local teenage blogosphere, and a fabulous wardrobe that's nonetheless coated with cooties. Which brings me to the question: What does a stale, nasty Tater Tot wear to school? Stale, nasty clothes, of course: in my case, jeans and sweaters and turtlenecks from freshman year. Ann the Astonishing had disappeared, replaced by a walking, miserable Tater Tot, and no one cared, except, of course, Justine, who was on my case about it, except that, ever since the blog bomb incident and our fight, even she didn't *really* care — or at least not enough to actually be friends again.

It may as well have been the beginning of the year again, with me in my bland clothes, hanging out with the Latins, and going through the motions of going to class and doing my homework and pretending that everything was just hunky-dory, when it wasn't. It wasn't AT ALL. As for Justine, she was mainly hanging around with Polly and Robin, and when I did see her, which wasn't all that often, we were like: *Hi. Hi. What happened to your fashion? I dunno. Well, see ya. Well, see ya. . . .* and that was all.

I was so depressed that I, me, Ann Eleanor Marcus, barely even talked until about a month later, when I was rumbling around my locker looking for my biology textbook. I felt a tap on my shoulder and turned to see Becka. She looked miserable, like she'd lost not only weight, but her personality, too. She'd never acknowledged my letter to her, but since it hadn't been returned to me, I assumed she'd gotten it.

"Hi?" I said.

"I didn't hate the blog."

"You didn't?"

"I thought your drawings were really good."

I didn't know what to say. She looked so angry.

"But then you went and . . ."

"I know," she said. "My accident."

"Right."

"For your information, it wasn't a suicide attempt, like everyone is saying."

"It wasn't?"

"No. I was just so — angry. I wasn't even thinking. It just kind of happened."

I was afraid to say it, but I said it anyway: "Because?"

"It's complicated," she said, "but it wasn't because of the blog."

"It wasn't because of the blog?" I had to say it out loud, just to make sure that I'd heard her right.

"Like I said," she said. "It was just a stupid blog. What do I care?"

I didn't know whether to be relieved or insulted, so instead, and for all the rest of the day, I was vaguely weirded out. When I found Justine to tell her what had happened, Justine told me that Becka had told her something similar, with that same flat intonation and nonexpression on her face. Polly, who was also there, just shrugged and said: "How do you like my varsity jacket?"

"I like it," I said.

"I know," she said. "You should blog about me. You can call it 'V is for Very Awesome.'"

"Ha ha. Funny. Not," Justine said.

"But I mean it!"

As it turned out, she *did* mean it. And she wasn't the only one. Even though she'd been in our first post, Robin had liked it, too. I know because she'd told Polly, and Polly had told me, and I told Justine, and the next thing I know, Justine and I were hanging out again. It was weird, though, hanging out with her like nothing had ever happened, when we both knew that things had changed. Big-time. And that my stupid blog was the cause of at least some of it.

Then one day, out of the blue, Robin herself sat herself down with us at the Latin Girls table, saying: "Do you have any clue how much I love clothes?"

"And?"

"No, really," she said. "I'm not just talking about your blog, either, which, by the way, everyone and their dogs know you did."

"I know," I said.

"We know," Justine said.

"Yeah, well, that's not all — you guys know my twin brother, Ben?"

Of course I knew Ben — everyone did. He was actually a pretty nice kid, but he had one of the biggest mouths in all of Western High, plus he was a supergeek, skinny and tall and smart, the kind who understands what black holes are and reads the *Wall Street Journal*. He hung around with Weird John. But Justine was like: "Ben's your brother?"

"My *twin* brother."

"OMG," she said. "That kid . . ."

"Tell me about it," Robin said. "I have to live with him. And you know that email that was going around about Becka? 'Teenage Tears and Fears'? The one that was like an article by her mother?"

The whole table nodded. Anything related to Becka was still considered to be good gossip.

"My brother sent it. He and my cousin, John, together. As a *joke*. He thought it was so funny."

"But it was stupid," I said.

"And mean," Polly said.

"I didn't see it," Justine said. "What article? What are you talking about?"

"My brother sent out a group email that was like a parody or something — something he wrote as a joke, but he said it was from the Daughter Doctor, which is what Becka's mother calls herself, and when I found out, which wasn't actually all that hard, I was so mad I wanted to kill him."

"How'd you find out?"

"John confessed. After Becka hurt herself. He thought you were going to go to jail, or something crazy like that, I don't know. He helped write it because he was so in love with you."

"I'm going to puke blood," Justine said.

"Seriously?" she continued. "And Ben thinks he's so smart, like he knows everything about everything. But he's not. And one thing he definitely doesn't know about is clothes. Which is where your blog comes in."

Justine and I just looked at each other.

"I want to write it with you," she said.

"You want to work with — us?" Justine gasped.

"Why not? When it comes to dressing it, you two are the best." Then, turning her attention to me, she said: "Except, I mean . . . I mean . . . Can I ask you a question?"

"I guess."

"What happened to you?"

"Huh?"

"Your fab fifties look. I mean, not that you don't look cute now, but it's just that I loved that look you started getting into, and now . . ." She let her sentence trail off.

"I know," I admitted. "Blandorama, right?"

"Yeah. Kind of."

"I've been telling her," Justine said.

"I know it's not my business, okay? But if I had clothes like yours — and your cute little figure to pull it off — I'd never wear anything but those old styles. God! I'm so jealous."

"You're jealous — of *me*?"

"God, yes," she said. "First of all, I don't know if you noticed, but my own wardrobe . . . How can I say this? I kind of feel homeless."

"You mean the PJ look?"

"It's awful, right?"

"Actually," I said. "I liked it."

"Really?" she said, turning slightly pink around the edges. Today she was wearing a more standard look: cords and a sweater, with clogs. "You didn't think I looked — just — totally stupid?"

"What can I say?"

"It's just — that I love clothes. I know they're just clothes. But I love them. I just do."

Right then, I knew what I had to do — what we all had to do. "Okay," I said. "You're hired."

"But we don't have a blog!" Justine said. "Remember how we're not allowed to do the blog anymore and will be put in prison for the rest of our lives if we do it again? Unless you want me to be grounded forever."

"Where there's a will, there's a way!" I said, and suddenly, I realized that I meant it.

The first thing I did when I got home was throw open my closet. Then I reorganized all my clothes — putting my Mama Lees in front, my weekend clothes in back, and my last year's bland, blah basics in a giant black plastic Lawn & Leaf bag for Goodwill. As for the red dress with the white flowers — I put it over to the side. After all, it was still too cold to wear it. I figured that I wouldn't even think about that dress again until it was warm again — and then, somehow, I'd figure it out. Afterward, I felt so good that I strode into the kitchen, where Mama was sorting the day's mail, and said: "What is the big deal about my wanting to be an artist?"

"Not now, Ann," Mama said.

"And about Mama Lee's clothes, which, by the way, fit me perfectly. I mean, so what if you wore the red dress in that painting? What does that have to do with me?"

Finally, and for the first time ever, my big mouth achieved something. Mama looked up and, squinting a little, said: "Who told you about that painting?"

"Er? Martha?"

"I should never have told that girl! Oh! What on earth is wrong with me?"

"But, Mama! So what? I mean, you were only a teenager yourself. You didn't do anything wrong."

"I didn't?" she said. "How about I humiliated my mother — and my father, too? How about I nearly threw my entire future away? How about I acted like a fool?"

"But, Mama!" I was nearly shouting now. "So what? That was — that was a million years ago."

"I never wanted you to find out," Mama said. "Oh! I'm still just so ashamed of myself."

"But, Mama!"

"I wanted you — you and your sister — to be proud of me."

I couldn't believe what I was hearing. Proud of her? I'd never really thought about it before, that she wanted us to be proud of her. I'd always thought it was the other way around, that I wanted her to be proud of me — but that she never would be, not with me being so like me, and so not like Martha.

"And not only that," I blurted out. "But you have to know something else."

"Oh, no."

But I was off and running, Ann the blabber-puss, back in business: "Because, and I hope you know it, and Daddy, too, but I'm never going to go to Princeton."

"I wouldn't put yourself down like that."

"It's not a put-down, Mama. It's reality. I'm just not that into it — school, I mean."

"Don't be ridiculous," she said. "Even if you don't like being a student, you have no choice. Going to school is your job, and Daddy and I expect you to do your best."

I couldn't believe it. After all that blowup and upset and blogging and mess, and she still didn't get it? Feeling like I'd been stabbed, I let out a long groan.

"What?" Mama said. "Is there something you're not telling me . . . again?"

"OMG! Mama! I really, really, really want to make sure that you know that even if I study twenty-four hours a day, there's no way I'm going to get into Princeton."

"Nobody said anything about your having to go to Princeton."

"Or . . ." I had to think a minute, because it wasn't like I had all the colleges lined up in my head in order of their prestige. "Or the University of the Midwest!" I finally burst out with.

"There is no University of the Midwest."

"Or even, like — I don't know. Mama, what I really want to do? I want to be an artist. I want to go to art school."

"You're too young to decide where you want to go to college. And you're certainly too young to decide to give up on a well-rounded liberal arts education."

"You're not listening to me. What's so awful about my wanting to be an artist? Just because that man — whoever he was — was a painter . . ." and I would have continued except that Mama shot me one of her "enough is enough" looks. Then, instead of answering me, she said: "Honey, you have some talent. I can see that. I'm not blind. But art school? That's the kind of dream that can only let you down."

"But why, Mama?" I was nearly crying by then. "What's the big deal?"

"The big deal is that you're still too young to understand that most dreams are just that — dreams. Life is a compromise, honey. It is for me, it is for your father, and one day, as you'll see, it will be for you, too."

"Why? Why does it have to be like that?"

Which is when Mama put her face in her hands and remained that way for a while. Finally, she looked up and spoke. "I don't want your spirit crushed, like mine was."

It took me a little while, but finally I understood.

◇◇◇◇◇◇◇◇◇

"Told you," Mama Lee said that weekend, when I took Justine with me to help her do her spring cleaning. Mainly that meant climbing up on her kitchen cabinets and dusting the parts she could no longer reach. That, plus raking up the last of last year's leaves. Mama Lee was a stickler about that kind of thing: Everything had to be perfectly neat. "Your mother loves you no matter what. And she believes in you, too. But I guess you just had to go learn it for yourself."

"But she's still kind of weird about my wearing your clothes."

"That's something the two of you will just have to work out, I guess."

"But why, Mama Lee? Why is she still so — so totally freaked out when I wear something that has some pizzazz?"

"Sounds to me like she already told you. "

"What did she tell me?"

"Your mother just wants to keep you a little girl a might bit longer," Mama Lee finally said, "you being the youngest and all. And how much you look like she did when she was your age. And also, I don't think she ever quite forgave me for allowing her to spend so much time with that man — and he was a friend of mine, too! I had no idea that something had started up between them. Oh! I was just stupid, letting her spend so much time with him. What was I thinking?"

"But," I said, "it wasn't your fault!"

"And you," Mama Lee said, ignoring me completely while

she turned her gaze on Justine. "I understand that you had a hand in this whole blog business, too."

"Yeah, but it was Ann who dragged me into it."

"Well, it could have been really good," Mama Lee said. "Next time, you girls just have to be sure that you go about it the right way: with kindness. Because I haven't met a teenage girl yet who doesn't like a little attention — just so long as it's the right kind."

"Told you," I told Justine.

Justine had never met Mama Lee before, and from the moment we'd walked in, I could tell she was kind of in awe of her — of how beautiful she still was, and how fashionable, in one of her lightweight pantsuits, of gray linen, with a scarf knotted jauntily around her neck. I'd never seen her haul her butt so readily before, either, letting Mama Lee order her around like she was a soldier in a private army of two.

"Do you really think so, ma'am?" she said.

I'd never, not once, heard Justine call anyone "ma'am," and nearly busted a gut laughing.

"I do indeed," Mama Lee said. "You've got a way with words. And your friend here has a way with a pencil. You make a great team. The way I see it, God wouldn't have put you two girls together just so you could mess up."

Justine's eyes were like two rocks underwater, swimming black in their pupils.

CHAPTER TWENTY-FOUR

An Original Libby Fine

• Robin •

On the night that it happened — that terrible night when Dad slugged me — Ben sprang out of the TV room and, brandishing the remote controls like guns, stood between me and Dad until Dad left. We both heard the sound of his car backing out of the driveway, and from there, racing down the hill.

"I'm taking you to the emergency room," Ben said as he lowered himself to the floor and drew me onto his lap.

"I don't need the emergency room!" I wailed.

"I'm going to call the cops."

"No!" I wailed even harder.

And we sat there, hugging each other, and rocking back and forth in each other's arms until Ben finally got up to get me some ice. Then Ben reached for the phone to call Mom, but Mom was already at the door, letting herself in. And when I say she freaked out, I mean it. But at least I didn't need to go to the emergency room, or even to the doctor. Dad had hit me pretty hard, but nothing was broken. At least, not physically. It was just my entire life that was broken. So broken that, in bits and pieces, as Mom applied more ice and then Neosporin to my face, I spilled the entire story — including pretty much everything, even how Becka had gotten drunk and ruined my work dress — and when I was done, Mom didn't say anything at all. Instead, she pulled me to her so tightly that I could hear her heartbeat and the sound of her blood moving through her veins and smell her smell of soap and fatigue and old red lipstick.

That was the night all three of us moved into our cousin's house. It was Mom's decision: She insisted that our safety came first, and even though I didn't think that Dad would do it again, and Ben said that he'd sleep on the floor next to my bed, Mom just kept saying: "Better safe than sorry." Which is how I ended up at my cousin Weird John's house, watching TV in the basement, with Polly and Justine. That was the night when I got to know Justine a little, the night when I realized that I didn't need Becka's approval anymore, that I could be friends with whomever I wanted to be friends with.

A couple of days later, Dad moved out of the house, and Mom and Ben and I moved back in. I didn't want to, though, and ended up staying over at Polly's for a couple of days. It was weird, but even with Dad gone, Mom was still there, and I just didn't want to deal with her. At all! I came home anyway. Ben told me I had to. He said that Mom felt so guilty her hair had turned gray. For the first time in his life, though, he wasn't exaggerating. When I finally came home, Mom's stubborn black hair was the color of tin.

The first thing she said to me was: "Let's go shopping."

"Very funny, Mom."

"Really," she said. "Want to?"

"Do you mean it?" I finally said.

"And maybe we can get something for me, too?"

I couldn't help it: It just jumped out of my mouth: "How about a trip to the hair salon?"

"Do I look that bad?"

"Yeah. Kind of."

"We'll do both, then."

So we did.

In March, Daphne called me to say that she needed someone to help out on Saturdays, as the girl who had been helping her just quit. This time, Mom didn't quibble, but instead said that she was proud of me. Even though I still wore an occasional semi-showing under-cami, or tight woolen leggings, I'd mainly upped my look to something I thought of as affordable-funky-classy, a redo of preppy, wherein I combined basic button-down shirts with, say, a wide belt and slim-cropped bright-pink pants, or a cord mini with my black boots and an oversized pullover sweater. (My mother had upped her look, too, and was actually wearing jeans that fit, sweaters that weren't covered with small granules of ancient pills, and dresses that didn't go down to her ankles.)

A week later, I was back at work, this time with a name tag and two more amazing dresses, which Daphne said were mine to keep for as long as I stayed. "But the minute you quit on me," she said, "these two babies come back to me. Understood?"

I understood, all right, and I also understood that I wasn't ever going to let Becka see me in my work dresses — a beautiful light-blue Kate Spade and a Theory printed charmeuse. These were the clothes, I thought, of my future, of the day when, instead of just being a salesgirl in a local dress shop, I'd inhabit an office in New York where, every day, I'd dress in beautiful silk or woolen clothes, in lace-trimmed shifts and colorblock dresses, in multistriped scoop necks with elegant black heels, and designer wool crepe.

But as it turned out, I didn't really have to worry about keeping the dresses in good shape. Now that it wasn't the pre-holiday rush, the job was pretty low-key, so low-key that at times there were no customers in the store at all. That's when, bit by bit, Daphne told me about herself, and she was amazing. Her husband had been killed in a car accident when their only daughter had been two, and Daphne had had to move home to live with her parents until she could work again. That's when she started in retail and eventually bought what became Daphne's Designer Digs. She was sending her daughter to college in the city. "And let me tell you," she said, marking down prices or taking inventory, "it costs me a pretty bundle, too. And it doesn't help that the girl has such uptown tastes."

She sighed. "She's my daughter, and I love her more than I can say. I just wish I saw her more. But she's growing up, and has her own life, in the city. She's my gem. Worth every late night doing inventory or pulling my hair out over taxes."

I just stared as Daphne's eyes grew wet.

"What? You don't believe me?"

Finally I found my voice. "Of course I believe you."

"I'm going to have you over for dinner sometime," she continued. "I want you two girls to meet. What do you say?"

But for some reason, I was too choked up to say much of anything, and turned away. "What is it, hon?" Daphne said. "Things still tough at home?"

I'd told Daphne pretty much everything, including the fact that my father had hit me and that Mom had kicked him out of the house and he was living in a sublet in the city.

"It's just weird, is all," I finally said.

"Because I'm your boss?"

"No, that isn't it."

"Or if you just don't like me . . ."

"But I totally like you!" I blurted out. "I like you. . . ." And again my voice trailed off, and then I was throwing myself into her arms. "I like you so, so much!"

"Then what is it, hon?"

But I couldn't tell her. Because how do you tell someone that you kind of wished that she, and not your mother, was your mother? Finally she patted me and said, "Good, then! I just know that you and Emma Beth will hit it off!"

I don't know why I simply didn't tell her the truth then and there — that the internship I'd told her about had been at Libby Fine, where Emma Beth and I hadn't exactly been best friends. Instead, I swallowed my pride and called the one person I could think of who I thought might be able to help me: That's right,

Becka. Things had slowly gotten better between us, or at least at school they had. One of the girls — it could have been any of them — had told her that Dad had hit me, and as soon as she'd found out, she'd come running up to me at school saying how bad she'd felt about not knowing. Now she said: "You just need to out-fabulous her."

"Like that worked out so great last time."

"But you're you, Robin. You can out-fabulous anyone."

"Are you being sarcastic?"

There was a pause. "I know!" she said. "You can wear one of my Libbys."

"Meaning?"

"Aunt Libby gave me some of her new line."

I had to ask: "Do they have poodles on them?"

"Poodles? Very funny. But you should come and see. There's something in particular that I think would look awesome on you."

I hadn't been to Becka's since the night she'd spilled red wine on me — oh, and once afterward, when I'd brought her some flowers after she came home from the hospital. So I thought it would be weird being there again, that there'd be so much left unsaid that it would be like a giant invisible ice cube sitting between us. Instead, when she opened the door, the first thing she said was: "I've missed you."

"You have?" I said after a little while.

"I really have!" she said. "And, Robin?"

"What?"

"I'm, like — I'm, like, so lonely!"

What do you expect after you've been such a bitch? I thought. Then I stood there, feeling as awkward as a freshman in a class full of seniors, and tongue-tied, like I'd never met her before, let alone been friends with her most of my life. It got worse when she looked at me like she could read my mind. So I was super-relieved when she lunged toward me and, giving me a hug, said: "I miss everyone!"

"You do?"

"I even miss Um!" she said, and in the first time for over a year, I saw her laugh. She laughed so hard she turned purple and had to bend over to stop from coughing. She laughed so hard that I couldn't help but laugh with her, hiccupping and drooling as I went into hysterics. Finally, when we'd both calmed down, she gestured toward the stairs, saying: "Shop my closet."

Daphne lived on the third floor of a redbrick building a few blocks from her shop, in an apartment filled with brightly colored Oriental rugs, slightly beat-up furniture, and silk pillows in lollipop colors.

"No way" was the first thing Emma Beth said when she saw me. It didn't surprise me that she looked amazing in tight black pants and a cropped black-and-white houndstooth jacket, with black ballerina flats.

"Way," I said, wearing my new Libby outfit, which was, and you're not even going to believe it, an off-white clinging blouse with a pair of gray silk pajama pants. Except that unlike my own pajama pants, Libby's looked like something you're supposed to wear to a party or a ball, and had a protective, well-made weight to them.

"This can't be happening."

"I work for your mom," I said, my voice shaking a little. "At the store."

"What's going on here?" Daphne said.

"Did you know about this, Mother?" Emma Beth said.

"I'm confused," Daphne said.

"How long have you worked for her?"

"Not long. I don't know. A month or so."

"*Would someone please explain what's going on here?*"

"You planned this, didn't you?"

"No."

"And what exactly are you trying to prove?"

"Would someone please tell me what's happening?"

So we did — both of us — Emma Beth narrating the crucial bits of information, which basically boiled down to the fact that we both had summer internships at Libby Fine at the same time — and me providing the footnotes, like how Libby Fine was my friend's godmother. And when we were done, Daphne, in her blunt way, said: "What's the beef between you two, anyway?"

"Jesus, Mother!"

"And why didn't you tell me that you knew my daughter?" Daphne said, turning to me. "Don't you think I might have wanted to know?"

Instantly, I felt like two-day-old cafeteria food: crusted-over macaroni and cheese, perhaps, or ancient boiled canned green beans. So much for showing Emma Beth up! So much for being fabulous in my Libby Fine *pajama pants*!

"I'm really sorry," I said, blushing to the roots of my hair and then some. "The truth is, I didn't want to let you down, and then when you said her name, it was already too late. Oh God! Sorry." Once again, I'd blown it. Once again, I'd be out of a job. Once again, I'd humiliated myself in front of Emma Beth, and even worse, Daphne would never want to see me again! When the heat began to drain from my face, I asked her if she wanted me to leave.

"Oh, dear," Daphne said.

"I totally don't understand what's happening here," Emma Bitch said.

I was so embarrassed that I just wanted to dig a hole in the floor and crawl into it. Then it just kind of burst out of me, like I had no control whatsoever on what was happening inside my own mouth, like I had lost control of my tongue, and all I could do was drool: "I just want people to like me!" I said. The next thing I know, I'm dribbling tears and snot all over Becka's beautiful Libby Fine.

"Here, hon," Daphne said, handing me a box of Kleenex.

"*Mother*," Emma Bitch said. "What the . . . ?"

Stroking my shoulder, Daphne said: "Okay, girls. Enough. What on earth happened last summer at Libby Fine? What's your issue with each other?"

"I should have never even been there!" I cried. "Everyone was right! Mom was right! I can't do this! I'll never make it in fashion! I ruin everything I touch!"

"Nonsense," Daphne said. "Stop feeling sorry for yourself!"

"I'm not," I wailed anew. "It's true. I suck! And everyone knows it!"

"Oh God," I heard Emma Beth say impatiently.

"Fine," Daphne said. "You suck. What about you, then, Emma? Do you think Robin sucks?"

A pause. Then: "No."

"I see. I don't, either. But I do think that something happened between the two of you last summer."

"Whatever, Mother. Why don't you ask *her*?"

"Do you have an explanation for me, Robin?"

"Not really," I blubbered. "Just that Emma Beth was — well, she was the real intern. I just got that job because my best friend's mother is friends with Libby Kline!"

"So what?" Daphne said. "How do you think Emma got through the door? That's right — connections. In her case, me. I do a lot of business with Libby Fine. In fact, I was one of the few boutiques that really supported Libby when she first began. But both of you, listen to me, and listen good. *Neither* of you got to Libby's because of connections alone. I know Libby, and she won't hire you, even for a summer internship — even to do nothing but step and fetch — if she doesn't think you've got the stuff. No one will. It's just the way it is."

"Really?" I said at the same time that Emma Beth burst out with: "Oh my God, Mother! Do you have any idea how embarrassing you are?"

As the two of them headed off into their own squabble, it began to dawn on me that perhaps, just perhaps, I hadn't made as big a fool of myself at Libby Fine as I'd thought I had. But before I had time to really think it through, Emma Beth turned to me and, her voice shaking a little, said: "You were like — like a little mascot or something, in your funky weird pajamas and your braids! And my God! Look how tall you are! I'm so short I look like a midget!"

"*What?*"

"Don't you get it, Mother? All my life, you've told me that the thing that matters most is hard work. But it isn't! In the end, even if I work harder than anyone, it's always people like your new little friend here who get the goodies — just look at the pants she's wearing! They're Libby originals! God! Libby loved her so much that she was ready to adopt her!"

I don't know what possessed me, but maybe it was Ben. I said: "She can't adopt me. I already have parents."

And for some reason, the minute I said that, I started cracking up. Not only was I channeling Ben, but I'd turned into him, too, with no ability to stop, and no borderline between being funny and just being stupid. "Get it?" I said. "I have parents already. Only, you know, my father's a total alcoholic. And my mom — she dresses like a bag lady. Or she used to. She actually bought some decent clothes so she only looks like a bag lady half the time now. Also, she's a control freak. Oh, and I have a twin brother, too? He's the one everyone thinks is going to grow up to be some huge success. I'm the one who everyone thinks is too stupid to do anything but work with two-year-olds."

"Two-year-olds?" Emma Beth said.

"Like in a day care?"

"I hate little kids," she said.

"Me, too."

"Only my mother here always made me babysit. I had to work in the store and babysit, too. She said I needed to learn the value of money."

"Me, too," I said. "Once, a little boy I was babysitting put Cheez Whiz in my hair."

"A girl I babysat wet her pants on me. She was sitting on my lap."

"There was this kid who hid my cell phone and wouldn't give it back to me until I let him be Facebook friends with me."

"I once babysat this kid who stole the toilet paper from the bathroom just before I went into it."

We fell into silence.

"I told you you had a lot in common," Daphne at last said. "You're both a mess."

"I think I ruined my outfit," I said, but Daphne assured me that tearstains wash away clean.

And maybe she was right, because after Dad started going to AA meetings, Mom let him move back in. He went to so many meetings that he was hardly home at all. But he was. I knew because every night, every night when he came home, the first thing he did was come upstairs to Ben's room, and then, a minute later, to mine, where he stroked my hair and kissed me good night.

CHAPTER TWENTY-FIVE

Five Groovy Chicks

• Justine •

For the first time ever, I wasn't freaked out about moving. But that was because, for the first time ever, we were only moving a mile away: to an apartment building on the same block as Polly's, in a part of town filled with antiques shops and cafés and a lot of little old ladies and dogs. It had three bedrooms, a big living and dining room, a forties-style kitchen with black-and-white tiles, and a view of the small park across the street. I pretty much liked the apartment about a million times better than I liked Homely Acres, except for one small detail: my room. Which had pink-flowered wallpaper. PINK. *FLOWERS*. Barf. My. Brains. Out. Even so, it was a whole lot better than any house we'd had since three houses ago, when we lived in Germany for a couple of years. In short, I was cool with it. The only part — the only part at all — that made me a little bit sad was that I was going to be on the other side of town from Becka.

Yes, I really did say that.

She wasn't so bad after all.

But I didn't know that until later — after the FOR SALE sign went up, and after I gave Becka that scarf; after it came out that Robin's dad had hit Robin (my dad wasn't exactly the world's greatest, but one thing I knew was that he'd never lay a hand on me) and that Ann didn't actually have to duplicate her sister's utter nerdhood-slash-perfection, that Polly's father had AIDS, and that Becka's mother made my own hover mother look laid-back. Because that was when, one day, she actually came over and knocked on our door, and when I answered it, she said: "Sorry I called you 'Um.'"

As usual, as I looked up into her dazzlingly perfect beauty, I was struck stupid.

"You are?" I finally managed to squeak.

"Look," she said, glancing at the tips of her perfect black boots, "the problem wasn't really you, okay? It was my mother. She — well, it's complicated. But — well, she writes about me all the time."

"She does?"

"Except for, like, movie stars, I'm the most famous teen in America."

"You are?"

"She's made a career out of writing about me."

"She *has*?"

Like I said, I was struck stupid, but then suddenly, I wasn't.

"That sucks," I said.

"Half the time, I feel like a walking, talking doll. Like a giant Barbie, made of plastic, but empty inside."

"That *really* sucks."

"By the way," she said, "that scarf you gave me? I love it."

That was the day I stopped being afraid of her. And the day that, weeks later, she said that she wanted to help write the blog was the day that I began to feel that life in West Falls would turn out to be okay after all. Not that we'd ever get around to writing it again. But it was a nice thought.

It was her idea to change the name of the blog. "*Fashion High* is okay," she said, "but kind of cutesy. You don't want to be cutesy, do you?"

"Do I look like a person who wants to do cutesy? I don't even like *cute*."

"Exactly my point, J-bird. So we need to find something more on the funky side of life."

"Since when do you do funky?"

"Since now," she said, closing her huge liquid blue-green eyes. (Really, it kind of sucked getting along with her even more than it had been being enemies, because every time I was with her, I felt like Miss America's homely cousin.) Then her eyes popped open: "I know! Let's call it *Five Groovy Chicks and a Dude*."

"Who's the dude?"

"Weird John."

"Weird John is *not* on this project."

"He told me he was."

"He lied."

It was getting to be a pain, how, ever since I'd showed up, in desperation, at his house, he followed me around. I already had one pathetic male in my life — that would be my father — and the last thing in the world I needed was another one. Who knew that the guy would turn out to be so, er, *loyal*?

Dad, however, wasn't so loyal. What he was, was pissed off. Like it was my fault when Mom finally confronted him. Like if only I'd been a better daughter, Mom wouldn't have been so furious, and hurt, and miserable. Like it was my fault that he'd fallen for some divorced thirty-year-old with a nose job and hair the color of a hot dog. Whose name, he told me, was *Ruby*. "Like the stone," he said.

"Like I could care."

"Can't you at least try to understand?" he said.

"Don't talk to me."

Of course, eventually I *had* to talk to him. And listen, too: about how he hadn't meant to start up with — kill me now — Ruby, how at first he really had thought that the job in New Jersey would be better both for his career and for our family life as a whole, and a bunch of other stuff I didn't believe. I didn't not believe it, either. It was just that it didn't really matter what he said. What mattered was that, in the end, it was Mom's decision to leave him. Which meant that I had to listen to her, too — *endlessly* — as she explained that she didn't want to do anything to make things even worse for me than they had been, but that she just didn't think she liked herself anymore. "I used to be someone," she said (over and over as Skizz rubbed himself against my ankles). "I want that back. I want to be someone again. Someone you can be proud of."

"Can you stop talking now?"

"What do you say that, instead of looking for another house, we get an apartment?" she then said.

"I thought I asked you not to talk."

"I'm serious, Justine. Would an apartment be okay with you?"

"Honestly, Mom, just so long as it's not pink, I don't care where we live."

"But I thought you loved your room."

"I hate my room."

"You do?"

"I hate pink."

"What color *do* you like?"

I pulled out my winter coat, the one she'd given me for Christmas. "I like this color," I said. "I like blue."

Two days after Mom and I moved to our new apartment on George Street, the doorbell buzzed: It was all four of the girls, along with Weird John. The girls were all dressed the same, in shorts and T-shirts and sneakers. WJ had on his usual black-on-black assemblage, complete with butt-crack visibility and bright-green fingernails.

"Reporting for duty!" he said.

"Hi, kids!" Mom said, popping her head out of the kitchen, where she'd been unpacking. "All the stuff you need is already in Justine's room. Go to it — and thanks!"

Earlier, Mom and I had gone to the hardware store and bought two gallons of high-gloss blue paint, along with buckets, rags, and paintbrushes, and as my friends started to paint my room, I realized that the color I'd chosen was the same blue of my dreams, with a hint of gray-green in it, like the sky over San Francisco when it was about to rain in the spring, and the color of my mother's eyes when she was happy, and how I thought about Eliza, when I missed her, and all the people who'd ever been kind to me, or took me into their confidence, or let me be sad. And when, later, we walked to the head of the trail that was to take us up to a waterfall, I saw that my blue was also the color the rocks made when they glittered in the sun.

"You mean there really is a falls in West Falls?" I said as we hiked up through the woods in the hot afternoon. I was wearing the same thing as all the other girls, shorts with a T-shirt — in my own case, the same Gay-Straight Youth Alliance T-shirt that I'd been wearing the first time I'd met Becka.

The girls laughed at me.

"Of course there's a falls, J-bird," Becka said.

"It's the best thing there is about this whole town," Polly added.

And suddenly I looked up, and there it was: a bright, crashing, roaring waterfall, dropping at least twelve feet from its pinnacle into a deep green pool before quieting down to join the quick, dancing flow.